MW00478758

RETURN
TO
PRIMORDIAL ISLAND

RICK POLDARK

SEVERED PRESS
HOBART TASMANIA

RETURN TO PRIMORDIAL ISLAND

Copyright © 2020 Rick Poldark

WWW.SEVEREDPRESS.COM

All rights reserved. No part of this book may be reproduced or transmitted in any form or by any electronic or mechanical means, including photocopying, recording or by any information and retrieval system, without the written permission of the publisher and author, except where permitted by law. This novel is a work of fiction. Names, characters, places and incidents are the product of the author's imagination, or are used fictitiously. Any resemblance to actual events, locales or persons, living or dead, is purely coincidental.

ISBN: 978-1-922323-88-0

All rights reserved.

ACKNOWLEDGEMENTS

Thank you, Alan Basso, for lending me your eyes, brain, and insights. Your feedback on early drafts was crucial and is greatly appreciated. Thank you to Severed Press for publishing this adventure. Finally, thank you to all the readers who made the first book a success. I hope you enjoy this installment.

PART I

GHOSTS, GUILT, AND BURDENS

CHAPTER 1

Dr. Tracey Moran bit her lip as she waited in front of her house for the limousine to arrive. It was a nervous habit she had developed as a teenager that always raged when she was under stress. David Lennox hadn't sounded surprised when he answered her call, and he was in some hot bother to get her to Poseidon Tech immediately. She barely had time to pack a bag.

Her mother was watching from inside the house from the bay window, but her father was standing next to her on the curb. He looked as if he wanted to hug her or put his arm around her, but he didn't. "We're proud of you, honey. I think it's a good thing, you getting this job. You've been sulking in the house for too long."

Tracey had told him she was being flown to a new dig site. She didn't have the heart to tell him where she was really going...to a trans-dimensional island filled with murderous dinosaurs, indigenous tribes, and Death Lords. And then there was the NDA she signed. "Thanks, Dad."

"Maybe you can patch things up with Peter."

Tracey frowned at the mention of his name. "Yeah, hopefully."

"Whatever happened between you two can be patched up, I'm sure." Her father knew the two were like bookends. When he inquired about Peter and why she wasn't talking to him anymore, she had to tell him something. She indicated a falling out and kept it vague, and her father respected her privacy enough not to pry.

A black limousine turned onto the block. Tracey looked at her watch. *That was fast. He's not messing around.* It pulled to the curb where Tracey stood and parked. The back door opened, and David Lennox hopped out wearing a ten-thousand-dollar suit and his patented phony grin.

Tracey turned to her father and hugged him. "Bye."

Her dad squeezed her. "Knock 'em dead, honey."

A driver stepped out and came around to take her bag. Lennox stepped forward, extending his hand to Tracey. She shook it.

He guided her into the limo as her father waved from the curb. Tracey was immediately enveloped in recycled, cooled air. When Lennox closed the door, he tapped on the glass divider.

Tracey waved at her father one last time as the limo pulled away, but she knew he couldn't see her through the heavily tinted glass. He waved back anyway, guessing correctly that she was waving at him.

"I'm so glad you changed your mind," said Lennox. "If you don't mind me asking, what *did* make you change your mind?"

Tracey glared at him. "You know what it was."

Lennox smiled, but it was genuine, or at least it tried to appear so. "He's still there, you know. We just received a transmission this morning. It looks like they're all there—Peter, Jason, Susan."

"Mary?"

Lennox cocked his head at her tone. "Yes, Dr. Tambini is there, too. They're all alive."

"Those other lifeforms in the photos you showed me...what are they?"

Lennox shook his head. "We don't know. They appear bipedal..."

"But not human."

He shrugged. "The photos are inconclusive."

"I want a better security team this time. Better armed."

He nodded. "Done and done. I think you'll be pleased with the expedition we've put together."

This time Tracey cocked her head.

Lennox looked amused. "What? What is it?"

"Funny, last time you called this a salvage operation. This time you used a different word...*expedition*."

Unflummoxed, he shrugged his shoulders again. "Well, we recovered the flight recorder, which was extremely helpful. Now we intend to recover our people...your friend, which is why time is of the essence."

Tracey sized him up. "That's never it with you people. The last time you didn't tell us there was another salvage operation before us."

Lennox extended his hands, palms up. "I'm an open book. Nothing held back this time."

Tracey leaned forward and narrowed her eyes. "Yeah? Why should I believe you?"

"Because you signed an iron-clad nondisclosure agreement. You leak any detail about these operations, the island, or our company, and we'll sue you into oblivion. Is that honest enough for you?"

She eyed him for a moment and then sat back, folding her arms. "What about the team? Who are the other consultants?"

"There are no other consultants this time, other than you. The last time they were a liability."

Tracey glared at the Poseidon Tech rep again. "A liability? People died. People with families."

"From the data we've gathered, it wouldn't appear so. At least not all of them."

"So, who's on the team?"

"Our staff...and a much bigger security team."

Tracey stared ahead of her, breathing in the stale air. "Your last one didn't fare so well."

Lennox shook his head emphatically. "This group has RPGs, grenades, and choppers. Lots of high-tech gadgets and gizmos." He leaned in, as if imparting a secret. "They have fabrics that bend light. Camouflage. Like in that movie, with the alien that runs around killing those soldiers."

"I just want to get Peter and bring him back. I mean, his parents and sister think he's dead. He's got a niece and nephew who wonder where the heck he is."

"We're going to bring him back," assured Lennox, flashing his smarmy grin again.

Tracey's eyes lit up. "Oh...really...I didn't realize you'd be joining us."

Lennox laughed. It was a hollow sound. "No, no. I won't be going."

Tracey smirked. "Oh, I see. I guess that makes you a liability." He offered no reaction. The dig rolled off him like water off a duck's back. "So, I'm an asset, not a liability?"

"You're the only one who's been on the island. You know what it's like...what to expect."

Tracey stabbed a finger into the air. "You mean I'm the only one crazy enough to have been there and return."

Lennox nodded.

"Where are we going now?"

He looked relieved the conversation was going in a different direction now. "Straight to the airport. We're flying you out to the off-shore oil rig. There you'll meet the new team and be debriefed."

Tracey decided to end the chit chat, as there was nothing more to discuss that was substantive or relevant with Mr. Lennox. He was the salesman, and he'd been effective in his pitch. He'd served his only purpose. Now it was time to meet with operations.

She used the rest of the car ride to the airport to mull over her conversations with Bill Gibson and Allison McGary. She had called them right after Lennox had left her house several days earlier. Bill chastised her for even entertaining his visit, let alone considering returning to the island. Regarding Peter, Bill had said that there was nothing to be done, it wasn't her fault, and there were plenty of fish in the sea.

Her conversation with Allison, however, had gone much differently.

"Allie, I was paid a visit by David Lennox yesterday."

Allison was silent for a moment. "He visited me last week."

"You're not considering…"

"No, I'm not," said Allison, almost snapping at Tracey. "I have a family. Apparently, you are considering going back."

Tracey sighed. "I think I might have to."

"Peter."

"Yes. I can't just…leave him there."

"Did Lennox show you the pictures?"

"He did. They look real. I know he's still alive. I feel it."

"You really care for him."

"Of course I do. We've worked so closely together."

"Oh, come on. What is it with young people today? Too chicken to say when they love someone."

"I have to go back, Allie."

"I know, hun."

This time it was Tracey that was silent. "I didn't expect you to agree with me. Bill sure didn't."

"If you were in Bill's shoes, you'd say the same. Tracey, Bill and I found our soul mates. We built a life with them, and we won't do anything to jeopardize that. Not again. We've moved on. But you…you are still finding that someone, and you're still building your life, your career. You need to come to terms with your feelings about what happened on that island, with your feelings for Peter, or you'll never move on. You'll still be stuck on that island, reliving it over and over in your own personal hell."

Allison was right. Tracey was still stuck on the island. She still woke in the middle of the night in cold sweats. She had been experiencing recurring nightmares, vivid ones, very lifelike. There was one recurring monster that haunted her in each and every one—the T. rex without the feathers. Sometimes, within the nightmare, he morphed into the feathered tyrannosaur.

He even appeared in nightmares that didn't feature the island. The other night she had dreamed that she and Peter had gone to a diner. She had forgotten her purse and excused herself to retrieve it from the car. In her dream, she had crossed the parking lot to her car. She opened the door, pulled it out, and when she turned around, it was standing right there, waiting for her, growling through its teeth, its mouth closed, dark eyes glaring at her from underneath sharp cranial ridges.

In another dream, she was at the beach, sitting on a blanket, watching Peter dip his feet in the water. Her eyes had drifted off to the left, where she saw down the shoreline the Tyrannosaurus stomping towards him. She stood and cried out to him, jumping up and down and waving her arms, but Peter couldn't hear her.

But *it* did. The T. rex lowered its head and bounded for her. She turned to run as fast as her legs would take her, but each time she looked over her shoulder, it was gaining on her, outpacing her with every thunderous footfall.

Every nightmare ended with it getting her, but right before it sunk its teeth into her body, she awoke, heart racing and drenched in sweat. She hadn't gotten a proper night's sleep without the aid of a glass of wine, which turned into cocktails and even pills. That monster was killing her in her real, waking life, and she knew she wouldn't find peace until she confronted her fears and returned to that primordial island.

She had seen a psychologist at one point, at the recommendation of her physician and the prodding of her parents. He was a patient man with a kind bedside manner. When she related her nightmares to him, he had inquired about Peter, and through some feat in mental gymnastics had identified the T. rex as her fear of commitment. That was the last time she entertained psychotherapy, but even now she knew that she was the one engaging in mental gymnastics.

She knew what she had to do, and she was ready to do it. She only hoped she'd return in one piece and with Peter.

* * *

On the Island
Date and Time Unknown

"Are you sure this is a good idea?" Jason bit his lip, eyeing his comrade, as they hid with several tribal warriors in the bushes about one hundred feet from the temple entrance.

"I have to," said Peter. "I woke them up. I have no idea why they're attacking us."

"They're not attacking you," said Jason. "You're their god."

Peter grimaced at the label. "I hate it when you call me that."

Mary placed a gentle hand on his shoulder. "Well, to them you are. Tell them to stop. Tell them we can all coexist on this island."

Peter wiped the sweat from his brow, which was in part due to the humidity and in part to the fact that he was terrified. "Man, talk about the law of unintended consequences. I was just trying to do the right thing, but by slaying one monster, I created another."

Jason swatted a mosquito feasting on his neck. "Yeah, and this one's worse."

Peter sighed. There was something even worse yet on this island—the something that had manipulated Mike Deluca. Peter caught a glimpse of it—or was it more of a feeling? Either way, he gleaned it was much older than this race of lizard men he woke up, and very evil. Peter didn't think these lizard men were evil; he believed they were acting according to their nature.

Then again, so was this other entity, whatever it was. Peter knew it was trying to get off the island. He was relieved when the island had phased out of his home dimension, trapping it here.

Jason elbowed him in his side. "Come on, mate. We need your head in the game."

Peter cleared his head. "Yes. Right. So, here's the plan. They won't attack me. I'm going to walk right into the temple and demand to speak to their chieftain."

"What are you going to say?" pressed Jason.

"I'll explain what Mary just said, that we can all coexist. I'll tell their chief. If I can make him understand, maybe he'll back off."

"And if that doesn't work?"

Mary leaned in and spoke softly into Peter's ear. "You know what you have to do."

"I know. I know," said Peter. He knew what she meant—using the death orb to wipe them out wholesale. "I...I just feel funny about it. I brought them back."

"And you can send them back into extinction," said Mary.

Jason shot Peter a sideways glance. "You act like they're your children or something. They're freaking lizards, man. Pests. Stamp them out if they won't listen."

Peter knew there was a better than average chance that his appeal would fall on deaf ears. When the lizard men raided the Umazoa village (that's what Peter called them, because the word they used to reference themselves as a group sounded like 'Umazoa'), Peter had tried to talk to them, to forbid them from ravaging a people that had become his friends. However, they had just ignored him, slaughtering men, women, and children in brutal fashion.

"They want access to the river," explained Peter. "They can have it, peacefully. If only I could explain it clearly. We can share it."

Mary leveled her gaze at Peter. "We're low on ammunition, and there's no more coming. Food is scarce because they won't let us hunt.

The dinosaurs are starting to figure out how to access the plateau, likely with the help of the lizard men. Something's got to give, or we're not going to survive."

"I'll see to it that we all do," snapped Peter.

"Not if we're eaten," said Jason. "Even you can't do that with your...powers."

Peter took a deep breath, steeling himself. He knew they were right. He also knew he bore the responsibility for bringing this down upon the Umazoa. "Then I guess I can't fail, can I?"

Mary and Jason both shook their heads.

The tribal warriors listened intently, trying to follow the conversation. In their time together, Peter and the Juwai (what the Umazoa called those from the other dimension) had learned some of the tribal language, and the Umazoa had learned some English.

Peter stood up. "Okay. Here I go. If I don't come back out, go back to the village and begin preparations to evacuate." When Jason shot him a look, he said, "If I don't return, it'll be your only option."

Mary stood up and kissed him sweetly on the lips. "Then you make sure you return."

Peter nodded.

"Are you sure you don't want me to come in with you?" asked Jason.

Peter shook his head. "No. If this doesn't work, you'd never make it out in one piece, and I can't risk that."

Jason pulled his handgun and handed it to Peter, who shook his head, waving it away. "I won't need that." Even he found his sureness to be strange. His newfound power had transformed him and was continuing to change him in ways he couldn't comprehend. He knew things at certain times with an uncanny certainty.

Jason nodded. "We'll be waiting for you right here."

Peter looked up at the sun, now low in the sky. While he sensed the lizard men were warm-blooded, for some reason they returned to their subterranean realm during the night. "Watch your backs. There may be some stragglers returning home."

"That's why I think we should wait till nightfall," said Jason.

"No," said Peter, "I'm counting on running into a few of them returning." There was a roar in the distance. "Watch out for dinosaurs. Remember, if I'm not back in a couple of hours..."

"Head back to the village," said Mary. "We got it."

Satisfied, Peter turned away from his friends and began to cross the clearing to the Umazoan temple. He wished Mary and Jason hadn't come along, but there was no dissuading them. As he approached the temple entrance, he looked at the posts driven into the ground once used for human sacrifice. However, since the lizard men started attacking the Umazoa, all worship and rituals had ceased.

The Umazoa thought that they had angered the gods, which resulted in this reptilian plague upon their tribe. They also believed Peter was imbued with the power of the sun, which they regarded as a deity, to right their wrongs. Peter, of course, had tried to explain to them what had happened, but much was lost in translation, and the Umazoa were resolute in their beliefs.

The entrance to the temple was dark, so Peter unbuttoned his shirt, allowing the glowing orbs in his chest to illuminate the way. The bushes rustled behind him and two lizard men darted out, dashing towards him. However, Peter was unconcerned as they shoved past him to enter the temple, leaving him unharmed. Peter smiled to himself.

He broke into a jog, attempting to keep pace with them. He remembered the room with the intertwining paths of multi-colored tiles and the side doors that unleashed velociraptors, as well as the Dilophosaurus cave. Surely, there was a more direct way to the lizard men's den.

He followed them to the door with the reptilian face crudely painted on it. They entered the room with the tiled paths, but instead of taking the paths, one-by-one, they jumped into the pit. Peter watched them, smiling. He knew this wasn't suicide. To be sure, he reached out and sensed their life forces, like lanterns in the dark.

Peter walked to the edge of the pit, keeping one eye on the side passages for any velociraptors. He felt their presence behind the rolling stone doors, waiting for a meal. He leaned over the edge of the chasm before him and squinted to see in the darkness, crouching for a closer look. There it was, a narrow shelf clinging to the sheer wall of the cliff. He reached out and felt their essences move away, and when they were far enough, he lowered himself down.

Clinging to the wall so as not to fall into the chasm, he side-stepped his way to a tunnel entrance. He thought of his tabletop role-playing gaming and smiled again—search for hidden passages. He entered the tunnel, using the two orbs that resided in his chest to illuminate the way. He crept along as it sloped downward, and he sensed the den of lizard men in the distance.

Before long, he was in the room with the massive pitcher plants. He looked up at the holes in the rock cavern above, remembering the horror of the Dilophosaurus cave. He walked around to the opening with the reptilian carving depicting the large, obsidian eyes and passed through. The subterranean city was drawing closer. He felt it, and the orbs in his chest pulsated in response.

He passed the reptilian statues and descended the stairs that led to the city below. The last time he saw these stairs, they were covered in dust from sitting unused for ages. This time, there was no dust. As he descended, he saw them—hundreds of lizard men traversing the city, walking the streets, entering and leaving buildings.

When he reached the bottom, two sentries grasping long spears guarded the entrance. However, when they saw Peter, they parted, allowing him admittance. They watched him with those large, black eyes, their faces cold and expressionless, except for the occasional flaring of the dewlaps on their throats. Their bodies, however, emanated heat. Peter mused how reptiles—at least in this dimension—must've evolved from these progenitors, becoming cold-blooded as an adaptation to living above ground in the sunlight in warm climates.

As he walked the streets, Peter sensed life all around him, but he was seeking out one life in particular—the chief. Unfortunately, his newfound powers didn't provide him the ability to distinguish between beings. He kept an eye out for a prominent building, one that looked like it might house the tribal chief.

The subterranean city looked different from the last time Peter saw it. Prior, when he had first discovered the orb of life, it was barren. Now, various multi-colored, floating orbs illuminated bustling streets. The lizard men had wasted no time in rebuilding. As he looked around, Peter wondered at their actual numbers.

He also wondered if he should have spent more time down here after reawakening this ancient race. He had figured he'd leave them alone to reacquaint themselves with an island that had moved on in their absence. He had believed a policy of non-interference was best, respectful even. Now, he realized his folly. His absence had made him less of a presence in these reptilian beings' lives.

Although he was viewed as a deity amongst them, the lizard men's concept of piety was somewhat unusual, at least to Peter. They acknowledged him, but chose to remain aloof. The distant clockmaker, he had set their civilization in motion and left them to their own devices, and now he was repaid in kind. This reaction, however, was preferable to the savage violence they typically greeted other humans with.

He paused at an intersection, where a black orb floated above the ground at waist height. Passersby would swipe a three-clawed hand over it, pausing, and moving on. Peter knew that the orbs served to transmit information. He figured if he touched one, it might provide a clue as to the whereabouts of the chief. He reached out, the two orbs in his chest brightening, and touched the top of the black orb with the palm of his right hand.

Visions conjured in his mind's eye of news, prominent figures, and ideas that he wasn't quite able to translate into human terms. Knowing he could interact with the orbs, he reached out with his mind, asking the orb about the chief in the best way he knew how. Countless visions toggled through his mind, and he swooned. Overwhelmed, he staggered but kept his hand on the orb. Finally, when it became too much, he released the orb, pulling back his hand. His surroundings blurred and his head rang as he tried to regain his bearings.

When his vision cleared, he was startled to find that the lizard men around him had stopped what they were doing and were staring at him, silent and statuesque, the way reptiles could voluntarily slow down bodily functions to attain an eerie stillness.

Peter looked around, wondering if he was in any danger. As if in answer to his silent query, a detail of what was apparently some kind of town guard approached him, spears in-hand but held point facing upwards. The throng of onlookers parted to let them through.

Peter realized he must've transmitted his desire to meet with the chief, and this was to be his escort. As if reading his realization, they turned and walked away from him in formation, and he knew he was to follow. As he marched behind them, onlookers continued to gawk in their cold, expressionless way with large, black eyes reflecting the crystalline illumination, and Peter's mind raced to decide how he was going to address the reptilian chief.

CHAPTER 2

Tracey stepped into the cafeteria at the off-shore oil rig for the second time in her life. She was exhausted from the long flight, and she had never been able to sleep well on planes. The room was already filled with various Poseidon Tech employees.

She walked over to a metallic table holding coffee decanters and grabbed a paper cup. She poured herself a cup of coffee, adding two artificial sweetener packets and a dash of powdered milk. She bypassed the finger sandwiches and found a seat at a table next to a woman approximately her age. She was dressed in a beige blouse and khaki pants, and her straight brown hair hung over part of her face as she pored over her notes on her laptop.

When she felt Tracey sit on the bench next to her, she looked up and smiled. "Hi."

Tracey returned the smile. "Hi." She looked around the room. At the front, a man stood, reviewing something on his laptop, the same laptop the woman seated next to her used, no doubt Poseidon Tech standard issue. Tracey figured he was the team leader. Fresh meat for the grinder. "So, what are we waiting for?"

The woman looked up. "We're waiting for a private consultant, some paleontologist who has experience on the island."

Tracey smiled. "Oh, wow. I can only imagine what she must've seen on that island."

"I know," replied the woman. "Isn't it wild?"

"That's a good word for it." She extended her hand, "Tracey."

The woman shook it. "Marcy, data engineer."

"Data...engineer."

Marcy smirked. "Yeah, nothing as exotic as a paleontologist, but someone has to collect and crunch the data."

Tracey leaned in, looking from side to side. "From what I hear, the data on this island will crunch *you*."

Marcy shook her head. "The last time was a trial run. This time, there's going to be more security."

Tracey frowned. 'Trial run?' She figured Marcy didn't know that the last expedition was not the first. It may have not even been the second or third, for that matter. Poseidon Tech apparently kept many of their employees in the dark. "Let's hope so. Many people died last time."

Marcy looked startled by that last revelation. Before she could respond, the man up front looked up from his laptop and saw Tracey. He cleared his throat. "Okay, let's begin. We don't have much time before the island phases out, so time is of the essence."

The din quieted down, except for the occasional cough and throat clearing, and all eyes were on the man up front.

"For those of you who don't know me, my name is Trevor Nielsen. I'm the team leader of this operation, and what I'm about to tell you will likely save your life. So, you'd better pay close attention."

People in the room traded glances, and murmured to each other. Nielsen let the weight of his words hang out there for effect before continuing. "Risk analysis from the last expedition has been compiled to provide a comprehensive threat assessment…although all of you have read the debriefing, some of what you're about to hear may still shock you. But, for the safety of this expedition, we must take these threats seriously."

He paused, looking around the room. Tracey thought he looked like a principal scolding a classroom of children. "The island is unstable. Not only does it phase in and out of this dimension, it emits energy that can interfere with scanning. It's played havoc with our satellites and radar. However, it is inconsistent. The EMI waxes and wanes, and it is during the troughs that we have obtained what little surveillance data we have remotely. However, the most reliable way to gather data is on the island itself.

"We do not expect the containment field to hold up." The murmurs started again, louder than before. "That's right, folks. We totally expect to be cut-off once on the island. Not permanently, of course. This isn't a one-way ticket. Our technicians, guided by data transmitted from our vessels circling the island, will do their best to raise a stable containment field when possible. However, our focus will be on the island.

"Once we land on the island, there are a variety of threats coming from indigenous flora and fauna. Firstly, I have provided you with a detailed list of dangerous plant life, as related by a botanist from the last expedition. There are plants that sting, plants that paralyze, and toxic plants that can kill with the slightest contact with the skin. Our expedition will have two scouts who will identify any of these known threats so they may be circumvented or negotiated safely.

"Secondly, as I'm sure you've read and may not believe, there are animals on this island that pose a significant threat, namely dinosaurs." He paused as the room erupted into a combination of scoffs, chortles, and gasps conveying everything from disbelief to mockery. When the room quieted down, Nielsen continued. "It's true, and we are fortunate to have a paleontologist with us here today who was on the last expedition. We will listen to her guidance on what we can expect once on the island."

Everyone looked around the room to see who the paleontologist was. Marcy leaned in and whispered to Tracey, "This is so exciting. My little nephew would freak if he knew I was going to see dinosaurs, if it wasn't for the NDA."

Tracey noticed a man dressed in camouflage enter the room and stand off to the side. She knew who this was going to be.

When the room settled down, Nielsen cleared his throat and continued. "There appears to be the presence of an indigenous tribe on the island. Data gathered from the last expedition indicates that they are not a significant threat. In fact, the last expedition had established a relationship with them, and several of our staff are still on the island, presumably with them. Our main objective is to locate and rescue our stranded employees. Our secondary objective is data collection for off-site processing."

"What about security?" blurted Tracey.

Nielsen nodded. "I'll leave that up to our security detail leader, Rudy Collins." He nodded, and the man in camouflage stepped to the front of the room and cleared his throat.

"Thank you, Mr. Nielsen. Hi, my name is Rudy, and my job is to keep the expedition safe."

"Funny," shouted Tracey, "that's what the last security team leader said, and none of his detail made it back."

Marcy nudged Tracey. "Come on. What are you doing?"

Collins scowled. "Yes, that was...unfortunate. I knew Mario. He was a good man. But he was unprepared. His detail was too small and underequipped. I assure you, we're larger and better equipped. Plus, we have learned from his mistakes."

Tracey stood up, indignant, forgetting where she was. "Mistakes? Mistakes?" Marcy grabbed her arm, but Tracey shook her off. "People died. People like you, Collins, who thought their training and weaponry would protect them, died. When the T. rexes came swooping in, they destroyed our helicopters and devoured Mario's men one-by-one."

She walked towards the front of the room as she accosted Collins until she was practically nose-to-nose with him. "How do you plan on dealing with a fifteen-foot tall eating machine with legs like tree trunks and teeth like hunting knives? What marvel of modern technology will you use then?"

Collins didn't budge an inch. "We're going to clear the Landing Zone with a cargo plane using 'Daisy Cutters.' We have two light squads of nine each and two weapons squads of twelve each. One weapons squad will remain near the staging base, serving as security and a reserve. They'll be equipped with AT4s and guided anti-tank missiles. We have Humvee-mounted anti-tank rifles and MK19 belt-fed automatic grenade launchers. This time we certainly won't leave our birds parked on the ground to be destroyed. In fact, they'll be mobile, Hueys with gunship configurations, able to track and take down a T. rex on the move."

"Hueys? Aren't they a bit old school?" asked Tracey.

"This is the private sector," reminded Collins. "We use what's available and whatever Poseidon Tech will pay for. They'll do the trick."

Tracey met his gaze with hers, her eyes burning with intensity. "How do you know this is all going to work?"

Collins didn't blink. "We are also equipping members of the team, including you, with the latest in camouflage, fabric that actually bends light." He nodded to a man standing at the back of the room, also clad in camo. The man stepped forward and handed Collins what looked like a folded tablecloth. Collins turned it in his hands, pinched an edge, and unfurled it. Suddenly, his legs appeared to vanish before everyone in the room. There were gasps and murmurs from the crowd.

Collins looked at Tracey. "May I?"

Tracey, stunned, nodded.

Collins addressed the group. "If a dinosaur penetrates our screen, you can find a spot to hide..." he draped the sheet of cloth over Tracey, "...and blend into the environment as a last resort."

There were oohs, aahs, and applause from the crowd of technicians and data analysts. Tracey wasn't able to see them through the material, but she pulled it off her head, balled it up, and shoved it into Collins' hands.

Nielsen quickly stepped up to the front of the room. "Thank you, Rudy. I have complete faith in your detail's training." He waved a hand in front of Tracey. "Ladies and gentlemen, I introduce to you the paleontologist who will be accompanying us, sharing her expertise and experience, Dr. Tracey Moran."

There were stunned looks and applause, as if her interjection was all part of the show. Marcy looked positively flabbergasted, and she clapped enthusiastically.

When the noise died down and all eyes were expectantly on her, Tracey leaned against the metal table and eyed the group with a combination of pity and contempt. "This is no pleasure jaunt, I assure you all. I was in the last expedition. I was awed when I saw my first dinosaurs, two T. rexes, but the effect wore off quickly when they ate our security detail and nearly killed the rest of us. They can see you, even if you remain still, and one damn near climbed a hill, using its little arms, to eat my group."

She turned to Collins. "With all due respect to your training and experience, your Hueys may take one down, but what about velociraptors? They're smaller and agile, and they picked off several of our group and the indigenous warriors who had experience with them.

"You can blow up the whole damned jungle, but there are other things…" she paused, pondering how exactly to explain, "…more preternatural, even supernatural elements of the island that your grenade launchers and 'copters can't touch."

Collins snickered and looked at Nielsen. "What in the hell is she talking about…supernatural?" His amusement faded when he saw the grave look on Nielsen's face.

Nielsen stabbed a finger into the air. "Funny you should mention that…" He pressed some keys on his laptop. "Our technicians analyzed the flight recorder your expedition recovered, Dr. Moran. They found something…unusual. Something strange."

"Something stranger than an island from another dimension with dinosaurs?" quipped Collins.

A chill shot down Tracey's spine, and her skin erupted in goosebumps.

"Let me play it for you," said Nielsen, pressing a button. A voice recording played out of his speakers. It was the pilot talking. His chatter turned to panic, then static, then an eerie, scratchy voice over the static, 'Cooooooome to meeeeee.' Then more static.

"What was that?" gasped Tracey.

Nielsen held up a hand, signaling it wasn't over yet. 'You're miiiiiine!' Then nothing.

Everyone in the room was silent, exchanging horrified looks.

"Maybe explain what else happened on the island," said Nielsen.

Tracey swallowed hard. "The island affected some people in rather peculiar and…unnatural ways. The previous team leader, Mike Deluca, found something in a temple, deep underground. It changed him. It allowed him to raise the dead. He…he created zombies."

"This is ridiculous," said someone in the room. "You expect us to believe all this?"

"Believe it," said Nielsen. "Your life literally depends on it. If anyone wants to back out, now is the time. If you're not on board with all of this, you're a liability. You have one hour to decide." He closed his laptop and thanked Rudy, shaking his hand. "Prep your team. We go in exactly one hour." Then he turned to Tracey. "Are you sure you're still up for this?"

"Do I have a choice?"

"You do, as a matter of fact. What do you think of our preparations?"

Tracey paused a moment. "Your intel is spot on. Do you think Collins and his men can handle it?"

"Short of using the actual military, his outfit is the best there is, and they are better equipped than Torres' men. We spared no expense this time."

Tracey's eyes narrowed. "What's Poseidon's interest in all this? You got paid for recovering the flight recorder."

"We still have people on the island. *You* still have people on the island, Dr. Moran."

"That's exactly what David Lennox said."

"He's correct."

"Come on," pressed Tracey. "There has to be something else. Some other reason."

Nielsen smiled, a strange departure from his permanent scowl. "You mean first dibs on the exploration of another dimension?"

"Yes, but to what end?"

He winked at her. "That's for us to worry about. You worry about bringing your friend home and helping keep our team safe." He bowed his head slightly and left the cafeteria.

Marcy approached cautiously, eyes wide in awe and apparent admiration. "Holy smokes. I had no idea it was you. I mean, you were her. Uh, you were you."

Tracey smirked. "Who else would I be?"

Marcy cocked her head sideways. "Come on. You know what I mean."

"Marcy, you don't have to do this. Go home."

Marcy raised her eyebrows. "No way. Are you kidding? This sounds..."

"Dangerous," said Tracey, finishing her sentence.

"I was thinking like an experience of a lifetime. Come on, Tracey. *You're* going."

"I have unfinished business on the island. I left someone behind that I care about very much."

Marcy gasped. "The other paleontologist?"

Tracey nodded. "You have your whole life ahead of you."

"Yeah, but I want to be a part of history. Another dimension, dinosaurs. This is huge."

"That island changes people. You may not like what you find out about yourself."

That remark clearly confused Marcy.

Tracey threw her hands up in exasperation. Her appeal was falling on deaf ears. "Listen, you stay close to me and do as I say. Understood?"

Marcy grinned from ear to ear and her eyes lit up. "Yes. Whatever you say."

"You know that nephew of yours?"

Marcy nodded.

"You might want to say goodbye to him."

* * *

Peter entered a large stone structure with impressive pillars in front. While the other buildings had windows, this one did not. He marveled at the architecture, which was amazing for a species with only three clawed fingers and no opposable thumbs. It was cold and dark, multi-colored orbs casting peculiar light. A strange, discordant music piped in from an unknown source. They passed through a large antechamber stocked with around a dozen guards, and he was led to a crude staircase. Two of the guards he followed stood aside, allowing everyone else to climb the stairs. When Peter passed them, they stood in front of the staircase, guarding it. Peter wasn't sure if it was to keep others out or him in.

When they reached a landing up above, they turned left and marched down a long hallway. On the walls, runes were arranged, set in the stone. The pattern, if there was any, seemed haphazard to Peter. At last, they brought him to a set of double stone doors. One of the guards waved a claw over a rune, and the door opened to the sound of stone grinding on stone.

The guards stepped aside, gesturing for Peter to enter. Not wanting to be rude, Peter did as he was asked and stepped into the dark room where the strange, almost cosmic music was louder. As the door closed behind him, he was enveloped in darkness. In the pitch black, Peter was unsure how large the room actually was. He focused on his power from the orbs embedded in his chest, and in response they grew in illumination. However, his light was snuffed out by the darkness around him, as if it was alive and hungry, devouring his light.

"Hello?" His voice echoed, indicating that the room was of significant size.

As if in answer, a single purple light emanated from twenty or so feet in front of him. It looked to Peter like one of those crystal orbs. He nearly jumped out of his skin when a figure stepped into the light.

Peter caught his breath, touching his hand to his chest where he found his heart beating like a drum. "You...you frightened me." He cursed himself silently as soon as he had said it. He was supposed to be a god, or at least a reasonable facsimile of one. He needed to project more confidence. He hoped whatever it was didn't understand English.

The reptilian man standing by the orb beckoned him over, curling its fingers towards itself. Peter stepped forward toward the crystal orb. As he drew closer, he saw that it was placed on a small pedestal, waist high. The reptilian man was shorter than the others, and dressed in a shimmering purple fabric. At least Peter assumed it was a man, but he wasn't certain.

The figure watched him with emotionless black eyes. Peter saw his own reflection in them cast in a purple hue. The cosmic music lowered in volume as he approached. The lizard humanoid gestured for Peter to touch the crystal orb. Peter knew it wanted to communicate, and he was sure this was going to be the modality.

He reached out with his right hand and lay his palm on the crystal orb, wincing as he braced his mind for a flood of images. He was surprised when none came. He took his hand off the orb and looked at his palm bathed in ethereal purple light.

Peter startled when the figure gently grabbed his hand and placed it on top of the orb. It then placed its claw on the bottom. A voice entered Peter's mind, or rather it was an idea. 'Why do you come?'

Peter opened his mouth to speak but figured it was unnecessary. He stared into the creature's eyes and thought. 'Peace.'

'No war with you.'

'You hurt my friends. Want it to stop. Peace.'

The lizard being cocked its head sideways a bit. 'Not me. Others.'

'Why?'

'They feed. They conquer. They take.'

'Are you their leader? Their chief?'

'I am...' Several notions without translation entered Peter's mind. He was unsure of their exact meaning, but he got the sense that this being wasn't a warrior or marauder. He was some kind of thinker. Suddenly the room around him transformed, like a dark movie theater when the projector came on, only the entire room was the screen. Peter knew simultaneously that what he was about to see was going to be projected from this being's mind, and the projection wasn't actually all around him but in his own mind.

The creature conjured scenes of the lizard men hunting other animals, bovine as well as reptilian. It also summoned scenes of being hunted by the larger dinosaurs, namely the Tyrannosaurus rex. Peter thought it was good they had a common enemy, an apex predator, that it might aid in diplomacy. The scene shifted, evaporating, replaced by one where the lizard men warred with a society of apes. The apes appeared muscular and fierce, wielding simple weapons like spears and clubs. However, on the battlefield they clearly communicated with each other. The scene was savage and bloody as the two races slaughtered each other.

Peter looked at the reptilian figure before him. 'Why do you show me this?'

However, there was no answer. Rather, the figure removed its claw from the bottom of the orb, terminating the playback.

Peter took his hand off the crystal orb. 'I...I don't understand. Help me understand.'

The door opened behind him, casting faint illumination into the room. Peter held his hand up over his face to shield his eyes. Several guards marched inside and seized Peter by his arms. He wriggled to escape, but their grip was tight. Claws dug into his skin, stinging him, as he cried out. "What? What happened?"

A figure strode into the room. It walked right up to Peter and glared at him with cold, lifeless eyes. It then turned to the figure in the purple tunic, and in some kind of display of emotion flared the flap of skin under its chin, extending it like a small sail. It hissed at the other creature. The two of them communicated in a most peculiar way, their bodies becoming rigid as they hissed at each other and whipped their tails behind them. Peter only watched in stunned silence. After this carried on for several minutes, the one that had barged in made guttural sounds at the guards, and they dragged Peter from the room.

"What? What did I do? What's wrong?" Peter cried out as he was dragged away.

CHAPTER 3

Mary and Jason crouched outside, waiting for their friend to emerge from the temple. Night had fallen on the island, and the moon was high and full. Jason checked his wristwatch and sighed.

"Are you kidding me?" chuckled Mary. "You know your watch is useless here."

Jason shrugged. "What? Old habits." He looked at the mouth of the temple. "He's not coming out, is he?"

"Dammit." Mary stood up and paced around. "I knew this was a mistake."

"No, you didn't," said Jason. "You told him it was the right thing to do...the *only* thing for him to do."

"I didn't see you try to stop him."

Now Jason stood up and faced her. "No, but I offered to go with him. Maybe if I had gone, he'd be back right now, and in one piece."

Mary balled her fists at her side, and she was about to deliver her retort when there was a stomping of feet and rustling of vegetation off to their right. They both instinctively froze, drawing their shoulders up to their ears and gritting their teeth. Jason grabbed Mary by the arm and pulled her down into the underbrush, shushing her. They crouched next to a large tree with a massive trunk and large, thick roots protruding from the ground, offering them cover.

A large animal ambled out of the bushes, hobbling along, casting a strange silhouette against the moonlight. Plates jutted from its back, and it swung a tail tipped with large spikes behind it.

Mary and Jason both released the breaths they were holding and sighed deeply in relief.

"It's a Stegosaurus," said Jason, rolling his eyes at how foolish they had been.

"We were lucky," said Mary, admiring the majestic creature as it mulled around, chomping on plants.

"Kind of like a big cow," winked Jason, trying to lighten the mood.

Mary put her hands on her hips. "It's nothing like a cow, you jackass."

Jason looked around. "Well, we should go before something nastier than a Stegosaurus decides to pop out and say hello."

They both stood up. Mary turned to head back to the tribal village on the plateau when Jason placed a firm hand on her shoulder. She wheeled around. "What now?"

Jason cupped a hand over her mouth and pulled her back against the tree trunk. "Shhhhh," he whispered into her ear. Her body went rigid against his as her eyes darted around the surrounding area. He knew when she saw it, because she held her breath. He released his hand from over her mouth and whispered directly into her right ear, "It's over there, in the shadow of that big tree."

Jason smelled it right before he saw it. He wouldn't have seen it unless it had shifted a bit, altering the contour of the tree's shadow ever so slightly. It stood, crouched, arms hanging down in front of it. A low, faint snort carried on the island breeze, barely masked by the wind.

Fortunately, it didn't look like it was facing them. At least Jason hadn't hoped so. "Be very still." He couldn't unshoulder his rifle without attracting its attention, so instead his hand moved to his handgun in its holster on his hip. He unsnapped the strap and grabbed the handle very slowly. Mary began to tremble against his body. He ever so slowly slid the handgun out of its holster, slipping it behind Mary's body for concealment. "If it runs at us," he whispered, "just run. Don't look back."

He thought it might have been a T. rex, but he knew they weren't ambush predators. Not like this. Its arms hung low and were too long for a T. rex. It was too big to be a velociraptor. It moved its head, and large, hornlike protrusions gave it away. It was an Allosaurus.

It darted out from the shadows, claws extended and spread, lunging past them. It was going for the Stegosaurus.

Jason watched as the Allosaurus opened its mouth at an insane angle. It collided with the Stegosaurus, blindsiding it, sinking its teeth into the flesh of its haunch. Mary tried to run, but he pulled her close into a firm embrace, his back against the tree. "Not yet," he whispered. He slid his back laterally along the tree trunk, positioning them so that they weren't visible. Then he pulled her into another crouch. "They can be pack hunters, remember?" he whispered.

Mary nodded. Jason's eyes darted around, searching the shadows for others.

The Stegosaurus cried out as the Allosaurus worked its articulated jaw, sawing back and forth with its teeth. The Stegosaurus bucked, turning and swinging its spiked tail.

The massive tree trunk behind Jason and Mary shook, and strange seed pods rained down from above, pelting their heads. Something had struck the tree. The head of the Stegosaurus jutted out to the right, as if it had tried to run for it, but it stopped, its right eye wide in horror. Its body jostled as the Allosaurus tore into its side with its jaws.

There was a loud thump, and the Allosaurus let out a high-pitched yelp. The Stegosaurus lunged forward as its tail swung around, this time missing its assailant and wrapping around the tree trunk, shaking the tree some more. The Allosaurus limped past the left side of the tree and cut right in front of Mary and Jason, lunging at its prey with massive jaws, only to get a mouthful of bony plates. Its own haunch was gored and its tail whipped behind it, just missing Mary and Jason.

Jason side-stepped, sliding his back along the rough bark of the trunk, dragging Mary with him, until they were on the other side of the tree, leaving the scuffle behind them. Crouched in front of them was another Allosaurus, and he was looking right at them.

"Oh, hell." Jason shoved Mary back around the tree trunk as it sprang at them, jaws open wide, just missing them and getting a mouthful of bark. Back around the other side, the first Allosaurus and Stegosaurus battled, shifting their feet and kicking up dirt and dust. The predator snapped its massive jaws, and the prey swung its spiked tail, each only finding purchase part of the time.

Jason now ran around the tree trunk, narrowly ducking a swipe of a spiked tail, pulling Mary behind him by the hand. The second Allosaurus sniffed the air. Smelling blood, it quickly became interested in the Stegosaurus. Forgetting about the two small morsels, it joined its fellow hunter in taking down the now outnumbered herbivore.

"Now we run," Jason muttered to Mary, and they took off in a mad dash away from the brutal scene and toward the tribal village.

* * *

Tracey lay in her cot in the cafeteria, trying to fathom the notion of getting rest before the expedition tomorrow. She turned on her side and stared at all of the other cots arranged in rows, filled with Poseidon Tech personnel. Collins and his men must've been passing the night somewhere else on the rig, as they were nowhere to be found.

Marcy turned over on her cot and smiled when she saw Tracey was awake. "Can't sleep?" she whispered.

Tracey shook her head.

"Me neither. Nervous?"

"Terrified. You?"

"A mixture of nervous and excited. What made you want to go into paleontology?"

"You've got to be kidding."

Marcy shrugged her shoulders. "Why? It's so interesting. I bet you'd never thought it'd lead you here."

"You got that right." Tracey saw that Marcy wasn't going to let it drop, and her interest seemed sincere. "I always loved dinosaurs since I was a little kid. When I was three, I was able to identify them by genus, species, and period."

Marcy giggled. "Holy crap. You read about dinosaurs at three? That's impressive."

Tracey shook her head, and a wistful smile crept onto her face. "No, my dad read it to me, repeatedly, because I asked him to."

"Is he proud that you became a paleontologist?"

Tracey smiled. "He told me he'd be proud of me no matter what I'd become because he knew I'd become something great."

Marcy slipped her arm, bent at the elbow, under her head as a pillow. "Your dad sounds cool."

"He is. How about you? How does a data analyst end up in a situation like this?"

"Data engineer."

"Oh, sorry. Data engineer."

Marcy smiled and shrugged. "I was always good with computers, and I'm super organized. It seemed like a good fit, and the pay isn't bad either."

Tracey smirked. "Pays better than a paleontologist. That's for sure."

The smile faded from Marcy's face, and she bit her bottom lip. "Is that why you signed on? For the money?"

Tracey sighed. "To be honest, it was a major factor the first time around. That and the adventure of it all. Now, I'm doing it for another reason."

"Dr. Albanese?"

"Yeah, but that's only part of it. The first time, I wasn't very principled or heroic. In fact, I was kind of a coward."

"So, you want to prove to yourself that you're not a coward?"

"Yeah, but it's not just about the dangers and pitfalls of the island."

Marcy shimmied closer and her eyes widened. "So, it *is* Dr. Albanese." She chuckled and covered her mouth with her hand to stifle the sound.

Tracey now realized that Marcy was a bit younger than her. She figured she was in her mid-twenties or so. "I had a good guy right in front of me, someone with whom I shared so much in common, and I was afraid to open up to him."

Marcy reached out and touched Tracey on the hand. "I haven't met someone like that yet. I didn't even start to date till the end of college. Grad school was a big commitment, so there wasn't much dating there."

Tracey smiled. This girl sounded like one of her students back at the university. She decided she was starting to like Marcy. "Same here. I didn't start dating until after grad school, but then I was travelling to dig sites…there just wasn't the time. On top of that, try finding a guy who understands what I do, let alone finds it interesting. It was always an empty spot in my life. I had accomplished so much, yet I was lonely."

Marcy arched an eyebrow. "So, did you and Dr. Albanese…?"

"Peter? Oh, no." Tracey chuckled. "I think he always wanted to ask, but… I don't know. The thought of dating a friend and co-worker was…daunting."

"Girl, you *are* a coward."

They shared a stifled chortle.

"We need to get our rest for tomorrow," said Tracey. "I have to keep my eyes peeled for carnivorous dinosaurs."

"And Dr. Albanese," added Marcy. "Good night."

"Good night." Tracey rolled over and closed her eyes.

* * *

Peter awoke, his vision blurry and his head pounding. His back was killing him, and as he got his bearings, he realized he was lying on a hard surface. He reached out and felt smooth stone beneath him. As his vision adjusted, he realized that he was in a dark room illuminated only by a red crystal orb embedded in the wall.

So much for being treated like a god. He sat up, fighting back a wave of nausea, realizing that he was likely concussed and definitely dehydrated. He closed his eyes for a moment, reached into himself for his special healing power, and allowed it to wash over him. When he opened his eyes again, the pain and nausea was gone.

He pushed himself to standing and saw that he was in a twenty by twenty-foot stone room that was sealed off by an iron gate. The entire room was cast in a red hue due to the crystal illumination. Peter wondered if the crystal was only for light. He stepped forward, gripped the bars, and peeked outside.

A reptilian guard clutching a crude spear patrolled the hallway. Peter figured he was in some kind of dungeon cell. He wondered what had gone wrong upstairs. They hadn't killed him outright, but he was being held prisoner. He thought back to the thinking lizard and the images projected within his mind, the historical record. What did he see that maybe he wasn't supposed to see? He wondered why he was being kept alive. Was it for interrogation? Would there be torture?

He heard sounds coming from somewhere down the hallway, and four guards marched down toward his cell. Peter dashed back toward his corner where he had been left, and sat with his back leaning against the wall. When the guards stopped in front of his cell, he rubbed his head and moaned, playing up his injuries.

One guard produced a large iron key and unlocked the iron gate. It swung outward, and three of the guards entered his cell. Two of them flanked him, pointing their spear tips at his chest. The third held a bag. It gestured for Peter to rise with its three clawed hand, eyeing him with those cold, black eyes.

Peter appeared to struggle to stand, clutching his back and groaning, playing the part of the weak and injured. Acting had never been his strong suit, but he figured these lizards' inexperience with human body language would smooth over the rough edges of his performance as nuances were often lost in translation.

The two flanking guards jabbed spear tips at him, menacing him. The third reached into his sack and produced a snake coiled around the lizard man's arm. It licked the air, tasting it, searching.

Peter knew this wasn't good, whatever it was for. The lizard man extended its arm towards Peter, and the snake stretched in his direction, its eyes glinting red in the crystalline light, flicking its tongue in and out of its mouth.

Peter wondered if it was a test. He decided not to flinch. His only option, flanked by sharp spear tips, was to remain still and calm. The snake hovered its face in front of Peter's, touching Peter's nose with its tongue, drinking in his barely concealed fear. Faster than Peter's mind could process, the snake lunged at his face and sank its fangs into his left cheek.

Peter instinctively grabbed the snake with both hands, but the toxin worked fast. His vision quickly blurred and his head swam. His muscles went limp, and he dropped to the floor, his head hitting the stone hard. Yet, he felt no pain.

The serpent handler placed the snake back into the bag and left the cell. The other two picked Peter up and followed the third, dragging Peter's legs across the hard ground. Peter was helpless as they dragged him out of the dungeon block. He felt nothing, which led him to believe that he had been anesthetized.

They brought him to another cold, dark room and lay him on a stone slab. It looked to Peter like an altar, and his mind raced with terrible notions of sacrifice. He lay face-up as the guards backed away. Another lizard man stepped forward, palming a small blue orb. Peter felt this being enter his mind, only this time there was no communication, no wordless voice.

Rather, this time it felt as if this creature was accessing his thoughts, more specifically his memories. Peter tried to resist, but he had no access to his muscles for fight or flight. He tried to control his thoughts, directing this lizard being away from anything sensitive, but to no avail. He felt it access his thoughts about the orbs that resided in his chest, his intentions regarding the lizard man race, as well as his feelings for the Umazoa, Mary, and even Tracey. He felt the creature probe his deepest secrets, specifically the plan to evacuate the Umazoan village should he not return. The reptilian inquisitor then toggled through more memories and impressions, settling on Peter's memory of the vision of the ape race. The reptile probed deeper. To Peter, it felt as if someone was scraping around the inside of his skull with a sharp implement.

At last, the reptilian inquisitor released Peter's mind. It motioned to the guards to take him away. Peter knew he'd served his purpose, whatever it was, and he wasn't going to like whatever came next. He immediately pondered his two possibilities. He could tap into the death orb and wipe all those out around him, but then he'd be left lying on the ground, paralyzed while more would surely come and kill him where he lay helpless. His other option was to heal himself quietly so when he took further action, he'd be strong enough to run.

He decided to heal himself, tapping his life orb within his chest. Unfortunately, it caused his chest to illuminate more. Worse yet, it pulsated as he healed, but he hadn't any other options.

He was dragged quite a distance through tunnels and eventually laid to rest on a crude raft made of long branches lashed together. Other lizard beings emerged all around him. Some appeared to be females, as apparent by their curvier appearances and the shape of breasts underneath their crude tunics.

As Peter pondered the perplexing juxtaposition of mammalian traits in the reptilian creatures, they arranged skulls and bones around him on the raft. The more he focused on what they were doing, the more his healing suffered from interruption, as the ability required intense concentration.

He decided to close his eyes and block out everything going on around him. He used all of his focus to expel the snake toxin from his body. His chest grew in warmth as he reached deep, tapping the power of the life orb. He felt his body's cells metabolize the toxin, gradually restoring agency over his own muscles.

He wasn't sure how much time had passed, but when he opened his eyes, he was blinded by sunlight. He felt every muscle of his body once again, and he felt the island breeze on his skin. He felt sweat trickle down his right temple, and he heard the burbling of running water. As he squinted and his eyes adjusted to sunlight, he processed the scene enfolding around him.

The thinking lizard from before loomed above him in some ceremonial garment, hands extended out, and it was making strange throaty sounds. Others stood around it, watching the thinking lizard. Peter wanted to lift his head to see what was at his feet, but to do so would have been to reveal his restoration.

Instead, he closed his eyes once more, this time tapping into the death orb inside his chest. He hadn't wanted to consider using this power, but he now felt as if he had no choice. If he didn't kill them, they'd kill him. At least he was outside, where he could make a break for it before reinforcements arrived.

It was his first time attempting to tap into this dark energy, so he was uncertain of how to proceed. He reached out and sensed their lifeforces. Their heartbeats, slower than those of humans, beat within his mind. He used the power of the life orb to accomplish this, but he'd have to access the death orb to quash their lives. He reached out, probing within himself, searching for the dark energy, straining.

His concentration was interrupted by the loud blowing of a horn and the sensation of being lifted. He opened his eyes and saw two lizard men standing over him, carrying his raft laden with skulls and bones like pallbearers hoisting a coffin. They took several steps forward, and Peter was lowered again. Only this time, the ground wasn't solid. He bobbed up and down. By the time he realized he was floating in water, they had released the raft, and the current took him away.

As he passed away from them and reached what he figured to be a safe distance, he lifted his head to look at his feet. He was, indeed, being sent down a river, away from the lizard hive. Again, he heard the blaring of a horn, over and over again. As he lay back, out of the corner of his eye he swore he saw movement. Startled, he sat up on his elbows and caught the crest of something dip beneath the water.

His heart raced as he reached out for signs of life in close proximity, and he found something. Something big. The sensation reminded him of fishing on his uncle's boat and the fish finder pinging something large. Only Peter wasn't fishing. He was the bait.

To his left, in his peripheral vision, he caught a swift movement and turned his head in time to see five feet of arched neural spines disappear under the water, followed by two feet of a longer run of spines. Peter saw a large shadow pass ahead of the raft.

He sat up on his raft, spilling bones into the river as the current gently swept him along. Up ahead, he saw a long rock rise out of the water. However, as he was swept closer, he realized it was no rock. It was a crocodilian head breaching the water's surface, elongated spines rising behind it. Peter rolled off the raft and into the water as a large mouth opened, chomping down on the raft with large conical teeth.

The raft immediately splintered under the force of massive jaws as Peter frantically kicked his legs, swimming sideways towards shore. Fifty feet of shadow passed under him. Its tail swept back and forth, propelling the predator through the water. Peter knew this theropod, and he knew that he didn't stand a chance against a Spinosaurus in the water.

He also knew, given the length of the Spinosaurus and the width of the river, he had a brief moment to make it to shore before it turned completely around to make another pass at him. As he swam, attempting a direct perpendicular route to shore, his trajectory took on more of a hypotenuse due to the river's current. He heard a massive splash behind him, and fear gripped his brain as he registered its meaning. It was coming for him. He had only seconds.

He felt the river bank ride up to meet him, and he shifted to a standing position. He ran, splashing, making a break for shore as he caught the massive theropod rising up out of the water behind him. He darted to the right as it dove at him, missing him. It, however, collided with him, spinning him sideways and knocking him off his feet.

It turned abruptly, pushing him back into the river. Its size made its movements on land clumsy and imprecise, and it struggled to snatch the tiny morsel. However, the current took Peter once more, rolling him past its hind legs. It spun around on its legs, roaring in fury and whipping its fanned tail, as it searched the river for its elusive meal.

Peter quickly held his breath and dipped below the surface of the water. If it couldn't spot him, he had a chance. If it spotted him, in the water using its fanned tail, it would close the distance within seconds.

Under the water's surface, rolling in the current, Peter was unable to see if the massive beast was pursuing him. Instead, he curled into a ball, bracing himself for large teeth closing in on him. At last, he had to come up for air. He breached the surface, gasping, his lungs burning as they filled with much needed oxygen. He rubbed the water out of his eyes as he heard another roar and saw the Spinosaurus slide back into the water.

Peter felt the current pick up, and the jungle on either side raced past him. The water gurgled louder now, and he turned to find that he had entered rapids. He looked over his shoulder and saw the arched spines racing towards him, closing in fast.

Suddenly, he felt the sharp pain of being slammed against a rock, knocking the wind out of him. He dipped beneath the surface, swallowing water, and popped back up again. He collided with another rock, slamming his head, and warm blood ran into his eyes. He moved faster now, merciless against the quickening current, bouncing like a pin ball against rocks, being rolled by dips and turns in the river.

Massive jaws opened and snapped shut, barely missing him, as the Spinosaurus was forced to stand up in the shallow depth, buying Peter just enough time to be swept away from it and out of its reach. He glimpsed that it only stood there, its chest heaving from exertion. Apparently, it had decided against pursuing such a small morsel through the shallow rapids.

Relieved, Peter's triumph was cut short by a massive blow to his head and the world going dark.

CHAPTER 4

Tracey saw the clearing made by the aptly named 'Daisy Cutters' out of the helicopter window. Her stomach lurched as the copter dipped, hovering over a spot in the clearing. She felt the landing blades touch dirt, and the pilot signaled for her and the others to exit.

As she hopped out, ducking her head, she saw the other copters and teams exiting their aircraft. The choppers took off immediately, and Tracey scanned the ground for animal prints, specifically theropod prints.

Her attention, however, was drawn to the sky, which was flickering. Discharges of electricity forked horizontally across the sky. It appeared as if a dome covered the island, and the atmosphere outside was hot pink in color. Nielsen walked directly to her.

"Do you see any prints?" he asked, looking up at the sky. He saw she was looking up at the show rather than down at the ground. "It's the containment bubble. It's unstable. The helicopters have to get out before it decompensates."

As the staccato chopping of helicopter blades grew distant, they were replaced by the gunning of Humvee engines. Tracey looked around and watched Collins' men assemble the staging base. Poseidon Tech staff melded with the paramilitary security detail, erecting tents and establishing com links. Collins' men set up a perimeter around base camp, while the weapons teams set up the Humvee-mounted weaponry. Pilots fueled the two Hueys for reconnaissance and potential air support.

Tracey noted this expedition was larger and better equipped than the last one. She had never heard of a belt-fed grenade launcher before, but it sounded promising. She allowed herself to feel cautiously optimistic. "It's a little big, don't you think?"

"What do you mean?" shouted Nielsen over the din.

"Don't you think this is going to attract attention?"

Collins strode up to the two of them, watching his men and shouting directions.

"Dr. Moran is afraid we're being too noisy," said Nielsen. "That we're going to draw the dinosaurs to us."

Collins shook his head. "Negative. We've got radar up and operational. Within minutes we'll have drones scouting the area." As if in response to his statement, several drones mounted with mini cameras buzzed into the air like bumble bees and scattered.

"Dr. Moran, what about the ground?" reminded Nielsen. "We need you to look for prints, anything that might indicate an imminent threat."

When Tracey looked hesitant, Collins added, "I'll send one of my men with you."

Tracey glared at him. "If a T. rex decided to barrel out of the tree line and attack me, your man would only be the appetizer to my entrée."

Collins nodded. He waved at one of the men operating one of the Humvees. The man shouted something at another, who then hopped in the back. The first man jumped into the driver's seat, turned the ignition, and threw the Humvee into gear. He drove over to where Tracey, Collins, and Nielsen were standing and stopped.

"This is Trevino and Roach." Each man nodded in-turn. "You'll go with them," said Collins, gesturing to the Humvee with his right hand. "They are more than equipped to take down a T. rex."

"We've got your back, ma'am," said Trevino.

"Yeah?" said Tracey. "I feel safer already." She lingered a moment, maintaining eye contact with Collins. She sighed and hopped into the Humvee. The man in the back manning the grenade launcher offered her his hand, but she ignored it.

"Follow her every instruction," said Collins. "She's the expert."

"Yessir," said Trevino and Roach, almost in unison. They took off.

As Trevino drove away, he looked at Tracey and smiled. "Where to first?"

Tracey looked around. "Take me out a ways."

"Sure thing."

The Humvee tore off past the tents and out into the clearing.

"Slow down," said Tracey.

Trevino dropped it into low gear and reduced his speed. She hung out over the open side, scanning the ground. "Stop. Here."

Trevino stepped on the brake and came to a stop. Tracey hopped out, her eyes darting back and forth all over the dirt. She walked twenty feet away from the Humvee and crouched.

"Keep your eyes peeled on the tree line," she heard Trevino tell Roach.

She reached down and probed the dirt with her finger. "I've got tracks!"

"Anything we need to worry about?" asked Roach.

Tracey followed the direction of the tracks, out further into the clearing. She squinted her eyes, extended an arm, and pointed her right index finger. "Take me there."

Trevino and Roach both turned to look where she was pointing. "What's there?" asked Trevino.

Tracey stood, dusting off her thighs with her hands. "That's where the tracks lead. There's something there."

"I gotta radio this in," said Trevino. He grabbed his radio. "Stallion to Chief. Come in."

"Stallion?" Tracey rolled her eyes. "I thought you guys were supposed to be like 'B2 to B7' and such."

Trevino winked at her. "This is private sector, doc."

His radio crackled. 'Yeah, what is it, Stallion?"

"Dr. Moran has found something."

'What is it?'

Trevino pulled his radio away from his mouth and looked at Tracy, waiting.

"There are prints," said Tracey. "They don't look like theropods, but I want to check it out anyway."

Trevino got on his radio again. "They're not theropods, but she wants to check it out."

'So, check it out,' said Collins.

"Copy that. Over and out." Trevino jerked his head, indicating for Tracey to hop in. "Let's go, doc."

Tracey rounded the Humvee and pulled herself inside, and Trevino took off. Tracey looked back at Roach manning the grenade launcher. His eyes were peeled on the terrain ahead while keeping an eye on the tree line. Suddenly, his eyes widened. "We've got dinos!" He trained the grenade launcher straight ahead.

Tracey turned around and saw what he saw. Trevino hit the brakes, and the Humvee skidded to a halt in the dirt. "We've got dinos," he gasped.

Tracey hopped out of the Humvee and darted off in their direction.

"Hey, wait!" Trevino called after her.

"Where the hell does she think she's going?" asked Roach.

Tracey didn't look back. As she was able to get a better look, her fast walk turned into a jog. Within minutes, she saw them, dozens of them, lying on the ground—most of them dead, the rest dying. "Jesus Christ."

Lying on the ground, strewn about, were the bodies of a herd of Stegosauruses. Most had been charred almost beyond recognition. If it wasn't for the tell-tale dorsal plates, she might not have recognized the species right away.

Trevino caught up to her, assault rifle trained at the dead stegosaur in front of her. "What are you, crazy, lady? Never do that."

"We're not in any danger," said Tracey, her tone impatient.

Trevino stepped next to her and nudged the charred body with his boot. "What is it?"

"Stegosaurus," said Tracey. "A herd of them. The work of your 'Daisy Cutters.'"

Trevino sighed. "Well, it could've just as easily been one of those T. rexes."

"We can't leave them here," said Tracey.

"Why not? There's nothing that can be done for them now."

Tracey turned to Trevino. "You've been camping, right, Trevino?"

"Sure?" He was unsure of where she was going with this.

"Well, you know how you're supposed to keep food buttoned up tight so bears don't smell it and come around?"

"Yeah. You're worried about bears?"

Tracey shook her head. "The Tyrannosaurus is a scavenger, not just a hunter. If any of them catch a whiff of Stegosaurus barbecue, they'll come running."

His eyes widened. "Got it." He grabbed his radio. "Stallion to Chief, come in."

'Chief, here. Go ahead, Stallion.'

"We're going to need a small detail to remove some Stegosaurus bodies. The doctor, here, thinks they might attract T. rexes."

'What bodies?'

"From the 'Daisy Cutters.'"

'Copy that. Re…'

It sounded as if Collins was about to say something more, but the radio cut out. There was a crackling in the sky, and with a bang the forcefield vanished, replacing it with crystal blue sky.

"We'd better head back," said Trevino. "Was there anything else?"

Tracey looked around. "No." Her eyes settled on the closest bit of tree line. "That's it for now. What was that in the sky?"

Roach looked up, squinting in the powerful sun. "The connection to our dimension was severed. We're on our own."

They drove back to base in the Humvee, where Nielsen and Collins met them. Tracey hopped out, but Trevino and Roach remained in the vehicle.

"Nice work, Dr. Moran," said Nielsen.

"Nothing nice about it," said Tracey. "Those poor animals didn't even see it coming."

He turned to Collins. "Do you think your men could see to disposing of them properly? The last thing we need is to be attacked by T. rexes."

"Do you really think that's the best use of our time?" asked Collins. "This'll delay the expedition. We're ready for anything that comes out of the jungle."

"I don't believe you," said Tracey.

"Pardon?" Collins looked irritated.

"I don't believe you could be so cavalier knowing what happened to the last expedition who didn't respect what we were up against."

"She's right," said Nielsen. "Why engage when we can avoid? Dump the bodies in the river. Use the Humvees to drag them."

"They're too big," said Trevino.

"Then cut them up," said Nielsen. "Or maybe we can burn them."

"That'll take precious fuel," said Collins. "Fuel we can't spare. We need them for the birds. You know… to keep us safe and all." He turned to Trevino. "How many bodies?"

"About a dozen, all torn up," said Trevino.

"Then we can take them to the river in pieces. The current will carry it all away."

"What river?" asked Tracey.

"The one we're going to follow right up to the plateau settlement where we believe Dr. Albanese and the rest of our old team are located," said Nielsen. "We leave in a few hours, after the Stegosaurus clean up."

"We're going to take three Humvees and a Huey with us," said Collins. "Dr. Moran, you and the other technicians will be riding in an INKAS Sentry Civilian."

Tracey arched an eyebrow. "An INKAS what?"

"An armored truck. We'll hug the river bank, which should make for easier travel. The rest will be left behind to guard base camp. We'll be in constant radio communication the whole time, with each other, our bird in the sky, and base."

"This island does strange things with radio communications," said Tracey. "What if there's too much interference?"

"We've anticipated that," said Collins. "We have a color-coded signaling system to communicate with the Huey."

Tracey had to admit, Collins was inspiring quite a bit of confidence. She thought about Peter, left behind to fend for himself. She wondered if they really stood a chance of finding him and the others.

"Let's move, people," said Nielsen. "Times a wasting."

"You heard him," said Collins to Trevino. "Take a small detail and handle those bodies."

* * *

Jason and Mary darted up the narrow path, deftly navigating massive boulders and the edge of the cliff, and made their way into the village. It was early morning, and the women and children were asleep, but the Umazoan men prepared their spears for an early hunt.

"Susan," cried Mary. "Susan, wake up."

Susan came stumbling out of her thatch hut, rubbing her eyes as Mary and Jason ran up to her, ignoring the concerned looks of the tribal hunters. "What? What is it?" She rubbed her eyes. "Where's Peter?"

"He never came out of the temple," said Mary.

Susan frowned. "I knew this was a bad idea."

"Yeah, well, we have to get the hell out of Dodge, like now," said Jason, out of breath.

"What's he talking about?" asked Susan.

Mary panted, trying to catch her breath. "Peter said we needed to evacuate the village if he didn't return."

Susan scrunched her nose, as if catching a whiff of something rancid. "Evacuate? Where are we going to go?"

"Peter said we're no longer safe up here," said Jason, "and I'm inclined to believe him. He thinks the lizard men are the ones sending the velociraptors up here. He thinks they're close to just invading this village." They had lost Molina in the last raid on the village. A soldier to the last, he had fought bravely but had been torn apart by the marauding velociraptors.

The hunters, led by the Umazoan chief, approached them. A small but well-muscled man, the newly appointed chief, named Hiu, looked concerned. The other chief had been killed in the last raid, resulting in his promotion, so hearing about lizard men and invasion grabbed his attention. "What?" he asked. "What happen? Liz?" His English was broken, but they understood him.

Jason turned and leveled his gaze. "Chief Hiu, we must leave. Big danger coming." Then he rattled off the few words that he knew in Umazoan describing the lizard men, raids, and velociraptors.

Hiu listened carefully. Wary from wave after wave of lizard men attacks on the village, he appeared receptive. He responded in Umazoan.

"River?" asked Susan, struggling to comprehend everything the chief was saying. "What river?"

Hiu elaborated, gesticulating wildly.

"Take us away…to another home," said Mary, translating. "We need to follow the river?" She undulated her hand in a serpentine motion over her other hand, palm facing up.

Hiu nodded emphatically, pleased she understood. He barked orders at the other men, who proceeded to fan out and rouse the rest of the village.

"Looks like we're leaving," said Susan, shrugging. "Are you sure this is the right thing to do? These people established this location for the village a long time ago."

Hiu listened and said in broken English. "Run and live…better than…stay, die." With that last word, he made a slashing motion with his hand across his throat. The chief before him had been proud and refused to give in to the new enemy. This one was clearly more pragmatic. The truth was, everyone was tired of the relentless attacks. Enough was enough.

The entire village mobilized. The men gathered weapons and cut down crops, loading them on drag sleds to be pulled. The women gathered clothing and tanned skins, packing them for transport while herding the children. The children carried out small tasks as directed by their mothers, anything from gathering up the animals to packing small items.

Within a couple of hours, the entire village had been packed up, leaving only the thatched huts and extinguished camp fires behind. Everyone congregated at the center of the village, where Hiu held court. As far as Mary, Jason, and Susan could tell with their limited language of Umazoan, he made some grand speech about survival against all odds, and he referenced other times in tribal history when an exodus was required. At last, he waved his right arm over his head, gesturing for the tribe to move.

Jason caught something out of the corner of his eye. Several velociraptors crept their way to the edge of the village. "Dinos!"

The tribe murmured and panicked, looking around. A few of them screamed and pointed when they saw the deadly therapods.

Jason turned to Hiu. "Move! I'll handle this. Just leave me a few of your warriors."

Hiu nodded and gestured towards three of the hunters, who nodded and hoisted their spears. They stepped forward, awaiting direction from Jason, who had become their lead hunter. Hiu also stepped forward, dispensing additional spears. These weapons would be thrown, as close combat with raptors was ill-advised.

"Not you," said Jason. "We cannot lose another chief."

"The tribe needs you," added Mary.

Hiu huffed, jabbed the butt of his spear into the dirt, and stood resolute.

"I'll lead the tribe away from here," offered Susan. In her home dimension, it was her job to manage large groups.

Mary nodded. "Go. We'll be right behind you."

Susan barked orders in English and broken Umazoan, and the tribe moved as a unit to the far side of the plateau, where they had constructed a platform out of branches and twine and a pully mechanism to lower it to the ground below. It wasn't designed for en masse usage, so Susan would have to coordinate it.

*

Jason looked to Hiu, who deferred to him. The Umazoa were accomplished hunters, but they acknowledged Jason's greater expertise.

Jason nodded, accepting the mantle. He unshouldered his rifle as Mary hefted hers. He put up two fingers and then karate chopped the air in several different places, signaling they had to disperse two-by-two. It was their go-to formation whenever velociraptors entered the picture. Raptors were clever hunters, using pack tactics, flanking and ambushing. Each pair of hunters would cover opposite one hundred-and-eighty-degree fields of vision, and the entire group formed a line, establishing a barrier between the raptors and the fleeing tribe while keeping firing corridors clear. When one was reloading or preparing another spear, the other would swing around and take over, and on and on.

The velociraptors spread out. Two walked down the middle of the village, moving like ostriches, their heads swiveling around, sizing up their prey. Another two crept through the fields to the left where the crops once grew, sniffing the ground and circumventing the line of humans. Two more slipped between thatch huts on the right, appearing and vanishing, making use of the cover while making their movements difficult to track.

"They're hunting in pairs," said Jason. "Just like us."

"They're learning from us," said Mary, watching his back.

Jason trained his rifle on the two walking through the center of the village. "The ones in the center want us to focus on them so we're taken off-guard by the flanks."

"I've got the flank covered," said Mary, training her rifle on the glimpses of velociraptors in between the huts.

Jason looked to his left and saw Hiu hoisting his spear, focusing on the center, but his partner watched the crops carefully.

One of the velociraptors bumped into a wooden stake drilled into the ground in the crop area, knocking it over. It turned and sniffed the stick before continuing on. Another investigated a crudely fashioned scarecrow designed to scare off birds and evil spirits from picking at the crops. It chirped and barked a couple of times, shrinking back as it expected a response. When it realized the scarecrow was no threat, it nudged it with its snout and continued advancing on the line of humans.

The middle raptors crept forward, heads lowered and teeth bared, claws splayed out in front of them. They walked in small, measured steps, leg muscles taut, primed for a sudden, explosive strike.

"Here we go." Jason took a shot at one of the center ones, striking it in the neck. It cried out, shaking its head. The other one sprung forward, dashing at him.

Mary saw one of the velociraptors running from around a thatched hut, becoming tangled in a clothesline Susan had erected. It writhed about, trying to shake the cord, pulling the stakes out of the ground in the process. Mary shot at it twice, hitting it once in the chest and then in its side.

The other velociraptor rushed out from two huts over, lowering its head and opening its jaws.

*

The two velociraptors from the farming area lunged at Hiu and his partner, a man named Ryo. Hiu hurled a spear at one, glancing its shoulder as it dodged. As he knelt to snatch another spear off the ground, Ryo swung around and launched a spear, striking one of the raptors in its open mouth. The wounded velociraptor veered off, shaking its head and swatting at the spear with its clawed hands. The other lurched forward, opening its mouth, targeting Hiu.

Hiu stayed in a kneeling position, pointed his spear at the advancing raptor, and braced the other end into the ground. The raptor shot forward, snapping its jaws. However, Hiu timed it just right, and it impaled itself on his spear with such force that it knocked the spear out of Hiu's hands. The raptor overshot and missed Hiu with its teeth. Its back leg, however, lashed out at Ryo, its curved claw slicing the man's thigh.

Ryo cried out and dropped his spear as blood spurted out of the gash. The raptor turned and latched its jaws onto his torso, sinking its teeth into his flesh between his ribs.

Hiu grabbed another spear and drove it into the raptor's side. It wheeled around, still gripping Ryo, the spear sticking up into the air. Ryo screamed as blood oozed from his mouth and down his chin.

The raptor slashed at Hiu with its foot, but the chieftain side-stepped it and grabbed another spear. He waited as the velociraptor wheeled around, trying to fend him off while it held onto Ryo. When the raptor stopped for a brief moment, Hiu lunged with his spear, hitting it in its right eye. He thrust it in, pushing with all of his body weight.

*

The raptor Jason shot dashed forward, somewhat unsteadily, as Jason fired another shot into its head, dropping it. The other rushed forward, teeth and claws out, moving too fast for Jason. Unfortunately for him, Mary was preoccupied with the right flank and couldn't back him up.

Jason struggled to aim, but it was too late. It snapped at him, but he staggered backwards, tripping over Mary. He fell on his back as the raptor pounced, pinning him down. It stood on his rifle, which he held horizontally across his chest, pressing it into him with its body weight. Its curved claws on its feet dug into his sides, and he groaned as they pierced his flesh. He felt his shirt mat up with his warm blood.

Mary took aim at the second raptor, missing it. She, too, lost her balance, tripping over the raptor squatting over Jason. She fell to the ground as the raptor lunging at her missed, colliding with the raptor pinning Jason.

The two raptors rolled around in a ball, and Jason wailed as the curved claws released him. He clutched his sides and rolled over to Mary, who was already getting to her feet.

Balled up and tangled, the raptors presented an easier target. She fired at them repeatedly, her shots finding purchase. As they wriggled to stand, they took fire, the bullets tearing into their flesh. Jason, from the ground, fired his rifle. When the smoke cleared, both raptors lay dead, bleeding into the dirt.

*

The third pair of Umazoan hunters broke formation and ran at the raptor assaulting Hiu and Ryo. They thrust spears at it, piercing its vital organs, until it fell to the ground, its tongue dangling limp from its jaws. The second raptor that had the spear lodged in its mouth ran off.

Ryo lay on the ground, clutching his chest. Blood pooled around him as his eyes grew dim. Hiu knelt beside him, clutching him, his expression desperate. He rocked the hunter in his arms as he died, the others watching in a mix of pity and horror.

*

Mary helped Jason up as he winced from the sharp pain in his sides. He struggled to stand, but she threw his arm around her shoulders to steady him.

"You're going to be okay," she said. "I'm sure you've suffered worse."

He remembered the time the wolves had cornered him. He remembered the sensation of being mauled, teeth tearing through his coat and sinking into his soft, young flesh. "Yeah, I'll be all right."

"Are you thinking what I'm thinking?" asked Mary.

Jason nodded. "Those velociraptors were sent." He and Mary traded looks, and then their eyes widened. "The tribe," they said in unison.

Hiu, covered in Ryo's blood, and the remaining two hunters joined them as Jason and Mary ran to the other side of the plateau.

"Wait," cried Jason. "Wait!"

Susan, sending the Umazoans down in small groups, looked at Jason. "What? What is it?" As he approached, she saw the blood stains on his shirt. "Are you all right?"

Jason swallowed and tried to catch his breath. "Fine. It's a trap."

"What do you mean?" asked Susan.

"The lizard men sent the raptors up as a distraction. They'll be attacking the tribe down below," said Mary.

Susan looked down as a tribesman turned the crank to lower a group of five down. Others waited at the bottom, looking up. "I don't see anything. I sent each group down with a hunter for security once down at the bottom."

"That was a good idea," said Jason, "but I'm afraid it won't be enough." He went to the edge of the plateau to look down. He didn't see anything out of the ordinary. He winced and clutched his side.

"You need medical attention," said Susan.

He shook his head, sweating profusely. "There's no time. I'll be fine."

"You'll get an infection," insisted Susan.

"Once we're away from all this, we can have a look," said Jason. "But right now, we need to get the hell out of here safely."

"He's right," said Mary. "That's our first priority."

Susan shook her head. "There's been no attack."

"That's because they're waiting for the whole tribe to go down," said Jason. "No one else goes down. Send me. I'll check for tracks."

"I'm coming too," said Mary.

Jason smirked. "Don't want to leave me all alone, huh?"

"Yes, that's because you're so damned irresistible," said Mary in sarcastic monotone.

"Okay," said Susan. "When the platform comes up, you two are next."

They all watched as the platform reached the bottom and the group of five got off. They joined the others as the hunters down below hoisted their spears, scanning their surroundings. The only problem was they were looking for dinosaurs, not lizard men.

Susan gave the order, and the man operating the winch cranked the platform back up slowly. It was a thirty to forty-foot drop, so it took a moment.

Jason looked around from his elevated vantage point and saw nothing. Dinosaurs, particularly the larger predators, would've been easy to spot. Lizard men, however, were too small. They could've been camouflaged and no one up on the plateau would've even known it.

When the platform reached the top, Jason got on, his rifle slung over his shoulder, steadying himself. He sat down, Mary helping him, and he flinched from the pain. Mary looked at Susan and nodded. Susan gave the order to the Umazoan man to lower them, and the man began to hand crank the winch.

As they began to sink in a jerky, disjointed motion, Jason looked up and said to Susan, "Wait for our signal, and watch your back."

Susan nodded and ordered a few of the remaining hunters to watch the village for any more invaders. They answered in Umazoan and ran off to keep watch for man, dinosaur, or lizard man.

*

As they descended, Jason unshouldered his rifle and used the scope to sweep the surroundings. Down below, the Umazoans gathered, milling around, awaiting the arrival of the others. Jason swept his scope across their flanks, looking for any movement or any sign of ambush. In the distance, off to the west, he saw the long necks of a brontosaurus herd breaching the canopy. To the east was a quiet stretch of jungle, or so it seemed. However, upon closer inspection, he saw monkeys swinging from branches, crying out to each other in warning. He looked south and saw the river Hiu spoke about snake by. He followed it down with his scope. It twisted and disappeared under the canopy.

"What is it?" asked Mary.

"The monkeys," said Jason. "They're agitated about something."

"Can you see anything?"

"No. But they're definitely reacting to something."

They were now fifteen feet above the ground. Mary's eyes darted around, searching. The Umazoans appeared completely unaware of anything out of place, even the hunters who kept a watchful eye.

When they reached the ground, Mary helped Jason up. He groaned as his sides stung. "We have to start to move everyone," said Jason. "They're all a bunch of sitting ducks bunched up like this."

Mary nodded. "I can set them up down by the river."

"That sounds like a good idea," said Jason. "I'll have Susan send the others down while I keep watch."

Underbrush rustled, and Jason held a hand up to silence Mary. "Did you hear that?"

"Hear what?"

Out of the side of the cliff, lizard men burst out from a cave covered by thick vines. They seized Mary and Jason, ripping their rifles out of their hands before they had time to react. They immediately surrounded the Umazoa, pointing spears at them. The hunters whirled around, ready to engage.

One lizard man stepped up to Mary and held a crude dagger up to her throat. He hissed, flaring the dewlap under his chin like an iguana, and the hunters looked on in horror. Their eyes darted from the knife-wielding lizard man to Mary, then to Jason.

Mary squirmed as claws dug into her arms, holding her still. "Fight! Don't worry about me!"

Jason tried to wriggle free, but he was weak and in too much pain to offer up much of a fight.

The lizard man holding the knife hissed louder, opening its mouth wide, pressing the blade to her throat. Mary whimpered as a rivulet of blood trickled from where the blade dug into her flesh. The hunters threw down their spears and surrendered.

"No," cried Mary.

"It's not their fault," said Jason through gritted teeth, sharp pain wracking his midsection. "They're outnumbered."

Susan called down from up above, but neither Jason nor Mary understood it. The rope attached to the wooden platform went slack, and the other end fell down to the ground, landing in a small heap, cutting everyone below off from the village above.

Jason only hoped Susan would lead the rest of the tribe to safety, whatever that meant on this island.

CHAPTER 5

Peter regained consciousness to the sound of gurgling water on the river bank, his body strewn across the mud, thankfully facing up. He turned his head and saw the river running past him. He realized he must've lost consciousness, as his head thundered with pain. He tried to move, but he felt strange. His limbs wouldn't respond to his brain's orders. As his eyes darted around, he caught glimpses of a pant leg and an arm, only they were in places they shouldn't have been…at angles that shouldn't have even been possible.

He tried to crane his neck to look at his body, but he couldn't do it. It didn't even feel as if his body was even there. Was he dead? Had he been decapitated, and these were the last moments of sentience? Had the Spinosaurus bitten his body off and feasted on it, leaving his head behind? He blinked his eyes and crinkled his nose. At least his head worked.

As his brain began to register the data his eyes sent, he realized that he was folded over on himself, contorted in a back-breaking position. Peter fought down panic, trying to analyze the situation. Then he remembered his powers.

He closed his eyes, reached deep within himself, and sought out his own life force. It was there, and it was fading. He sensed it in his mind's eye through the power of the orbs embedded within his chest. He must've sustained a spinal injury and become paralyzed from the neck down. He was thankful to even be alive, even as a human pretzel, and he knew he had to heal himself.

He looked around, scouting out for carnivorous dinosaurs lurking about, but with his limited range of sight, the coast appeared to be clear. Satisfied he was alone, Peter closed his eyes and reached into his essence, tapping the power of the life orb. He felt the orb glow inside of his mind as he focused on healing his damaged spinal nerve.

His eyes opened to splashing in front of him, breaking his concentration. He tried to crane his neck to spy what caused the disturbance, but to no avail. It, however, slithered into his view. A massive snake had slipped out of the river and was eyeing him for a nice meal.

"Shoo! Git!" he shouted at it. He wanted to swat at it with his arm and kick at it with his leg, but those weren't options.

It slinked through the mud, bringing more of its body into view. Its head was massive, like that of a cow, a black tongue slipping in and out of its mouth, tasting the air…tasting Peter. Its scales were deep brown, its body two feet thick. However, as it revealed more of itself, it appeared to be three feet thick towards its middle.

Peter forced his eyes closed and did his best to re-establish his link with the life orb. He really wanted to use the death orb to kill this monster, but he had no idea how. Desperate, he fired up his inner power, creating a neural handshake with the cells of his spinal cord. He injected his warmth into them as his body rattled. The massive boa, likely a Titanoboa, had just latched onto his feet. As he felt life and healing trickle through his nervous system, he had the faint sensation of teeth piercing his ankles and lips massaging their way up his calves. He didn't feel it as much as he knew it, as if he watched it happen to someone else.

His eyes opened to a much louder splash. *What now?*

A beautiful woman stood waist-deep in the river, watching him. Peter thought he was hallucinating, but as he fixed his eyes on the woman in the water, he could've sworn it looked like…

"Tracey?" He asked it out loud knowing full well it wasn't Tracey.

'I assumed this form as it would be pleasing to you. We haven't much time.' Peter felt its voice inside his mind, wordless as the intelligent lizard man, only this thing wasn't using an orb to communicate. He knew, however, what is was.

"What do you want?"

'There is quite a large snake consuming you, feet first. It has already worked its way up to your thighs.' Its voice was thin and hollow, like a hissing whisper in his mind.

Peter felt himself being turned around and sensed the peristaltic movements of the boa's throat muscles, guiding him into its esophagus. However, at the moment what stood before him in the river was much worse. It was pure evil. "I know what you are."

'You know nothing of what I am. I am as powerful as I am old, and I walked these lands well before the thunder lizards.'

"You corrupted Mike Deluca. Turned him into a monster."

'I offered him power over death. What he chose to do with it was his responsibility.'

"Leave me alone."

'The snake is now at your waist. You cannot feel it, but it's pulling you in, further and further, until you will be digested slowly, in agony every second of the remainder of your life.'

Peter wanted to heal himself, but he knew he didn't have enough time. "Leave me alone."

'I can help you.'

"I don't want your help."

'I can teach you how to use the death orb.'

This caught Peter's attention, and it must've sensed it, because an eerie smile crept across its face, flashing rotten teeth. The sight jarred him out of whatever enchantment it had cast upon him. "No. I don't want it."

'The snake is now working its way up your torso.'

Peter strained to look and saw the top of its massive head on top of his chest, its curved teeth digging into his flesh, yet he felt nothing. He thought about Tracey. He felt how much he still cared for her, and the orbs glowed within the boa's mouth. "She's here," he gasped.

'Yes. She is. You want to see her again. You want to be with her.'

Peter shook his head as he slid further into the jaws and throat of the Titanoboa. "No! Why did she come back?"

'She came for you.'

"No. You're playing tricks on me. I don't believe it."

The boa's lips now touched his chin, and the force of the rhythmic muscle contractions forced his head back.

'You are too late. Her death is your responsibility.'

Peter was swallowed whole, and the world went dark. He struggled to breathe as the boa's muscles tightened around him, working him into its digestive tract. What little air he could inhale was tinged with the odor of stomach acid, and his lungs burned with each limited draw of breath. He heard muffled shouts outside, and he was rolled around. He heard the pop of gunfire, and the peristaltic contractions around him slowed and then ceased. Sharp objects pierced the sides of the snake, poking Peter's body, and the walls of the snake were pulled apart as he was rolled over and over, gasping for air.

Just as he was about to pass out, fresh air and sunlight hit his face, and he felt hands grabbing at him, pulling the top half of his body up and out of the massive serpent. When Peter opened his eyes, he saw Tracey looking down at him. "Screw you. Leave me alone."

Tracey shook her head, looking confused. "Peter, what are you doing inside that huge ass snake?"

Now *he* was perplexed. "Tracey? Is that really you?" He furrowed his brow. "This isn't a trick, is it?"

A rather stern-looking man stood next to her. "Hello, Dr. Albanese. I'm Trevor Nielsen from Poseidon Tech. We're here to rescue you."

Peter turned his head towards the river. "But...but...did you see her?"

Tracey turned to try to see what he was looking at. "Who?"

"You...I mean, not really you. Not the real you. The fake you."

"He's delirious," said a man dressed in camos, toting an assault rifle.

"I don't even know how he's alive," said Nielsen.

Peter eyed the man with the large gun.

"That's Collins," explained Tracey, crouching by his side. "Head of security."

Peter met eyes with Tracey. He was overwhelmed to see her. "You came back."

"Of course I did," she said, her voice soft and warm. It was a complete contrast with the voice of the thing in the water.

Peter frowned. "You shouldn't have come."

The other men in camos pulled the snake apart from either side, cutting through muscle, freeing his legs. He made to push himself up, but he felt strong hands reach under his arms, hoisting him up. Peter staggered as he regained his balance. He looked at each of the men holding him up. "Thanks. You're a lifesaver."

Tracey threw her arms around him. He once again felt squeezed, but he welcomed it this time. He closed his eyes and drank it in. He heard shouts, weapons being drawn, and then Tracey's voice, "No! Wait!"

Peter opened his eyes. Collins and his men had their weapons drawn on him.

"What's wrong with him?" Collins pointed the barrel of his rifle at Peter's glowing chest. Peter's wounds from the snake and errant knife tips healed over, leaving his shirt tattered and stained but his flesh intact.

Nielsen smiled and stepped between Peter and Collins' men. "It was in the briefing. He gained some kind of power being on this island."

"Is he dangerous?" asked Collins.

"No, he's not dangerous," snapped Tracey, standing next to Peter.

Peter put his hands up, slowly. "I assure you, I'm no threat to you or your men."

Nielsen looked him up and down. "You look pretty damned good for a man we pulled out of a giant snake."

Peter suddenly felt self-conscious. He was filthy, his clothes were ragged, and he sported a bushy beard. He looked like a castaway, which really wasn't that far from the truth.

"Titanoboa," corrected Tracey.

"I knew it," chortled Peter.

"Stand down," said Collins to his men. They all lowered their rifles.

"Where are the others?" asked Nielsen.

Peter's expression changed from amused to grave. "I told them to evacuate the village."

"Evacuate?" said Nielsen.

"What happened?" asked Tracey.

"It's a long story," said Peter.

Collins looked uneasy. "Mr. Nielsen, I hate to cut this reunion short, but we need to get back into our vehicles. We're sitting ducks out here."

Nielsen nodded. "He's right. You two can catch up in the truck, and we can hear about the village."

Peter looked around. "Truck? What truck?"

Tracey led him over to the convoy, arm-in-arm, supporting him. "That convoy."

Peter took in the Humvees with mounted weaponry and the armored vehicle. The truck was black with a back window and four windows on each side. The front two side windows were larger than the rear window set in the back door. The tires were huge, set in angular wheel wells, lending it an aggressive appearance. "Whoa. You guys came better prepared this time."

A Huey buzzed overhead, and Collins' radio crackled. 'Eagle to Chief, we've spotted three T. rexes heading your way, three clicks south.'

"Chief to Eagle, copy that," said Collins. "Move to intercept. Chief out." He turned to address the group. "Let's move!"

Everyone dashed to their vehicles. Peter hobbled his way to the armored truck, and Nielsen helped him inside. Nielsen then waved Tracey in and hopped in himself.

"Three T. rexes?" said Peter, his eyes wide. "They're going to tear through this convoy."

Nielsen shook his head. "We've got helicopter support, not to mention belt-fed grenade launchers on those Humvees."

A young technician inside the truck beamed when she saw Peter, as if she'd recognized him. However, Peter didn't recognize her.

Marcy leaned in to Tracey. "Is that him?"

Tracey's face flushed, and she nodded.

Peter didn't understand what the exchange was all about, but he had other things on his mind. "Yeah, but three. The chopper said three T. rexes." His protest was interrupted by the buzzing of a minigun and angry roars. "What...?"

"That would be the chopper tearing through your T. rexes," said Nielsen, beaming.

As the vehicle lurched forward, Peter felt the percussion of tyrannosaur footfalls growing closer. "Yeah, but can it handle three?"

Tracey slid to the back of the vehicle to look out of the small window. "Peter, you have to see this."

Peter slid in next to her, while Nielsen looked over their shoulders. Peter saw the Humvees fall behind, trailing the armored truck. "What are they doing?"

"Getting ready to engage," said Nielsen.

Three tyrannosaurs burst out of the tree line behind the convoy. The Huey followed overhead, laying cover fire from above. Bolts of light erupted from the minigun, pelting the beasts below.

The gunners on the Humvees swiveled around in their ring mounts and fired at the advancing predators. The tyrannosaur leading the charge took the brunt of the attack. It sustained a direct hit to its mouth, and it slowed down, staggered, and dropped, blood oozing from its jowls. The other two picked up the pace.

"I thought T. rexes didn't run," said Tracey.

"These do," said Peter.

The one to the right lowered its head and extended it out, snapping at the Humvee in front of it. The gunner, panicked and thrown off by the tyrannosaur's sudden change of posture, fired several shots but missed most of them, only tagging it on its right shoulder and blowing off its tiny right arm. Furious, the T. rex pushed forward and roared at the gunner.

The other Humvee picked up speed as the pursuing tyrannosaur snapped at it. However, the predator pumped its muscular legs, keeping pace.

The now one-armed T. rex took several direct hits to its open mouth, the grenades devastating its soft palate and rattling its brain in its skull. It slowed to a walk as it shook its head, its mouth smoking, and toppled sideways into the river with a large splash.

The Huey above redirected focus on the remaining Tyrannosaur, barraging it with bolts of light. It roared in frustration as it dove at the Humvee in front of it.

"See," said Nielsen, inside the armored truck. "The situation is well in hand."

Peter, Tracey, and Nielsen startled as two tyrannosaurs came out of the tree line to the right, flanking the two Humvees. Having focused entirely on the rear, the drivers and gunners were taken by surprise. Before they had time to react, the flanking tyrannosaurs pounced on the vehicles, crushing tires under their massive weight. Peter watched in horror as the gunners were plucked from their mounts and voraciously consumed.

"Jesus Christ," said Collins. He got on his radio. "Chief to base, we're under attack. Weapons team down, requesting assistance." His radio only registered static. "Chief to base, we're under attack, requesting assistance." There were other strange noises, like distortion.

The chopper hovered over the two Humvees, firing at the two monsters tearing into them. The remaining original tyrannosaur deftly dodged the tangle and continued after the armored truck.

"He'll never catch us," said Nielsen.

The armored truck fishtailed, hitting a patch of soggy riverbank. Losing speed as the driver attempted to overcorrect, it slipped in the mud, spinning its wheels as it lurched forward, pushing its way through the soft, muddy embankment. The pursuing T. rex gained on them, closing the gap.

Marcy snarled at Nielsen. "You really need to shut up now."

It caught up, lowered its head, and rammed the side of the vehicle. Inside, Peter and the others were thrown about as the vehicle slid sideways. Outside, the T. rex staggered on its feet having injured itself with the blow. It was as if it thought the truck was an animal and hadn't expected it to be so hard on the head.

Peter reached out and stabilized himself as Tracey fell into his lap. Nielsen and Marcy fell on the floor. Tracey pushed herself up.

"Are you all right?" asked Peter.

She held her head. "I think so."

Nielsen helped Marcy up. "Are you okay?"

Marcy looked shaken. "Yeah, I'm okay."

The driver gunned the engine, throwing the vehicle into low gear for traction. The wheels spun underneath them, and the back vibrated with the spinning of the axles.

Peter slid over to the slits and peeked outside. He only saw its tail. The T. rex was alongside them, between the armored truck and the river. Peter darted to one of the side windows, Tracey behind him. Nielsen looked out of the other side window. Marcy curled into a ball on the floor, too terrified to look and praying the monster outside would go away.

The T. rex shook its head, like a wet dog trying to dry off. It swept its head back and forth, sizing up the strange, solid prey. It lifted its massive right leg and pinned the hood of the truck with its claws. The driver hit the gas, and the Humvee tried to heave forward, but the weight of the enormous, clawed foot drove the tires deeper into the mud. The truck's frame groaned under the weight of the theropod.

"We need to get out of here," cried Tracey.

"We're safe as long as we're in the truck," declared Nielsen. "He can't get us in here."

Collins got on his radio, calling for backup. "Chief to base, come in base." There was static on the line. "Chief to base, come in base." This time they heard fragments of words. "Damned island."

The T. rex nipped at the front of the vehicle, its teeth crunching down on metal. Peter heard the driver cursing up front. The vehicle bounced on its suspension as the tyrannosaur pressed down on it with its foot. The tires blew from the pressure as the truck sank into the mud.

"Great," muttered Collins. "Now we're stuck."

"It won't get us in here," repeated Nielsen, sounding panicked now. "It can't get us in here."

The Tyrannosaurus nipped at the metal a few more times and then backed off, releasing the truck. It stepped away from the metal box, lowering its head so it could sniff it.

"We can't move," said the driver from up front, grabbing his rifle. "We're sitting ducks."

"Maybe it'll lose interest after a while and go away," offered Tracey.

The T. rex stomped around the vehicle, viewing it from all sides, calculating how to get at the tasty morsels inside. It roared at it in frustration, the sound deafening at close range. Marcy crouched on the floor, covering her ears, the roar drowning out her cries.

Tracey noticed Marcy was in distress and sat on the floor next to her. She placed an arm around her. "It's all right. He can't get to us in here. We're safe."

"For the moment," added Collins.

Tracey shot him a stern look, but she softened as she stroked Marcy's hair. "It's okay. He can't get us."

The poor girl had tears streaming down her face. "We're all going to die."

"No," said Tracey. "No, we're not. We're safe in here."

Marcy looked up at Tracey, her eyes big and wet. "What if it doesn't go away?"

"It'll go away," said Nielsen, panting from terror. "It has to."

Collins glowered and looked out the side window at the circling thunder lizard. "It doesn't have to *do* anything."

"We can wait him out," said Peter. "We have provisions on this rig, right?"

"We have a dozen go bags," said Collins. "I hope you like jerky and granola bars."

"Dehydration will get to us before hunger," said Peter.

"We have water," said Collins. "But what we need right now is a plan."

"We'll wait it out," said Nielsen. "Like we said."

"What if our friend out there doesn't get bored?" said Collins. "We need a plan."

"I'm not going outside," said Marcy, trembling. "No way. Not me."

Tracey stroked her hair. "Not until it leaves. I promise."

"Well, I suppose we have to wait," said Nielsen, turning his back on the pacing predator outside and sinking to the floor. "Dr. Albanese, why don't you tell us about what prompted the evacuation of the village?"

Peter turned away from the tyrannosaur and leveled his gaze at the Poseidon Tech team leader. "There are things on this island other than dinosaurs. I appeared to have...awakened a race of reptilian humanoids, who proceeded to wage war with the Umazoa."

Nielsen squinted. "The Umazoa?"

"That's what we call the indigenous tribe we're staying with."

Nielsen nodded. "How did you reawaken this race?"

Peter shrugged. "The lizard men, who reside in a subterranean temple, communicate and store information for historical purposes via these crystal orbs. Mike Deluca had stumbled upon an orb that merged with him, allowing him to control death."

Collins grimaced. "Merged?"

Peter nodded and pointed at his chest. "Yeah, I merged with an orb that allows me to control life. I can heal myself and others. In some cases, I can even reverse death."

"Did you...revive any of your team?" asked Nielsen.

"Only those that were still bodily intact. Those eaten by carnivores or totally dismembered weren't salvageable."

Collins shook his head. "I don't believe this. I don't believe any of this."

Tracey ignored Collins' commentary. "Peter, tell him about what was controlling Mike Deluca."

Peter nodded. "There was something...supernatural that was guiding Mike Deluca, tricking him, influencing him. It wanted off the island. It posed as his deceased wife."

Nielsen traded knowing looks with Tracey. "The voice on the flight recorder." He shook his head. "Jesus. That poor man. Mike was devasted by her passing. Cancer."

Peter hesitated a moment. "It made contact with me."

Tracey looked startled. "When?"

"Right before you found me inside that Titanoboa. As the snake was swallowing me whole, it offered to help me."

"Why would it do that?" asked Tracy.

"Because I have something it wants...the death orb. I absorbed it after I killed Mike."

Nielsen shook his head, struggling to keep up. "Wait a minute. You killed Mike Deluca?"

"He had to," blurted Tracey. "Mike was murdering everyone."

"He was barely human anymore," said Peter, his tone pensive. "He had become a monster. He created living dead out of the Umazoa and even members of our team. Cannibals. It was a nightmare."

"So, now you have the death orb?" asked Collins.

Peter nodded. "I have both inside me. That's what you see glowing."

"How do we know he won't use it on us?" asked Collins.

"That's just it," said Peter. "I don't know how to use it. That was what that…demon was offering me—the knowledge needed to tap into its power. It saved my life."

"To what purpose?" asked Nielsen.

"I don't know," said Peter. "There's something else."

"Oh, this'll be good," said Collins.

Peter explained how he entered the temple to attempt to negotiate with the lizard men, to strike a peace accord or truce. "I ran into a particular one who was different than all the others. He was their historian. He was more intelligent than the others I'd encountered. He showed me something, visions of their past. As it ends up, there's another species on this island, or at least there was. A simian species of ape-like men."

"Have you ever encountered one?" asked Nielsen.

Peter shook his head. "No, I haven't. I've never felt their presence on the island, so I think they're also extinct."

"Why do you think he showed you that?" asked Tracey.

Peter shrugged. "I have no idea."

"So, let me get this straight," said Marcy, following the conversation. Her voice sounded mousey. "Not only do we have to contend with dinosaurs, but there are also murderous lizard and ape men out there?"

Collins looked out the window. "Hey, looks like our friend is getting bored."

They all stood up and looked out the windows. The Tyrannosaurus rex stomped off into the trees.

"Great!" said Nielsen. "We can get the hell out of here." He made for the back door.

"Wait just a minute," said Peter, grabbing his arm.

"If we're going to leave, now's the time," insisted Nielsen. "Don't forget, the other two are not far behind."

"Let's hear what he has to say," said Collins. "It's why he's here, isn't it?"

Nielsen huffed in exasperation. "Okay. What?"

"I don't think it's really left," said Peter. He closed his eyes and reached out with his senses. His chest glowed under his tattered shirt. "I can feel it."

Everyone looked out the side windows facing the jungle. "I don't see him," said Nielsen.

"Doesn't mean he isn't still out there," said Collins.

There was an explosion in the distance behind them.

"What was that?" asked Marcy, trembling.

Collins frowned. "That was likely our air support."

"They took down a helicopter?" cried Nielsen, incredulous. "Impossible."

"They're smarter than we realize," explained Peter. "They hunt in packs. They used a flanking maneuver on your Humvees."

"Pack hunting?" Nielsen looked stunned. "T. rexes?" He turned to Tracey. "You never mentioned anything about their hunting in packs."

Tracey stammered, taken off-guard and defensive. "It was only a theory...one I didn't subscribe to."

Peter came to her rescue. "It's not her fault. We operate on data and theories derived from digs in our dimension, Mr. Nielsen. The dinosaurs here behave differently."

"Or your theories are incorrect," added Collins.

"That's equally possible," said Peter, conceding the point.

"Okay, you think it's still out there," said Collins. "How do we test that theory?"

Peter looked around the back of the truck at the equipment.

Tracey turned to Marcy. "What kind of equipment do you have on-board?"

"All kinds of sensory equipment, measuring changes in climate...barometric readings, temperature, seismic activity."

"Do you have an infrasound detector?"

Marcy nodded. "Yes. It's an app on my laptop, but I need to hook up the microphone."

"Of course," said Peter, obviously amused by something the others weren't getting. He knew what Tracey was getting at.

"Hook it up," said Tracey.

Marcy nodded and began to rummage through her equipment strewn all over the back compartment.

"Someone want to fill me in?" asked Nielsen.

"T. rexes use what's called closed mouth vocalization," explained Tracey. "They can emit low frequency sound without opening their mouths. Birds can do it."

"If we can stick a microphone out the window, we might be able to detect it," added Peter.

"Which would mean it's out there, waiting for us," said Collins.

"Here we go," said Marcy, fumbling with a large, corded microphone. She unraveled the cord, plugged it into her laptop, and opened the infrasound detector application. "Okay…we're live."

Tracey reached out and took the microphone from Marcy. She paused, looking at everyone and biting her lip. "Okay, here goes."

She turned the back handle slowly and opened the back door gradually, wincing as it creaked on its hinges. Everyone held their breaths, waiting for the Tyrannosaurus to come bounding back out of the jungle. Tracey slipped the microphone outside, keeping her eyes peeled for movement.

"I've got something," said Marcy. All eyes were on her. "I'm picking something up…"

"Is it the T. rex?" asked Nielsen.

Marcy shook her head. "No…it's the river flowing outside. Let me try and filter that out." Her fingers darted around her laptop keyboard. "Okay…wait a minute…there's something else."

"Can you play it on the speakers?" asked Peter.

"Okay." Marcy hit a few keys, and the sound played over her laptop speakers. It was a low, vibrational sound.

"That's nothing," said Nielsen.

Peter and Tracey exchanged knowing looks. Tracey pulled the microphone inside and closed the back door.

"That's it," said Peter. "That's what it sounds like."

"Horror movies use the sound as part of their soundtrack, in the background, underneath all the other sound," said Tracey. "It's used to induce feelings of dread. We're kind of hardwired to respond to it, from an evolutionary standpoint."

"Okay, so he's still out there," said Nielsen. "What do we do about it? We can't stay here."

"We can take the river back to base camp," offered Collins.

Peter shook his head. "The current is flowing in the opposite direction. Besides, I almost got eaten by a Spinosaurus earlier."

"There was a Spinosaurus in the river?" Tracey sounded more excited than horrified.

"We have the light-bending camo," said Collins.

When Peter looked perplexed, Tracey said, "It's really cool. It's a fabric that bends light. Makes you almost invisible."

"Yeah, but what about its other senses, like smell?" asked Peter.

"There's not much we can do about that," said Nielsen, casually sniffing his armpit. His shirt was drenched with sweat. "How do we get back to base? The other T. rexes are back there, feasting on our weapons team."

"We could cross the river," said Collins, looking out the windows facing the river. "It looks deep. The T. rexes are all on this side."

"It is deep," said Peter. "The Spinosaurus swam in it, and they're quite large."

"Everyone here know how to swim?" asked Nielsen. Each person nodded. "Good. Then we have a plan. We cross the river and return to base camp on the other side."

"What about the other men?" asked the driver, who until now had been listening quietly.

"There's nothing to be done for them," said Nielsen, his tone grave and only slightly dismissive.

"Maybe *he* can do something," said the driver, pointing to Peter. "He said he can heal people."

Peter shook his head. "Only if they're bodily intact. If they're mutilated or eaten, there's nothing I can do for them."

"We can check for any survivors on our way back," said Collins. "Are we ready to do this? I feel if we wait too long, something else might come along, like a Spinosaurus or a giant freaking snake."

"He's right," said Nielsen. "We need to return to base camp and regroup."

"We need to get off this island," said Tracey.

"Not without the others, we don't," said Nielsen. "We haven't even established contact with the others."

"I told you," said Peter. "They'll have evacuated the village. There's no telling where they are."

Tracey squeezed his arm. "You can use the orb, can't you, Peter? To find them. You said you can sense everything on the island."

Peter raised both eyebrows. "That option hadn't occurred to me."

"Well, can you do it?" pressed Nielsen.

"I-I think so," said Peter. "I suppose I could locate them that way."

Nielsen nodded his approval. "Good. We don't leave until we have everyone."

"When we exit the truck," said Collins, "we have to all leave together and make a break for the river. If our friend is still out there, he's going to come right at us, fast and hard."

Nielsen looked around the back of the truck. "What about all the equipment?"

Collins shook his head. "We'll be lucky if we get out of this with our lives."

Nielsen swallowed hard and nodded. "Right. Are we all ready?"

Everyone nodded.

Collins turned to the driver up front. "Are you ready, Castillo?"

"Yup."

Collins hefted his assault rifle. "Okay, let's do it."

PART II

NEVER SPLIT THE PARTY

CHAPTER 6

"We have to go," demanded Susan, watching her friends be taken prisoner by lizard men down below. "There's nothing we can do for them."

Hiu's body went rigid, his chin held high. It was the posture he took when he dug his heels in. "Help friends."

Susan, too, knew how to be obstinate. In fact, one might have said it was her defining characteristic. "They wouldn't want us to help them. We need to get what's left of the tribe to safety."

"Hunter Jason and Mary need we."

Susan let out an exasperated growl. "How do we help them? Too many lizard men. More than us. They have all of our warriors."

Hiu stamped his foot on the ground and puffed his chest out. "Not all. I warrior."

Susan gesticulated wildly. "You're the leader, and your tribe needs you to lead."

Hiu looked at what remained of his tribe, and all eyes were on him. Some understood the exchange, and although they viewed Susan as a friend, they grimaced and pulled faces when she challenged their chieftain.

"What us do?" Hiu asked the group of thirty tribespeople, mostly women and children, some farmers.

They clearly looked stunned that their chief asked for their opinion, as it was not usual Umazoa custom. Susan was no stranger to office politics, and she realized she was putting Hiu on the spot in front of his people.

To help him save face, she bowed to him, something she'd never done to anyone in this dimension or her own. It pained her to do it, but she knew that she needed to repair whatever damage her arguments may have caused. If the tribe fell into chaos, they'd be finished for sure. "Okay, okay. We help the others. But how?"

Hiu smiled at Susan's deference. He gathered his people together. There were still a couple of warriors amongst them. He issued instructions, just like he did before a big hunt. What Susan understood was, after the lizard men below left, they were going to trek to the bottom of the cliff where the others were ambushed, checking for tracks. They would then follow the tracks and mount a rescue attempt.

Hiu turned to Susan, handing her a spear.

Susan put her hands up. "Oh no, I'm not a fighter." At least she wasn't in the physical sense. She preferred her sparring to be verbal.

Hiu insisted, shoving it into her hands.

Susan wrapped her hands around the long, wooden shaft. She had never had to engage in combat before. There were always others who did the fighting—warriors, Jason, Mary. She abhorred violence, but she was in a primitive land where violence was a part of existence. It was how the strong fed off the slow and the weak. Susan realized she didn't want to be the injured animal away from the pack, first to be picked off by astute predators.

She met Hiu's eyes and nodded.

Hiu huffed, but it was admiration rather than derision. It was what the Umazoa did when they were impressed.

Susan followed Hiu as he led the remnants of his tribe down the narrow path and through the jungle. Careful to avoid areas known to them to be prime spots for the larger predators, they tread through difficult terrain, as the road less travelled was indeed the safer one.

At last, they reached the bottom of the cliff where Jason, Mary, and the others had been ambushed. The place was empty. Everyone, human and reptile alike, had moved on. Hiu and the few hunters in the group immediately scoured the ground, squatting on their haunches from time to time, probing the dirt with their fingers.

Susan attempted to look for traps, seeing many sets of footprints leading in different directions. It all appeared a disorganized mess to her, and she struggled to make sense of it. The only detail she discerned was the human vs. lizard men tracks. The lizard men's tracks were larger and three-pronged for their three-clawed feet.

Hiu and the other hunters engaged in a lively conversation about their findings. They spoke so fast and with such emotion that Susan found it difficult to follow. They seemed to be in disagreement about something. The only meaning she gleaned from familiar Umazoan fragments of speech was they were discussing Jason and Mary as separate from the others.

Finally, she couldn't take it anymore. She agreed to follow Hiu, but she hadn't agreed to be kept in the dark. "What? What is it? What's wrong?"

Hiu turned to Susan, gesturing with his hands, moving them in divergent directions.

Susan shook her head. "I don't understand." She repeated the sentiment in Umazoan, as it was a familiar phrase of tremendous utility to her.

Hiu looked up, gathering his thoughts. "Jason...Mary..." He gestured south. "Us tribe..." He gestured north.

"Oh," said Susan, finally comprehending. "They split up." She moved her hands in divergent directions.

Hiu nodded. "Yes. Yes."

Susan realized what they were debating—who to rescue. Hiu went on to pantomime walking with his fingers, and he indicated there were many more tracks going south than north. Then, he indicated through pantomime that the tracks going south belonged mostly to lizard men, while most of the tracks going north belonged to Umazoa.

She cleared her throat. "Tribe...they go to temple...not many lizard men?"

Hiu nodded.

This meant that a small detail of lizard men brought the tribe back to the temple, whereas a larger detail took Jason and Mary south.

Susan didn't believe what she was about to offer, but she couldn't ask Hiu to abandon his tribe to save Jason and Mary. It just wasn't right. "I will go and find Jason and Mary."

Hiu paused and exchanged looks with the other warriors. Susan was uncertain if he understood what she was trying to convey.

The chieftain stepped forward, arched his back, puffing his chest out, and emitted an emphatic huff. The other hunters followed suit. He understood, and he was conveying his admiration.

Susan figured it was the only way. He had to see to his tribe, and she had to see to hers. Hiu squatted and spat on his right index and middle finger. He squatted, dipped them into the dirt, stood, and approached Susan.

Susan blanched, taking a few steps back. "Oh, gross...no...what are you doing?"

Hiu stamped his foot and held his chin high.

"Okay..." was all Susan could manage as the diminutive chief advanced. He smeared the dirt moistened with his saliva under each of her eyes. He was telling her she was now a hunter. He told her in Umazoan to follow the river, gesturing with his hand, and she would find her friends.

He placed both of his hands on her shoulders, bowed forward, and touched foreheads with her. It was something she'd seen him do to others before he left for a hunt. Then, he and the rest of the tribe went north to the temple.

Susan stood there, alone, with dirt and spit smeared under her eyes, wondering how she was going to find her friends. What's more, she wondered what she was going to do when she found them.

* * *

Mary held onto Jason, as their captors led them on foot deeper south into the jungle, following the river. He muttered something incomprehensible every so often, swatting at what she thought was flies, only he appeared to be reacting to hallucinations. As they walked with spears to their backs amongst twenty or so lizard men, Mary slipped a hand under Jason's shirt, a move he would've normally relished but now was oblivious to. His wound felt hot. She slipped her hand back out and placed it on his forehead. "My God, you're burning up."

She received a shove from the butt of a spear, causing her to stumble. This placed her off balance, and she was unable to steady Jason. He tumbled to the dirt.

Mary turned on her captors. "He's sick! Don't you understand?"

The lizard men looked at each other. One who appeared to be the leader stepped in front of her and hissed, flailing his dewlap under his chin.

Another stepped forward, clad in a blue tunic, holding a small orb. He made strange sounds at the leader, and there was a brief exchange before he approached Mary with the orb. He held out the orb.

Mary had heard Peter's stories about the lizard men's orbs and how they used them to store memories. She wondered why he extended one to her now. He waved it at her, inviting her to touch it.

Unsure of what to do but wary of jabbing spears, she reached out and palmed the sphere with both hands. She was surprised when the nicely dressed lizard man slid his three-clawed hands underneath the orb but didn't let go. She was even more surprised when a wordless voice entered her mind.

'What is wrong?'

Mary gasped and almost released the orb, but she held on, intuiting that releasing it would break the connection. 'Let us go. Please.'

The lizard man made small motions with his mouth, his retracted dewlap bobbing as it swallowed. 'I cannot do that. What is wrong?'

'My friend is sick. He can't walk in this condition.'

The lizard man paused. 'He requires medicine?'

'Yes. He has an infection from velociraptor wounds. What do you want with us?' She privately wondered why they hadn't killed her or Jason.

'If you cooperate, you will not be harmed…'

Mary's skin went cold. She hadn't meant to transmit that thought. She also didn't like the way it trailed off, thought unfinished, as if there was a 'but' to follow.

Jason grabbed her ankle on the ground and looked up at her. "Help me, Mary. Please."

Mary gazed into the cold, dead eyes of the lizard man holding the orb. 'You need us alive. He will die and cannot go any further in this condition.'

The lizard looked down at Jason, its dewlap extending a bit. It made several swallowing motions, as if something was caught in its throat. 'There's nothing to be done for him. We must leave him behind.'

Mary wondered if the strange body language was a display of emotion. Reading her thought, the lizard man flinched.

Mary cocked her head sideways, chuckling softly. 'My goodness. It *is* an emotional reaction. This upsets you.'

The lizard man flared his dewlap. 'We don't need him. We need you.'

'Why would you need me?' Mary's eyes lit up. 'It's Peter, isn't it? That's why you've all spread out, combing the jungle. You're looking for Peter.'

The lizard man made strange vocalizations, and one of the others stepped toward her, jabbing its spear at her but falling just short of actually piercing her side.

Mary retained her grasp on the orb. 'I'm your insurance policy for when you find him, aren't I?'

The lizard man pulled the orb away from her, thus severing the connection. The others corralled Mary away from Jason.

"We just can't leave him here," she shouted at them. "He'll die."

Jason reached up for her as she was shoved away from him. "Mary…wait…where are you going? Mary…"

*

Jason watched as Mary was led away. His muscles ached, and his body felt as if it was on fire. The whole thing seemed like a fever dream to him. As he lay back, his mind swimming, waiting to die, something approached him.

In his current delirium, he no longer cared if he lived or died. It loomed over him, looking down at him, but Jason's vision was so blurred and his mind so incapable of processing what he saw, it might as well have been a hallucination.

The wraith lowered itself to his level in a single, deft, fluid motion, as if it were made of smoke. 'Jason, the great hunter.' The voice was like fog in his mind, empty, reedy, and haunting all at once.

"Wh-what? Who...?"

'I am here to help you, Jason." It said his name in an odd kind of hiss, like air escaping. "Your friend has left you.'

"Mary...Mary, come back. Please...come back."

'She has abandoned you for the one named Peter.'

"No...she wouldn't...Peter is my friend."

'Would a friend leave you alone to fend for yourself? Would a friend, who has the power to heal you, leave you here to rot on the jungle floor?'

Jason started laughing and singing to himself. The infection had taken hold and was affecting his cognition. His blood was poisoned, and now he was dying.

'I would never leave you in such a state,' hissed the voice. 'I can help you, right here, right now.'

"Pl-please...please." Jason hummed musically to himself, choking on his own laughter as if he was drowning in it.

The wraith wrapped itself around him and infused itself in him, entering his eyes, ears, nose and mouth simultaneously. He felt it coursing through him, and as it moved throughout his body, he felt the infection yield to it. However, he wasn't quite being healed. Rather, this entity had placed the infection on pause. Within minutes his mind and body cleared. As he felt his body recover, the entity left him, swirling and reforming outside his body until it stood over him once more.

Jason lay on his back, his clothing drenched in his own sweat. He sat up and looked around. His mind and vision were clear. Yet, when he saw the wraith standing next to him, it remained shrouded in smoke and fog.

'Peter is not the only one with power. I have spared your life, and I seek only one thing in return. Peter must go to the Temple of the Simian King.' The idea swirled around like vapor in his mind, and the apparition dissipated in the sunlight, carried away on the island breeze.

"The Temple of the Simian King," repeated Jason to himself. He had no idea what that even meant, but he knew it was imperative he make it happen.

Jason heard a whisper. 'I will always be with you,' but he swore it was the island breeze playing tricks on his mind. It was only the breeze.

* * *

Susan slipped into the river, letting the current take her south. The lizard men who took Mary and Jason had a lead on her, and the only way she could make up the distance was to let the river take her. She would move swiftly while conserving energy—energy she'd need to mount a rescue.

* * *

Tracey pulled the handle and slowly opened the back door to the armored truck, bracing it with her other hand grabbing the edge. It creaked, regardless, but her efforts mitigated the noise. The ambient noise of the river hopefully drowned out the sound.

She slipped out, Peter and Marcy right behind her, followed by Nielsen and Collins, all wearing backpacks. The driver's side door, facing the jungle, creaked as Castillo stepped outside. The others froze, ears pricked for any sound and eyes on the jungle to their right.

"Crap," was all Peter could get out when the Tyrannosaurus bolted out of the jungle and descended on Castillo. The driver managed to raise his rifle and get off a single shot before he was snatched up in its jaws. He cried out as foot-long teeth pierced his camo and body armor like a hot knife through butter.

"Run!" shouted Collins.

The group dashed for the river as the T. rex chomped on the poor mercenary, his blood dripping from its jaws as it swallowed the pieces of meat. Peter and Tracey dove in first. He heard splashes behind him, but he didn't dare look as he pumped his arms and legs furiously, swimming for the other side. Rather, he kept his eyes on the river for large shadows.

As he and Tracey swam with all their might, the river carried them southbound, so their trajectory was more of a diagonal. Past the halfway mark across, Peter heard the T. rex roar behind him, but he was fairly certain it wouldn't cross. He kept one eye on the opposite river bank and one on the water below, praying there wasn't a Spinosaurus lurking about.

When he reached the opposite side with Tracey, they both stood up and slogged their way, splashing in the shallows until they reached the other side. They stopped, panting, catching their breath as the others joined them on the river bank.

Peter saw the T. rex pacing back and forth on the other side, furious they eluded it. It roared a couple of times and stomped off, disappearing back into the jungle. "That was close."

"Castillo was a good man," said Collins. "He didn't deserve to go out like that."

Peter shook his head, agreeing. "No one does."

Nielsen placed a hand on Peter's shoulder. "Do you sense anything around here? Any others?"

Peter closed his eyes and reached out with his senses, igniting the orbs in his chest. After a minute, he opened his eyes again. "Nope. The coast is clear for now."

"Can you keep that up as we follow the river back north?" asked Nielsen.

"He's not some kind of machine," snapped Tracey.

"I never said he was," said Nielsen. "In fact, he's some kind of magic."

"The answer is 'no.' I can't," said Peter. "It has to be a conscious effort. I can make periodic checks, but I have to stop and concentrate. It might slow us down."

"Better safe than sorry," said Collins. "Just let us know when you're going to do it, and we'll stop in as safe a place as possible."

Peter nodded. Just like the tabletop role-playing games. Searching for danger as he went, but each check would constitute a turn.

They stuck close to the river, making their way back to base camp. Collins tried his radio every so often, but to no avail. The island was interfering. The sun rose high in the sky, and at midday Collins unshouldered his pack. "We have to eat and hydrate."

The others slowed down and followed suit, grabbing granola bars and bottled water from their packs. Wrappers crinkled and the group ate, taking swigs of water between bites.

"I have to take a leak," said Peter.

"That's not a bad idea," said Nielsen.

Tracey looked down as she rubbed her stomach with her right hand. "I have to...do something else."

"We stick together," said Collins.

"There's no way I'm doing *that* in front of you," said Tracey, grimacing at her stomach upset.

"I don't want you wandering off," demanded Collins. "Who knows what's out there?"

"Sounds like it's time for one of my checks," said Peter. He closed his eyes and reached out all around them. He felt the plants around them, birds in the trees, several monkeys, but no clear and imminent threats. "The coast is clear right now."

Collins nodded. "Okay, let's make it quick."

They each split up, as privacy was apparently still important, even on an island in another dimension. Peter wandered off away from the river. He heard Collins warn Tracey not to go too far. He didn't hear her response, but he could've imagined it. He would've gone with her, but not for what she was about to do. A tinkle was one thing. Dropping the kids off at the pool was another.

He picked a good spot and unzipped his fly. He took a look around, checking over his shoulder. Satisfied he was alone, he relieved himself. It felt good to empty his bladder. Just moments ago, he was too terrified to know he had to urinate, so this small moment came as a welcome relief. As he zipped back up, he was startled by a rustling in the bushes off to his left. He meant to close his eyes and reach out with his senses, but he didn't get the chance.

Six lizard men emerged from the vegetation, five of them holding spears. One held an orb in his hands.

Oh crap, thought Peter. He wondered how they evaded his detection and if they'd searched for him after his narrow escape down river. He put his hands up, surrendering, as he was unarmed. He cursed himself for not asking for a weapon back in the armored truck.

He heard the voices of his friends chattering behind him. Nielsen told everyone to hurry up. Tracey shouted something back. Peter weighed his options. He could either shout for help, but his friends would have to face off against six lizard men, five of them armed. Or, he could let the lizard men take him and spare the others being taken captive or worse. Only Collins was armed. With an automatic rifle, he stood a fair chance.

The lizard man with the orb flared his dewlap and approached Peter, holding out the orb. He knew this meant it wanted to communicate. The others stood there, holding their spears, but otherwise posing no immediate threat. Peter reached out and palmed the orb.

A familiar wordless voice entered his mind. 'I see you are unharmed.' It was the one he'd encountered underground. The one who showed him the visions of their history.

'No thanks to you. You can have me. Leave the others alone.'

'If that is what you wish.'

'What do you want?'

The lizard man swallowed several times, his tongue flittering out between his lips. 'I need your help.'

Peter didn't expect this response. '*My* help? *You* need *my help?*'

'My people are warlike, bold, and equally foolish.'

Peter didn't know what to say to that. 'You speak as if you're not including yourself with them.'

The lizard man waved a clawed hand as it spoke. 'Unfortunately, I share their grim fate if I do not intercede.'

Tracey came bounding into Peter's small clearing, laughing to herself. "Jesus, Peter, how long does it take to..." Her eyes went wide when she saw the lizard men, "...drain the lizard."

The lizard men bobbed their heads, extending their dewlaps at full mast. A few wielded their spears, pointing them at Tracey.

She screamed, but Peter waved his right hand at her while keeping the other on the sphere. "Tracey, wait."

She looked at Peter, his hands on the orb, confused. "What's going on here?"

Collins and Nielsen burst into the clearing.

"Oh my God," gasped Nielsen, jaw hanging open.

Collins raised his rifle, training it on the lizard men. "Dr. Albanese, are you okay?"

The lizard men with the spears hissed at them, waving their sharpened spear tips. One produced a bolus and was twirling it in the air above its head.

The lizard man holding the orb made strange guttural sounds at the others. Because Peter's hands were still on the orb, he caught the order—*Now.*

Two of the lizard men attacked the other three. The three attacked appeared just as surprised as everyone else. Collins held his fire, appearing unsure of what to target. One victim took a spear to the chest and went down immediately. The remaining two victims fought back. However, one took a spear to the side and had its throat ripped out by a clawed hand. The remaining victim killed one of the traitors but was finished off by the other one.

Collins trained his weapon on the one survivor. "Will somebody tell me what the hell is going on?"

'Grux will not harm you,' said the lizard man holding the orb to Peter.

"Wait," said Peter.

"Tell me what's going on," demanded Collins.

"Why did they attack each other?" asked Nielsen.

'Why did your men turn on themselves?' asked Peter.

'Grux and Drok are among those sympathetic to my cause. Drok was a good man. Pity he had to die.'

'What cause is that?'

'The cause of all of us on the island, including the Uminami.'

Peter wondered at the reference, but soon realized he meant the Umazoans.

The lizard man cocked its head sideways. 'You are not like the other Uminami.'

'And you are not like the other lizard men,' retorted Peter.

'That is because I am not. My name is Ghenga. I am one of the higher evolved of what you call the lizard men. We are the Zehhaki. My people are in grave danger.'

'Why should I care about your people when they attack mine? I woke you from extinction, and you choose to hurt my friends.'

Collins stepped forward, training his gun on Grux. Grux looked to Ghenga, who croaked something to him. Grux bowed and laid his spear on the ground.

"These aren't like the others," said Peter over his shoulder.

"What do they want?" asked Tracey.

"Hold on," said Peter. "I'm trying to find out."

"How?" asked Collins.

"He's communicating with him somehow," said Tracey, "using the orb."

"Remarkable," gasped Nielsen, watching with great interest.

'Unfortunately, it is Zehhaki nature to wage war and pillage. It is what led to our extinction so many cycles ago. And now, given a second chance, it looks as if they are going to repeat the same mistakes again. If left unchecked, they will destroy the balance in this place. Without a natural predator, they will destroy the entire food chain.'

Peter cursed himself. He hadn't intended to awaken them. His carelessness was going to bring down a whole ecosystem. 'What can we do about it?'

'*You*,' said Ghenga. 'You possess the power of the two orbs. You possess dominion over life and death.'

'I could send you all back into extinction using the death orb.'

'That is one option...'

Peter felt Ghenga rummaging around his mind, searching through memories...recent memories. 'You do not yet know how to wield the death orb, but you have received an offer to learn.'

'What was that *thing* that offered to teach me?' asked Peter.

'That is Nazimaa. She is a dangerous presence in our land, a demon spirit of a common enemy of all life. She has dominion over sickness and healing, water, and darkness. She is entombed, sleeping...waiting to be reawakened in bodily form.'

'Okay, so she's someone to stay away from.'

'Yes.'

'I've pretty much gathered that. So, if I can't send the Zehhaki back into extinction, what is my other option?'

'There is another race that, if awoken, can bring balance.'

'The ape men,' said Peter.

'You must go to the temple of the Simian King and awaken them from their cycles-long slumber. Only then will the Zehhaki be counter-balanced.'

Peter didn't like this prospect. He had awoken one race and unleashed war and death upon the rest of the island. Was awakening yet another race the answer? What would they be like? 'Is the other race—the Simians—good?'

'Good?'

'Will they hurt life?'

'They will wage war with the Zehhaki. It is in their nature.'

'So, they are good.'

'There is no good,' said Ghenga. 'There is no evil. We each act according to our nature. The Zehhaki are not good or evil. Some wage war, and others are charged with using thought and strategy—both for the survival of the race.'

'Why should I do this? Why should I trust what you say? Why don't I just go to Nazimaa?'

'I have not threatened you in any way. I come to you offering balance...a chance for your people.'

Peter removed his hands from the orb. He didn't want Ghenga to have access to his thoughts at this moment. Balance? A chance? The Umazoa weren't even his people, but Ghenga didn't know that. Yet, he felt some responsibility for them. He even, in some twisted way, felt some responsibility towards the Zehhaki. Some deity he turned out to be. He woke an ancient race, and his children were the scourge of the island.

Tracey appeared by his side. "What is it, Peter?"

Peter held up a hand. "Hold on a second." He placed his hands back on the orb, re-establishing the connection. 'What if I refuse to get involved?'

Ghenga's dewlap twitched. 'You are already involved. The other Zehhaki are searching for you. They know what you saw. They know I showed you historical records of the Simians. They know what I want to happen, for the good of the race. The leadership disagrees.'

'You didn't answer my question. Why should I help you?'

'Because the others have your friends, the hunter and your mate.'

'Jason and Mary?'

'They will use them to get to you. To stop you before you awaken the Simian race.'

Peter shook his head. 'Go to them. Tell them I won't do it.' However, he knew that wouldn't work. The Zehhaki wouldn't respond to negotiations. That much was abundantly clear. 'What about the others? I'm sure there are others that believe as you do.'

'There are, but they are in the minority.'

'What do you care? Extinction would take generations. You wouldn't live to see it.'

Ghenga swept his head around, repeatedly pumping his dewlap as he swallowed hard. It was a major emotional response. 'The Zehhaki were once a great people. The large reptiles, the ones you call *dinosaurs*, are the descendants of the Zehhaki. They are what we devolved into. We are their progenitors. I do not wish that for my ancestors.'

Peter thought he sensed a sentiment like pensive nostalgia. As Peter felt responsibility towards the Umazoa and even the Zehhaki, Ghenga felt the same responsibility towards his people.

Peter released the orb. He had much to think about.

Tracey squeezed his arm. "What is it? Is everything okay?"

Nielsen looked astounded. "You spoke with him, didn't you? What did he say?"

"More importantly, is he friend or foe?" asked Collins.

Peter looked at each of them. "Okay, you want to know? You're not going to believe this…"

CHAPTER 7

Jason followed the lizard men's tracks along the riverbank, wondering if what he'd experienced was some kind of dream. He remembered being sick, Mary being taken away, and feeling totally powerless to do anything about it. He remembered talking to someone…was he really talking? The whole exchange was lost in a fog inside his mind.

He stopped every so often, squatting and examining the tracks. The lizard men's tracks started out numerous; Jason estimated thirty or so sets. However, as he progressed down the riverbank, keeping a careful eye out for predators, he noticed some veering off to the right and into the jungle, and others veering off into the river.

The ones leading into the river grew deeper and deeper, with the final sets of prints for each individual pressing down a few to several inches into the soft silt. This indicated to Jason that they crouched and dove into the river. Those things could swim.

As he squatted, examining the prints, he thought he caught something downriver in the corner of his eye. When he looked up, he saw a head bobbing in the current.

"Help! Jason, help me!"

He squinted, trying to see who it was. It was Susan. "Susan, swim towards me. I've got you."

She doggy paddled to the right as the river carried her toward him. Jason stepped into the water, waist-deep. "That's it, Susan. Swim to me."

But she was coming too fast. Within seconds she was swept past him. He reached out for her, but she was still too far out. Jason ran back up onto the riverbank and ran alongside the river. He was able to catch up to her and keep pace. The current wasn't exactly rapids, but it was too strong for her to fight it. "Swim to the side," he called out. "Swim to me. I'll get you."

"I can't," she cried. "It's too strong." She dipped below the surface for a moment, spitting up water upon resurfacing. Jason saw several splashes around her. She looked down into the water, screeching. "Something's grabbing…" She slipped under again.

Jason sprinted ahead of where she went under and ran into the water, splashing loudly. He unsheathed his massive hunting knife and dove under the water. He saw flashes of green writhing about and Susan kicking and waving her arms, trying to escape.

Jason kicked his way over to the underwater tumult and reached for one of Susan's feet. Her right foot had a three-clawed hand wrapped around it. He lashed out with his blade, slashing at it until her foot was shrouded in a cloud of crimson. He pulled at her ankle, and it was free.

Running out of air, he worked his way up her body, grabbed her waist, and pulled upward, kicking his legs. She rose with him, the both of them breaching the surface, gasping for air. Something pulled at his feet as Susan screamed, and they were both pulled under again. Jason curled up, bringing his hands closer to his feet, and he slashed at the arm grabbing his ankle. The lizard man recoiled, releasing him. He turned to Susan and pulled his way around her body towards her feet. A spear thrust up at him, narrowly missing his side.

He slashed at the two lizard men, desperate to grab either of them and pull them down. He dodged a couple of spear thrusts as they recoiled from his slashing. Jason shoved Susan to the surface. He burst up into the air, took a deep breath, and dove back down.

As he kicked, propelling himself down, the other two lizard men swam up to meet him. They each thrust a spear at him. He deflected one with his knife and was grazed by the other just under his ribs. Blood trickled out of his wound in a cloud. As they grappled, the cloud expanded, obscuring their vision. Jason reached out and grabbed a scaled wrist. He pulled himself close and knifed the surprised lizard man in the neck.

As he pulled his knife out of its throat, a claw struck out to his left and then a spear between his legs. The other lizard man was close. Jason swam out of the bloody cloud and to the side. The remaining lizard man lunged at him, gliding through the water, but a long, thick shape shot up from underneath it.

The reptilian attacker stopped short of colliding with Jason and was pulled under by a massive snake chomping down on its legs. The lizard man turned its attention to the massive boa as he sank, and Jason shot up to the surface. He filled his lungs with air and wiped the water out of his eyes. He saw Susan drifting closer to shore.

Jason swam over to her as fast as he could. She was exhausted from fighting the current and barely treading water. Spent himself, he grabbed her and swam sideways toward shore. When they felt the bottom rise up to meet them, they crawled, sloshing through the shallows, until they reached land.

Susan rolled over on her back, catching her breath. Jason lay on his side, panting, re-sheathing his knife.

"Wh-what…are you…doing here?" he asked.

She turned her head toward him. "Rescuing…you…of course."

They shared a laugh, a welcome dissipation of the high anxiety of moments ago.

"Where's Mary?" asked Susan.

Jason swallowed, his breathing equalizing. "They took her."

"You *left* her?"

"No! I didn't *leave* her. I was hurt from the velociraptor attack. They decided I was dead weight and left me behind."

Susan frowned. "You look all right to me."

Jason sat up, grunting. "It's a long story. I had…help."

Her face lit up. "Peter? He's here?"

Jason shook his head as he pushed himself to standing. "No, something else."

"What?"

"We need to focus on finding Mary." He walked up onto land and scanned the ground for tracks. "They split up into groups…we met the ones waiting in the river…but Mary's tracks continue to follow the river."

Susan stood, brushing herself off. "I didn't even see them coming. Do you think they can breathe under water?"

Jason shook his head. "Probably not. But, many reptiles can slow their breathing and heartrate to stay under for extended periods of time. Hell, I had an iguana that could stay submerged in the bathtub for half an hour."

Susan grimaced. "Yuck. Gross."

"He was a great pet, actually. Smart fella."

"I'll stick to dogs," said Susan.

Jason snickered. "Yeah, they're not gross at all. They just eat their own poop and use their tongues as toilet paper."

"That's charming," said Susan. "The ladies must be lining up to go out with you."

Jason's eyes lit up. "There she is."

Susan stood next to him as he crouched. "Who?"

"Mary. I see her tracks."

"What do you think they're up to?"

"They're keeping Mary alive. I think they wanted me alive, but in my condition, I was slowing them down."

Susan wrinkled her nose. "How do you know they wanted you two alive?"

"They could've killed us at any time, but they didn't," said Jason. "One of them spoke to Mary."

"Spoke to Mary? How?"

He moved his hands in a circular motion. "It used some kind of a crystal ball. If Mary and the lizard both touched it simultaneously, they could hear each other's thoughts or something. At least that's what it looked like."

Susan raised her eyebrows and let out a big sigh. "Well, now I've heard everything."

Jason was lost in thought. "They're tracking someone. They're keeping Mary alive as a bargaining chip."

She snapped her fingers. "Peter."

Jason nodded. "He's still alive. It has to be him. He must've escaped their lair." He looked around. "You're alone. What happened to Hiu and the others?"

"They went to rescue those taken back to the underground city," said Susan.

"With most of the warriors taken captive? They won't stand a chance."

"Not if most of the lizard men are out combing the jungle for Peter," said Susan.

Jason looked around and then at Susan. "Something happened. They want him badly. I've never seen them come above ground in these numbers before. We'd better get moving if we're going to help Mary."

"Maybe we'll run into Peter along the way," said Susan.

Jason picked up the trail, focusing on Mary's tracks. "The good news is she's still walking and not being dragged."

Susan walked alongside him. She had lost her spear in the river and was completely unarmed.

Jason looked over and saw she was wringing her hands. He unsheathed his hunting knife and extended it to her.

She was surprised by the gesture. "I-I couldn't."

He chuckled. "What? You're afraid of a little knife?"

Susan laughed. It was a nervous sound. "I wouldn't know what to do with that. Besides, you'd be completely unarmed. I'd feel safer if you had it."

"Are you sure? I can fashion a spear out of a tree branch."

She shook her head. "No, but thank you."

"When we find Mary, I'm going to need your help," said Jason. "I can't do it alone."

Susan's shoulders slumped.

He looked over at her. "What's wrong?"

"Nothing."

"Come on, out with it."

Susan bit her bottom lip. "I feel...useless."

"What do you mean? You led the rest of the tribe to safety."

"Only to have them go on a half-assed rescue mission where they're totally outmatched."

"Not your fault," said Jason. "It was Hiu's choice to do that."

"I don't know...back in the world—our world—I was someone important. I ran projects, managed people."

Jason stared at the ground as he spoke, following the tracks. "You still do. You helped the Umazoa improve their village. Even though you're an outsider, they look up to you."

Susan shook her head. "I screwed up the first expedition. People died. *I* died. Still can't wrap my brain around that one."

"And Peter brought you back," said Jason. "He brought me back, too."

"Honestly, I was a screw up back home, too. My marriage was falling apart because I devoted so much time to getting to this damned island. None of it was worth it."

"Well, we all make mistakes." He paused a moment, dwelling on his own. "All we can do is learn from them and live with them."

Susan smiled, looking at him sideways. "Pretty philosophical for a big game hunter."

He smiled. "When you've devoted your life to taking life, you get pretty philosophical. Metaphysical, even."

She opened her mouth to speak but stopped short, as if wanting to ask him something but thinking better of it.

"Out with it," he said.

"Have you...ever...you know, hunted a person?"

"You're asking if I'm a murderer?"

Susan quickly averted her eyes as they walked. "It was just how you said it...taking lives. Sounded like you were referring to human beings."

"I'm not a monster, you know."

"I'm not saying you are," she stammered. "You're a complex guy. A real mystery wrapped in an enigma."

Jason guffawed, breaking the tension. "Where do you come up with this stuff?"

They continued on, following Mary's tracks in a comfortable silence. Jason hadn't noticed that they were being watched, but it wasn't by dinosaurs or lizard men. It was something that left no tracks.

* * *

"We need to return to base camp," said Collins. "We can discuss side missions later."

"I made this mess," insisted Peter, "I need to clean it up."

"I'll go with you," offered Tracey.

"No, you won't," said Nielsen. "You're an employed consultant of Poseidon Tech, and you'll stay on mission, Dr. Moran."

Tracey shook her head. "I left him all alone to deal with all of this. I need to help him fix it."

"Who's to say that this thing is telling the truth?" said Collins. "It could be leading you right into a trap."

Ghenga watched the exchange, occasionally flicking his tongue out to taste the air. Grux stood by his side, waiting patiently.

"I don't think so," said Peter. "He basically wants me to awaken an old rival race."

"How do we know this Simian race won't join forces with them and kill everything else on the island?" insisted Collins.

"Why do we even care about this when we're all going to be leaving this island?" said Nielsen. "It's a moot point, because we won't be here long."

"In all good conscience, I can't leave everything like this," said Peter.

Tracey placed a hand on his shoulder. "Maybe Nielsen's right. I came to get you and bring you back, not help you fix unintended consequences."

Peter met her eyes with his. "I can't go back. Not yet, anyway. You have to understand, I set things in motion that need to be corrected."

She nodded, eyes welling up. "I'll back whatever decision you make. I need to correct my mistakes as well."

Peter arched an eyebrow. However, before he could query as to what she meant, Nielsen stepped in front of him. "If it was your interference that caused these problems, do you really think more meddling will help? We came for you, to bring you back home."

Tracey turned on him. "That's not really why you're here."

Nielsen took a step back. "Well, we're here to bring back all of the old team."

Tracey put her hands on her hips. "Is that why most of our current team is back at base camp?"

Nielsen laughed, but it was bitter and joyless. "What are you talking about? We brought a full weapons team and a helicopter. I came in person, for crying out loud. And I brought Collins, the head of security, with me."

Everyone looked at Collins, who shifted his feet, looking uncomfortable. "Can we argue this back at base camp? We're sitting ducks out here."

"No," demanded Tracey. "We discuss this now. You brought a team of technicians but only bring one on this mission, and she's a damned kid."

"Hey!" protested Marcy. "I'll have you know I'm damned good at what I do."

"I don't doubt that," said Tracey, "but what are all the others doing back at base camp?"

Marcy turned on Nielsen. "Now that you mention it, she raises a good point."

"We're making a lot of noise," said Collins, annoyed, his eyes darting around their surroundings. "This really isn't the place to discuss this. We really need to return to base camp."

"He's right," said Nielsen. "I'd be happy to discuss this back at base camp."

"What about him?" said Peter, gesturing to Ghenga.

"He can come with us," said Nielsen.

Collins stepped forward, putting a hand up. "Now, wait a minute. I didn't approve that."

"You don't need to," said Nielsen, sounding imperious. "I'm the project manager and team leader."

"I'm in charge of keeping base camp secure, and bringing lizard men back constitutes a major security risk," said Collins. "What happens when the others track him back to our base camp?"

Nielsen waved a dismissive hand. "Your men can handle a bunch of lizards with spears."

"What about Mary?" asked Peter. "They have her."

At her mention, Tracey appeared deflated.

"We can launch a rescue mission once we regroup," said Collins.

Peter glowered. "She could be dead by then."

"Now, we don't know that, Dr. Albanese," said Nielsen. "We can't go off into the jungle half-cocked without support."

"He's right about that, Peter," said Tracey, her voice small. "It's too dangerous. We'll be no good to Mary or Jason."

Peter felt guilty. All this time he only focused on Mary; he'd almost forgotten about Jason. He turned away, angry at himself and the situation. "Maybe you're right."

"Send them away," said Collins, gesturing to Ghenga and Grux. "Tell them you'll go to that Temple of the Simian King, but you need reinforcements."

Peter knew he was right. He didn't trust Nielsen as far as he could throw him, but he respected Collins' judgement. The man seemed like a straight shooter. He turned to Ghenga and reached out, palming the orb. 'Ghenga, I have to return to my people.'

Ghenga flared his dewlap and retracted it in a swift motion. 'What about the Temple of the Simian King?'

'I will go and awaken them, but I cannot do it alone. I need my people.'

'If you do not do this, your people will die. All of them.'

'You have my word, Ghenga. I will fix my mistake.'

Ghenga cocked his head. 'You gave the Zehhaki a second chance at existence. It is their mistake that threatens all life in this land, including their own…I will lead them away for now, to afford you time.'

'Thank you. How will I know where the Temple of the Simian King is?'

'I will show you.'

Without warning, a map flashed in Peter's mind with such force it nearly knocked him off his feet. It depicted his current location and the path to the Temple of the Simian King. The map extended even further. Peter's mind meandered, exploring, but the mental image was cut short by Ghenga.

'Now you know how to get there.'

'Thank you, Ghenga.'

'Remember, Peter, beware of Nazimaa and what she offers.'

'I'll stay away from her.'

Ghenga flared his dewlap. 'You cannot. She will follow you.'

'Follow me? Why?'

'She is entombed within the temple. She was separated from the life and death orbs to prevent her resurrection.'

'Well, that's an important detail.'

'Yes. She will try to manipulate you into freeing her from her prison.'

"Let's go, doc," pushed Collins. "We don't want to get ambushed out here."

Peter nodded. He released the orb. Ghenga croaked something to Grux, and they both turned and disappeared back into the jungle.

"Let's go," said Tracey.

"I'll take point," said Collins.

*

Collins and Nielsen took the lead, discussing future plans. Nielsen appeared to dislike having his authority challenged by the security chief.

The two hashed out their differences as Peter, Tracey, and Marcy lagged behind.

"I think you're right," said Marcy, keeping her voice low.

"About why you're really here?" asked Tracey.

Marcy nodded. She shot a nervous glance at Peter.

"I won't bite," said Peter.

Marcy averted her gaze a moment. "What does it feel like?"

"What?"

"Those orbs...the power."

Peter shrugged. "It's all very...alien. They are a part of me, yet they feel different from me."

"How do you bring people back to life?"

Peter considered this a moment. "It's like I reach out with my life force or soul, and I can feel the souls or life forces of others. Then, I just focus on them, making them stronger. Kind of like turning a dial to brighten a light."

"That's amazing," said Marcy, gazing at Peter with obvious admiration.

It made Tracey a little uncomfortable. She remembered Petra, their graduate student, and her kiss with Peter. "That must be some burden to carry."

Peter nodded. "The consequences more so than the powers."

"I shouldn't have left you," said Tracey, her voice thick.

Peter smiled. "You didn't leave me, Trace. I told you to go."

"Yeah, well, I didn't have to listen."

His smile faded. "Have you been beating yourself up about this the whole time?"

Marcy apparently decided to hang back and spectate rather than interject. She fell a couple of steps behind, allowing Peter and Tracey space to talk.

"It's been eating me up for the last year."

Peter appeared nonplussed. "Is that all it's been? A year?"

Tracey nodded. "Yeah. Why? It feels like longer?"

"It feels like it's been years." He unconsciously glanced down at his wristwatch, long broken, a force of habit. It didn't matter anyway. The island had a peculiar effect on time.

"That's a long time," said Marcy, chiming in.

Both Peter and Tracey glanced back at her.

"That must've been awful," said Tracey.

"Not all of it," said Peter. "In that time, we've gotten more familiar with the Umazoa."

Marcy scrunched her nose. "The who?"

"That's what we call the indigenous tribe. We've actually learned some of their language, and they ours."

"That's amazing," said Tracey. "What are they like?"

"They seem like good people. Very family-oriented." He hesitated. "Then, there are the Zehhaki…"

"The lizard men?" said Tracey.

Peter nodded. "They seem more primitive, animalistic, but not entirely. They make use of orbs to record memories and history, and to communicate with humanoids."

"What do you make of that intelligent one who spoke to you?" asked Tracey.

"I believe him. I believe that they'd wipe everything out, exhausting their own food supply. Which leads me to something else…something I saw in my mind when he showed me the location of the Temple of the Simian King."

"What did you see?" asked Marcy.

Peter paused, gathering his thoughts. "Something has always bugged me about this island. We've encountered way more predators than prey. Tracey, you know that in a stable ecosystem there needs to be an optimal ratio between predators and prey."

Tracey nodded. "That's right. That bothered me from last time I was here, but I just figured I hadn't seen enough of the island."

"Well, I've been here a while," said Peter, "and I still haven't seen enough prey to sustain the predator population. And you're right. We haven't seen enough of the island. In fact, this isn't even an island."

Tracey and Marcy both answered in unison, "What?!"

He nodded. "When Ghenga showed me the location of the other temple, I saw the land extend out past what we thought to be the boundaries of the island."

"Maybe it's just a bigger island than we thought," offered Tracey.

"Either that, or it's a continent with only part of it phasing into our dimension," said Marcy, "making it appear to be an island to us."

"You didn't sense any of that?" asked Tracey of Peter.

He shook his head. "I guess my powers have a range."

"So, this island may actually be a continent," said Marcy.

"Which brings us back to the original question," said Peter. "Why is Poseidon Tech here?"

Marcy now kept pace, re-inserting herself into the conversation. "I've overheard conversations about locating some kind of metal ore. For what purpose, I'm not sure. A bit above my paygrade."

"A kind of metal," repeated Peter, thinking out loud. "A precious metal, perhaps?"

"I didn't notice any mining equipment in the expedition," said Tracey.

"I don't think we're here for mining either," agreed Marcy. "We've brought mostly sensory equipment."

"Something's been bothering me," said Tracey. "Why did Nielsen pick that landing site for our base camp?"

"Because it was close to the village and by a river," said Marcy.

Tracey shook her head. "No boats or rafts. If we were going to use the river, we would've brought watercraft. Not only that, why go through all the trouble of clearing out jungle with bombs when Nielsen could've just picked a natural clearing?"

"Maybe he wanted to chase away or kill any predators in that area," said Peter.

"Why are you here, specifically?" Tracey asked Marcy. "What's your specific job or objective?"

"To use the sensory equipment to map the island as we searched for Dr. Albanese and the others."

"You mentioned seismic measurements in the back of the truck," said Tracey. "Do you think that was part of the search for this metal?"

Marcy shrugged. "I don't think so."

"What other use would a metal have to Poseidon Tech?" asked Tracey, thinking out loud.

*

Their speculation was interrupted by Collins, who called back over his shoulder, "We've found the Humvees."

Peter, Tracey, and Marcy ran forward to catch up with Collins and Nielsen.

"Holy smokes," gasped Marcy, taking in the scene before her.

"You can say that again," added Tracey.

Peter winced. "Poor souls."

The Humvees were torn apart. Pieces of jagged metal and parts lay strewn about the riverbank on the other side of the river. The tops of the vehicles looked as if they had been peeled open by a massive can opener.

"Look at all the blood," whispered Marcy, her face turning green.

"I wonder where the chopper is," said Collins. He got on his radio. "Chief to base. Come in, base."

His radio crackled. 'Copy that, Chief. You've been radio silent. What is your location?'

"It's radio interference," said Collins. "Heading back to base camp. We were attacked. The weapons team was wiped out. Have you seen our Huey?"

'Negative. We've lost radio contact with the Bravo Huey. Alpha Huey is still in the air."

"That's the one guarding base camp," said Collins to the others. "That means we've lost ours."

"How the hell does a T. rex take down a Huey?" asked Nielsen.

"Maybe it wasn't a T. rex," said Peter.

"Are there predatory birds on this island?" asked Collins. "Pterodactyls or something?"

"I haven't seen any," said Peter. "Then again, I really haven't ventured out this far before. The Umazoa like to stick to their territory, keeping a close proximity to their plateau village. But that doesn't mean there aren't any."

Instinctively, everyone's eyes darted up to the sky.

"We need to keep moving," said Collins. "Whatever took out the Huey could return." He got on his radio, "Base, be advised there may be airborne bogies. Over and out."

"Copy that, Chief. Over and out."

They continued along the riverbank, unaware of the top of a spiny fan breaching the river surface a hundred feet behind them and disappearing quickly under the water.

CHAPTER 8

The afternoon gave way to evening, and the sun waned in the sky. Jason and Susan walked in comfortable silence as they tracked Mary and her reptilian captors, stopping only to drink from the river. Susan's stomach growled, and it was audible. Jason jutted his left arm out, stopping Susan from walking further.

"What is it?" she whispered, looking around, hand rubbing her stomach.

Jason scanned the dirt. "They've slowed their pace."

"Are they close by?"

Jason nodded. "They probably had to stop on account of Mary growing tired."

"How do you know that?"

Jason pointed at the ground. "Her stride changed, and she's now dragging her feet."

Susan's shoulders sagged. "I know I'm tired, and I'm freaking starving."

Jason stepped away from the river. "The tracks veer off into the jungle." He looked up at the sky. "We'll wait till dark. The lizard men don't normally come out after dark, so they should be off their game."

"What do we do in the meantime?"

Jason watched her rub her stomach. "We need to get some food in you, or your stomach's grumbling will give away our position." He pointed to some nearby trees. "Why don't you find a long branch I can use as a spear? I'll scout the area for some food."

She nodded and stepped away to search for sturdy branches.

"Stay close," said Jason. "Scream if you're in trouble." He looked around, checking for animal tracks, specifically for something edible. There weren't any, and he preferred to stay out of the jungle, as he didn't know exactly where the lizard men had stopped.

He walked back to the river's edge and saw large fish swimming around. He watched them, darting about, feeding on things between the stones at the bottom.

Susan returned with a few straight branches. "How about these?"

Jason looked them over. "Let me see." He reached out with his hands.

Susan handed them over. He hefted each, gaging its weight. After examining each, he selected one and dropped the remaining two on the ground. "This'll do. This'll do just fine." He took out his knife and began whittling the tip to a sharp point. "There're fish in the river. Big ones. Good eating."

Susan looked over at the river. "You're going to spear fish?"

He nodded, smiling. "I've done it before. When I was growing up in Alaska."

"I didn't know you grew up in Alaska. I figured you were from somewhere else."

He stripped bark and then wood off the tip in smooth motions, steadying the branch under his armpit. "I lived there with my mother and brother." His knife strokes became faster. "My little brother was killed by a pack of wolves."

Susan gasped. "Oh my God. I'm so sorry. That must've been awful."

Jason grunted a little as he shaved off the final strips of wood. "I was left alone with my mother, who wasn't exactly 'Mother of the Year.' I eventually tracked down the pack that killed my brother."

Susan's eyes widened. "Did you kill them?"

Jason re-sheathed his hunting knife and took the spear in his hand, holding the newly hewn tip up to his face for inspection. "Nah, they almost killed me. A local Native American hunter took me in, saved my life. He taught me how to hunt all different kinds of prey and to live off the land."

"He taught you how to spear fish?"

"That's right. And now I'm going to teach you."

Susan took a step back. "No. Not me. That's not my thing."

Jason arched an eyebrow. "You want to eat, don't you?"

Susan's expression softened. "Well...I am hungry."

"I thought you said you were 'freaking starving.' Or did I hear wrong?"

"No, you heard right."

Jason thrust the spear into her hands. "Here. I'll make one for me." He reached down and snatched up another branch. It was also sturdy and straight. He slipped it under his armpit and unsheathed his knife again. He began whittling down the tip.

"So, is that why you kill animals? Revenge?"

Jason shook his head. "No. Respect."

"Respect?" She clearly hadn't expected that response.

"Yeah. The wolves that killed my little brother were hunters. So are a lot of the other animals I hunt. Taking a life is a sacred act. In order to do it correctly, one must have respect for both hunters and prey."

"Yeah, but you got into trouble for shooting those lions in Africa." When he shot her a withering look, she blushed. "Well, that's what I read in the newspaper. You take rich folks out to kill animals."

"That I do," grunted Jason as he finished the tip of his spear. "They're going to hunt anyway. I try to teach them respect for the lives they take. Besides, what happened to my brother and I is an explanation, not an excuse. I didn't exactly say I was Mother Theresa."

Susan chuckled. "Oh, you're not so bad...and you're a lot deeper than you let on."

Jason slipped his knife back into its sheath and smirked. "Susan, are you warming up to me?"

Susan waved her hands in front of her. "I wouldn't say that now." They shared a laugh. "But seriously, thank you."

He hefted the spear, thrusting it down in front of him in a few practice strokes. "For what?"

She laughed, as if his question was ridiculous. "For helping me, stupid."

Jason waved her toward the river. "Let's spear us some fish."

*

Susan watched the mighty hunter walk to the river's edge. She felt something stir within her, a feeling she hadn't had in quite some time. He was attractive, in a rugged sort of way. He was well-built, and she liked his square jaw covered in rough stubble.

She shook her head, as if to clear it. She was still a married woman. Then again, she probably wasn't going to see her husband again. The thought made her sad. Her mind engaged in mental gymnastics, toggling between justifications for entertaining her attraction to Jason. The one she liked best was her marriage wasn't all that great anyway. In fact, Chris had left her. Did that make her a free woman?

Jason waded into the water, the current brushing up against him, until he was knee-deep. "Come on, what are you waiting for?"

What *was* she waiting for? He extended a hand, beckoning her. She hefted her spear and waded into the river, joining him. The cold water felt good on her legs. It was a relief from the relentless sun. She stood next to him, looking sheepish. "Okay, now what?"

He took several steps away from her. "Okay, now we wait, very still and very quiet. After a while, they'll swim near us, and when they do..."

He thrust the spear into the water with a speed that startled her. "Just like that."

"Just like that? You say it as if it's so easy."

He winked at her. "That's because it is."

They stood, waiting in silence, as Jason watched the water. He was positively statuesque. Susan, on the other hand, found it difficult to remain completely still. Her eyes widened when she saw the fish start to swim close by. She looked up at Jason, who fixated on the approaching fish.

In an explosion of action, he thrust his spear into the water, barely making a splash, and withdrew it, cursing under his breath.

Susan chuckled.

"Shhh," he admonished. "You're going to scare the fish."

She put a hand on her hip. "Are you sure you know what you're doing?" she whispered. The mighty hunter. She was amused, which seemed to annoy him.

"Of course I do," he whispered. "You don't hit every time."

Susan saw a fish swim in front of her. Her body went rigid. She watched as it meandered over towards her feet. She lunged at it, driving the spear straight down, striking a rock and missing the fish entirely. The fish darted away. "Dammit."

Jason smirked. "Not so easy, is it?" he muttered.

"I'll get one," she whispered. "You'll see. I'll get one before you."

He winked at her. "You're on."

They spent the next half hour stabbing at the shallows, occasionally changing position. Finally, Jason speared a couple of fish. He called her to shore, and he sat on the ground, crossing his legs. The fish flapped their tails, skewered on the makeshift spears.

"I hope you like sushi," he said, pulling out his knife.

Susan shot him an incredulous look. "You're kidding, right? You're going to cook the fish?"

Jason shook his head. "Negative. A fire will give off smoke, and we'll give away our position to any lizard men or predators in the area." He started cutting the fish open, removing the guts, leaving the flesh behind. He handed one to her, and she accepted it in open hands.

She looked down at the raw, torn open fish. "There's no way I'm eating this."

Jason pulled a piece of fish away and popped it into his mouth. "Aw, come on," he said between chews. "It doesn't get fresher than this. I thought you said you were hungry."

Susan's stomach growled loud enough to frighten a T. rex. "Well..." She pulled away a piece with her fingers, her face contorted in disgust.

"Watch out for bones," he said.

The truth was, she loved sushi. There was no difference between restaurant sushi and this, except for presentation. At least that's what she told herself. She looked at Jason, who tore one piece off after another, popping them into his mouth and chewing.

She popped her piece into her mouth. It was fishy and slimy, but she chewed and swallowed. It felt good hitting her empty stomach. Her mouth began to salivate. She tore off another piece, eating it, and another.

"There you go," said Jason, grinning as he chewed.

They passed twilight feasting on their catch, careful to avoid the bones. When they finished, Jason wiped his mouth on the back of his forearm, and Susan washed up in the river.

Jason stood up and stretched. "Ah, feels good to have fuel in the tank. I'm going to drain the lizard."

Susan pulled up the corner of her mouth. "Charming."

He went into the jungle to relieve himself and was back in two minutes. "Okay, let's find Mary. She's somewhere nearby."

"It's dark," said Susan. "Can you still track her?"

"I know the direction they went in," said Jason. "I think they won't be too far in. Let's go. Follow me, and be very quiet."

Susan nodded and followed him into the jungle, clutching both fishing spears. He wielded his knife, pushing vegetation aside as they walked. They crept in the dark, their only illumination the sliver of moon up in the night sky and the myriad of stars.

Jason put his hand out, signaling for her to stop. He pointed at his eyes with the index and middle fingers of his right hand and pointed at the clearing ahead. Mary lay on the ground in a heap. She was surrounded by several lizard men.

"Is she dead?" whispered Susan into Jason's ear.

He shook his head. "I don't think so," he whispered back into her ear. His breath was hot and fishy, but she didn't mind.

"What are we going to do?" she whispered back.

He thought about it for a moment. Then, his eyes brightened. "They know about me, but they don't know about you. I'll cause a diversion, get them to follow me. You go get Mary. Follow the river. I'll take the long way around to lose them and catch up with you."

"I don't like this plan," whispered Susan.

"Why?" he whispered back. "Do you have any better ideas?"

She didn't like the plan because it placed him in danger and it separated them from each other. She felt safer with him, and she didn't like the idea of Jason running off into the jungle pursued by several lizard men. "It's dangerous."

Jason shrugged. "Honey, this whole island is dangerous. It's our only option. I'll draw them away, and you get Mary out of there. Easy peasy."

Susan looked back at the clearing. Bathed in monochromatic light, it was difficult to determine exactly how many lizard men were present. She nodded.

Jason began to creep off to the right, but Susan grabbed him by the arm. He turned to look at her, his expression questioning. She looked into his eyes, hesitating. Surprising even herself, she planted a wet kiss on his lips, closing her eyes and lingering for a moment. When she pulled away and opened her eyes, she saw that his eyes had been closed a second longer than hers. She liked that.

Jason winked. "Thanks, honey." He crept in the vegetation off to the right. This time she let him go. She skulked off to the left, careful to remain as hidden as possible using the flora, making her way to where Mary lay. She prayed Mary wasn't dead. If Jason was correct and the lizard men had stopped to rest, chances were, she was still alive.

As she drew close, she looked across the clearing to search for Jason, but she was unable to spot him. *Damn, he was good.* Trusting he was going to carry out his part of the plan, she crept in behind where Mary lay. The lizard men lay all about. One lay right next to her. Another was standing guard, looking around.

Susan crouched in the bushes behind a fallen tree, clutching her spears, waiting for something to happen, though she didn't know what. Suddenly, she saw Jason moving across the clearing. Slipping in and out of the shadows, he made his way to where the one lizard man stood watch. The guard didn't appear to notice him.

Be careful. Her hands clenched her spears tightly in anticipation. She looked at the other lizard men, sleeping. They lay so still, they looked as if they were dead, but she knew better.

Without warning, Jason burst out of the vegetation and brought his knife down into the chest of the lizard man on watch. Taken by surprise, it flared out its dewlap and emitted something between a croak and a hiss. Jason pulled his knife out of its torso, the blade dripping a thick black syrup in the monochromatic moonlight.

Susan covered her mouth, stifling a gasp, as the other lizard men awoke in alarm. They scrambled to their feet and dashed after Jason, tails whipping behind them, propelling them in their savage fury.

Mary sat up, moaning and holding her head. "Wha-what's happening?"

Susan watched as the stabbed lizard man dropped to the ground, clutching its wound. It rolled over on its side, facing away from Susan, and stopped moving. The other lizard men followed Jason as he dashed into the jungle, howling like a mad man.

Susan looked around. She didn't see any other lizard men, except for the one lying dead on the ground in a pool of its own blood. She emerged out of the bushes and climbed over the fallen tree trunk. "Mary...Mary, it's Susan." She crouched down, next to Mary. "Are you all right?"

Mary looked dazed. "Susan? What are you doing here?" She appeared groggy.

Susan lay her spears down on the ground beside her. She smiled, working on untying Mary's wrists which were bound with a crude twine. "I'm here to rescue you, silly."

Her hands free, Mary rubbed her wrists. "Who was that?"

"That was Jason, causing a diversion so I can get you out of here. Can you walk?"

Mary looked up at Susan. "I-I think so. I'm so tired."

"You've been walking all day," said Susan. "You're probably dehydrated."

Movement in front of them caught both of their attention. It was the fallen lizard man. He was on all fours and looking right at them.

"Crap," said Susan. "Come on. We have to get you up." She reached under Mary's armpits, pulling her up, trying to get her to stand. However, in her weakened condition, Mary stumbled, trying to regain her footing. Susan thought she felt a bit heavier than she looked.

The reptilian man crawled his way over toward them in the dirt, blood oozing out of the wound in its chest. Despite its injury, it moved with a purpose and closed the distance faster than Susan had anticipated.

"Kill it," said Mary, dropping to her knees. "Kill it, Susan."

Susan didn't know what to do. Mary was having difficulty standing up, and the lizard man was almost upon her, hissing in rage. She released Mary and snatched a spear from off the ground. She turned it in her hands, pointing the sharp end at the advancing lizard man. It reached up and snatched the tip of the spear in its one clawed hand. Susan pushed the spear down, but the reptilian man's grip was firm, preventing the thrust.

Susan gripped the shaft of the spear with both hands and pushed down with all of her body weight. The lizard man's grip buckled for a moment, and the spearpoint slid down closer to its face, but stopped again.

"Kill it. Kill it, Susan."

Susan grunted as she pushed down with all her might. The lizard man swept its tail and caught her leg, throwing her off balance. She went down hard on one knee, but she didn't let go of the spear. It slid a bit more through the monster's grip, the tip now only a couple of inches from its face.

On its knees, it reached up and grabbed the end of the spear with its other clawed hand, reinforcing its grip. Mary crawled over to Susan and pulled herself up on Susan's back.

Susan groaned under the weight of her dehydrated friend as she continued to push the spear down against the creature's vice-like grip. Mary gripped the bottom of the spear shaft and added her weight to the effort, leaning on Susan.

The lizard man flared its dewlap, its arms trembling from exertion, blood cascading out of the wound in its chest. It let out a high-pitched whistle as the spear slid through its fingers, the point hitting it in the throat. The sharpened tip slid into its flesh, and its whistle turned into a whine. Blood poured out of its neck as Mary and Susan collapsed on top of it, all three falling into a heap in the dirt.

Susan lay face-to-face on top of the creature, Mary lying on top of her. It let out a deep breath and became still underneath her.

"Off me," grunted Susan.

Mary rolled off Susan's back and onto hers. Susan rolled off the lizard man, panting. She looked over at it. Its dewlap flopped to the side, unfurled and inert. Blood continued to leak from its two wounds, but after a couple of twitches, the body remained completely still. At last, it was dead.

"I think...we got it..." wheezed Mary, catching her breath.

Susan pushed herself to standing, her chest heaving as she caught her breath. "We need to get out of here. They may return."

"What about...Jason?" asked Mary.

Susan stood over her, extending a hand to help her up. "He said he'd lead them around the jungle and then circle back, meeting us at the river. We need to follow the river."

Mary nodded and accepted Susan's hand. This time she helped push herself up. She steadied herself by throwing an arm around Susan's shoulders. Together, they hobbled their way out of the clearing, heading for the river.

"Where are the Umazoa?" asked Mary.

"They went with Hiu to rescue the others." Susan explained her exchange with Hiu.

Within minutes they heard the river's current, and they saw it glistening in the pale moonlight.

"Water," gasped Mary. She released Susan and got down on all fours. She crawled to the river's edge and thrust her face into the water, taking in large gulps. Susan, anxious to leave the area, waited patiently as Mary gasped, coming up for air, only to dunk her head back into the river for more.

When Mary had drunk her fill, Susan helped her up. "Come on. We have to go." Susan turned to walk south, but Mary didn't follow.

"Where are you going?" asked Mary.

Susan gestured in the direction with her hand, as if the answer was obvious. "South."

"Why south? Shouldn't we go back to help Hiu?"

Susan shook her head. "Jason said he'd meet us down river."

"It doesn't make sense," said Mary, lost in thought.

"What doesn't make sense?"

"The lizard men left Jason behind because he was too weak to continue. He was succumbing to infection from his wounds. But now I just saw him stab one of them and run off into the jungle."

"Maybe he just needed a rest," said Susan.

Mary shook her head. "No, he was burning up, and he couldn't even stand."

"So, maybe the fever broke."

"Without any kind of intervention? Fevers like that don't just break."

"Well, we can discuss first aid as we walk south," said Susan looking around, uneasy. "If we stay here, we'll be discussing it with the lizard men. There's nothing we can do for Hiu. For all we know, he could be dead already. Or maybe he succeeded. Who knows?" She started to walk.

Mary fell in next to Susan, and they both headed south, clinging to the riverbank.

"Why are we headed south?" asked Mary.

"That's where Hiu wanted us to go. He said there would be a habitable area for the tribe."

"How do we know when we find it?"

"Good question," said Susan. "When we meet up with Jason, maybe he'll have an idea."

*

Jason dashed through the tangles and underbrush, scraping his shins and forearms. He heard thrashing from behind him as the lizard men pursued him in earnest. He zig-zagged, attempting to throw them off his trail. However, the rustling of flora appeared to fan out behind him, keeping pace with his changes in direction.

The jungle terrain all looked the same in the monochromatic moonlight, and he had to be careful not to get turned around. He began to arc towards the south, giving his reptilian pursuers a wide berth. The left flank of their skirmish line nearly caught up with him, so he widened the arc. Although the immediate threat was the team of lizard men, he was wary of the potential presence of predator dinosaurs ambling about in the dark. He didn't want to be blind-sided.

Just as that thought had occurred to him, he skidded to a stop in the dirt before running headlong into a herd of large shadows milling about in a clearing. About twenty to twenty-five feet long with curved backs and short, fat tails, the creatures stirred at his sudden appearance. In the moonlight, Jason noticed rows of knobs serving as armor on their backs. One turned and groaned at him, its skull wide with two horns jutting backward and a beak for a mouth.

"Whoa there," said Jason, noticing its alarm at his sudden arrival. He placed his hands up in front of him, palms out. "Easy, girl. Easy."

He caught a sudden movement in the periphery of his vision and dodged just as a massive bulbous knob at the end of a tail swung at him, narrowly missing him. He rolled away on the ground and sprung back up to standing.

The herd of ankylosaurus shifted, reorienting themselves to deal with this pest. Jason backed away as several lizard men burst into the clearing behind him, pointing the sharp ends of their spears at him.

"Oh, hell." The bigger threat now behind him, he dashed forward into the herd with such speed, they were not able to react in time. The lizard men bolted after him. The ankylosaurus swung their wrecking ball tails, missing Jason but catching a couple of his pursuers, knocking them to the ground.

The ankylosaurus shifted about on their feet, kicking up dirt, colliding with each other in the process. Jason deftly changed direction, darting through openings between armored backs and under tail swings. He was nearly crushed between two massive bodies in the shuffle.

He glanced over his shoulder in time to see one of the lizard men being crunched between two ankylosaurs turning in opposite directions, only to then be trampled underfoot. Jason ran the gauntlet, narrowly evading trample himself, only to run right into two lizard men who had apparently circumvented the herd altogether.

They thrust spear tips at him. Jason wielded his hunting knife, parrying and side-stepping, as he didn't want to re-enter the confused herd at his back. Within a few moves, the lizard men had him surrounded, and he cursed under his breath.

Past the lizard men, Jason thought he saw the small silhouette of a child step out of the underbrush and into the clearing. He figured it was one of the Umazoa tribe, or perhaps a member of another tribe. The child stepped right past the lizard men without being noticed and stood in front of Jason.

The hunter gasped as he recognized the face looking up at him in the moonlight. "Joey? Is that you?"

The lizard men flared their dewlaps, hissing at him and snapping their jaws as he spoke. They didn't appear to notice the small humanoid child who had entered the circle.

'It's me,' said a wordless voice in his mind. 'I missed you, Jason.'

Jason shook his head, tears welling up in his eyes, blurring his vision. "No. It's not real." He wiped his eyes with the back of his forearm. "*You're* not real. You're dead."

'Are these monsters bothering you, Jason?'

The lizard men closed in, moving slowly and with great caution.

"They don't see you," said Jason. "Why don't they see you?"

'They're getting closer,' said Joey. 'Do you want me to help?'

"Yes," said Jason, desperate. "Yes, help me."

The lizard men traded confused looks.

Joey's eyes began to glow like hot coals in the darkness. He raised his hands, palms facing up, until they were shoulder height. The lizard men thrust their spears at Jason, but Joey quickly dropped his hands. The lizard men fell with Joey's hands, landing in the dirt in heaps, lifeless.

Joey's eyes dimmed back to their original state. 'There you go, Jason. They won't bother you anymore.'

Jason looked around at the lifeless lizard men. "Wh-what did you do?"

The apparition of Joey cocked its head sideways. 'I took care of them.'

"You...you killed them. How?"

'Remember, the Temple of the Simian King, Jason. You must bring Peter there.' Joey started to back away into the underbrush.

Jason stepped forward after him. "No! Where are you going?"

'We will be together soon,' said Joey. 'At the Temple of the Simian King. Don't forget. I will see you there. Then we can be together again. I have so much to show you.'

Jason took another step forward, reaching out for his brother, but the apparition evaporated in the night air like fog, leaving Jason to question if he ever really saw what he thought he saw.

One thought reignited in his mind, playing and replaying like a catchy song, 'Bring Peter to the Temple of the Simian King.'

CHAPTER 9

After walking much of the night, Collins, Nielsen, Peter, Tracey, and Marcy encountered the outer perimeter guard at base camp. "Chief, is that you?" asked one of the guards.

"Yeah. We're back."

"Where're the Jeeps and the truck?"

"It's a long story." Collins checked his watch. "It doesn't make sense."

Nielsen looked at his watch. "Mine's been acting screwy, too. Time seems to have passed at rather uneven intervals. I couldn't even tell you how long we've been walking."

"It's the island," said Peter. "Time, the way we measure it, is different here."

"My feet are killing me," said Marcy, shoulders slumped and eyelids heavy.

"Do you want me to get a Humvee to take you back?" asked the guard.

Collins looked at Tracey and Marcy, who both looked exhausted. "Yeah, that sounds good."

The guard got on his radio, and a Humvee was there within minutes. The driver stopped right in front of the group.

"Are we all going to fit?" asked Marcy.

Collins shook his head. "You go ahead. I'll debrief the perimeter guard and head back on foot."

"You don't have to tell me twice." Nielsen hopped into the front passenger seat. Peter, Tracey, and Marcy all got into the back.

Peter scanned the grounds as they drove through, trying to ascertain Poseidon Tech's true purpose. However, the ride back passed quickly, and Peter hadn't gleaned any new information. When they reached the center of base camp, everyone got out.

"I'm going straight to bed," declared Marcy. She placed a hand on Tracey's shoulder. "Good night."

"I think that's a good idea," said Nielsen. "We need our rest. We have a lot to figure out tomorrow."

Marcy was gone before he could finish his sentence.

Peter and Tracey headed back to the tents. They saw Marcy disappear into hers, and Nielsen walked over to the main tent. Peter supposed Nielsen wanted to oversee whatever was currently happening. "Where are we going?"

"To my tent," said Tracey.

Peter did a double take. It hadn't occurred to him until this very minute that he wasn't a part of this expedition, and as such didn't have an assigned tent. "I-I...Nielsen can give me a tent..."

However, his stammering was cut short as Tracey pulled him into her tent by the front of his shirt. Kneeling on the ground, she pulled him down to his knees and close. He felt her hot breath in his face.

"We have to be very quiet," she whispered.

"Wh-why? What's going to happen?" squeaked Peter.

She shushed him, stuck her head back outside of the tent, and popped it back inside. "Okay, we're alone."

Peter's palms became sweaty, and his heart was beating out of his chest. *Was this it? Was this really happening?* "Tracey, I had no idea...you felt this way."

She looked at him cockeyed. "What do you mean...? Oh, no. I-I don't..."

Peter's face flushed hot with embarrassment. "Oh, no. I'm sorry. I mean...that's not what I meant."

She arched an eyebrow. "That's exactly what you meant. You thought I brought you here for..."

Peter shook his head emphatically. "No. Absolutely not. Why would you want to do...*that* with me?"

Now Tracey's face turned red. "Don't say it like *that*."

"I-I-I figured maybe you liked me. I'm stupid."

"I-I do like you," stammered Tracey.

"I know. I'm your friend."

Tracey stamped her foot. "No. For Christ's sake, it has to come out. I have to just say it." She turned around, pacing back and forth, gesticulating wildly. "Why am I such a damned coward? Why can't I just say it?"

Peter looked perplexed. "Say what? I don't understand what's happening here."

Tracey turned and faced Peter, locking eyes with him. "For crying out loud, Pete, I came back to a dinosaur infested island in another dimension for you. If that doesn't say 'I love you,' I don't know what does?"

Both of them appeared stunned into silence. There it was. It was finally out, and the words hung out in the night air between them.

Peter broke the silence first. "You...you love me?"

Tracey waved her hands around. "Of course I do. I always have. At first it was as a friend, but then we got to know each other. We worked together on the same projects, taught in the same department. The feeling just grew and grew, and now I can't stand it anymore."

Peter looked staggered. "Why didn't you tell me this?"

She looked down at the ground. "Because I was afraid."

"Of what?"

"That you didn't feel the same, or if you did and it didn't work out, I'd lose you."

Now Peter paced back and forth, running his hand through his hair. "Holy smokes. That's crazy." He turned and met her gaze. "You'd never lose me, Tracey. You mean too much to me."

Tracey's face lit up. She let out a big sigh. "Well, that's a relief. I should've done this a long time ago."

Peter withered.

"What? What's wrong?" Her eyes were searching, pleading.

"Tracey, there's something I have to tell you."

"What?"

He swallowed hard. There was only one way to tell her, and it was by being direct. "I'm in a relationship with Mary."

Tracey stared at him, dumbfounded. She didn't appear to process what he had just relayed to her. Then, as it dawned on her, she appeared crestfallen. "Oh, I see." She turned away from him in embarrassment.

"I didn't know how you felt," pleaded Peter. "You were gone. I thought I'd never see you again."

"You?" she spat. "You?"

"Tracey..."

"I could see her ending up with Jason. But, *you*?"

Peter shrugged his shoulders. "It all kind of just happened. She came back for me."

"When everyone else left. When *I* left."

"That's not what I meant. You didn't leave me. I told you to go, to save yourself."

"I can't say I blame you, Pete. She's beautiful."

"So are you." He winced after saying it. It sounded pathetic.

"Do you love her?" Tracey's voice was small.

Peter threw his hands down at his side. "I don't know."

Tracey turned around to face him again, her jaw set. "What do you mean you don't know? What kind of answer is that?"

Peter raised both eyebrows. "To tell you the truth, she kind of scares me."

"She scares you?"

"Yeah. A lot."

Tracey shook her head, as if to clear her thoughts. "This isn't why I pulled you in here. We're getting sidetracked. There's something we need to do."

"Now I'm really confused. What the heck are you talking about?"

She looked at him, eyes determined. "They're up to something."

"Who?"

"Poseidon Tech. They're not here for you or the others. Come on, you know how these guys operate. There's something else."

Peter threw his hands up in exasperation. "Yeah, but we don't know what."

She stepped closer to him, lowering her voice to a whisper. "Exactly. That's why we have to find out."

"Find out? How?"

"We have to sneak around and get a look at the main tent. Whatever is going on, it's happening there."

"It's late, Trace."

She popped her head out of the tent. Her left hand reached out for him and pulled him towards the opening. Now his head was also sticking out of the tent.

"Look," she said.

Peter saw Nielsen walking back to his tent. He disappeared inside. "What am I looking at?"

"Nielsen turned in. Collins is walking back from the edge of base camp. We don't have much time. If we're going to do this, we have to do it now."

"Even if we see something, how do we know what we're looking at?"

Tracey snapped her fingers. "We'll need help." She dashed out of the tent, yanking Peter with her. She crept over to Marcy's tent, dragging Peter along.

She squatted in front of the tent. "Marcy...Marcy, are you awake?"

Marcy's head poked out. "I'm trying to get some sleep."

Tracey shook her head. "We need you. We're going to see what's going on in that main tent, but we need you to recognize whatever it is."

Marcy shot her an insolent look. "Can't this wait till morning? I'm dead on my feet."

"No," whispered Tracey. "We have to do this now."

Marcy scowled. "All right. All right. Hold on. Let me get my shoes on." She disappeared back inside her tent.

Tracey stood straight.

"This is a really bad idea," whispered Peter, leaning in.

"No, it's crucial to getting off this island in one piece," insisted Tracey.

"What if we get caught?"

"What do you think they'll do to us?" asked Tracey. "Feed us to the dinosaurs?"

Before Peter could answer, Marcy emerged from her tent wearing her tank top, khakis, and her boots. "Okay, let's do this so I can get some damned sleep."

The three of them walked casually across base camp, Peter casting a wary eye at Nielsen's tent. There was no light on within. He was probably sleeping, something Peter believed he should be doing at the moment, but once Tracey got a notion in her head, she was very tenacious.

Collins' men all but ignored them, going about their business, keeping the camp secure.

"Look," said Marcy, pointing.

Several technicians in Poseidon Tech jumpsuits fanned out, sweeping the ground with long apparatuses ending in what looked like a steering wheel in a cordoned off sector of base camp.

"What are they doing?" asked Tracey.

"Metal detectors," said Marcy. "Part of the geological survey. Look over there." Off to the right, a technician was manning surveying equipment and jotting notes onto a digital pad with a stylus. "That's a total station. He's recording distances."

"What for?" asked Tracey.

"He's marking coordinates," said Marcy.

"There's something significant about this site, other than being a landing zone," said Tracey.

Peter pointed at a large red vehicle on metal treads surrounded by portable flood lights. A large drill was mounted on the front as two technicians shouted instructions, guiding the operator. "They're taking core samples."

"Part of our geological survey," shrugged Marcy. "Nothing strange about that."

"They're going to draw an awful lot of attention."

They saw a Humvee circling the survey area, the gunner scanning the jungle. Peter knew it wasn't going to be enough if something large decided to amble out of the tree line.

"Let's check out the main tent," said Marcy.

They made their way to the back of the main tent. Marcy held up her index finger over her lips, telling Peter and Tracey to be quiet. She placed her ear up against the side of the tent. Tracey shrugged and did the same. Peter looked around, shifting his feet. Finally, he joined them, placing his ear up to the canvas.

They all heard voices from within the tent. One of them was clearly Collins. He'd returned faster than expected. Tracey cursed under her breath, and Marcy shushed her silently. Peter clenched his teeth and balled his hands into fists, terrified.

Marcy's eyes lit up as she listened. Tracey touched her arm and mouthed, 'Do you understand what they're saying?'

Marcy shook her head. "You stay here. I'm going in to get a closer look. Don't move. I'll be right back." She disappeared around the corner.

Tracey leaned forward, listening.

Peter was lost. He heard multiple people speaking, now including Marcy, but he only made out a few of the words—metal, phase shift, lock on.

"Can I help you?" The voice came from behind Peter, and its sudden appearance made him and Tracey jump out of their skin. Peter wheeled around and saw Collins standing there, glaring at them.

Peter looked around. "Uh…I was just trying to find my tent."

"Well, it isn't over here," said Collins. "You were listening in."

"No we weren't," insisted Tracey, sounding like a stubborn child.

"You do realize we can see you through the tent," said Collins. He gestured up with his right hand. "You're standing in front of the flood light."

Tracey stepped forward, going for broke. "Yeah, well, we want to know the real reason why Poseidon Tech is here."

Before Collins could answer, automatic gunfire erupted off in the distance. He whirled around.

"What's that?" asked Tracey, but she had a feeling she knew.

"It's coming from the direction of the river," said Collins.

Peter had closed his eyes as soon as he heard the shots, reaching out with his senses using the power of the life orb. He opened them. "A dinosaur. A Big one. Spinosaurus, I think."

Tracey looked at him sideways. "Wow, Pete, you can actually tell the species now?"

As if in answer, a thundering roar filled the night air, followed by more gunfire.

Collins got on his radio. "Chief to perimeter guard, report." He waited, no answer. "Perimeter guard, report."

The radio crackled. "It's coming through. It's huge. We can't stop it…" The pops of gunfire filled the background, and the call terminated.

Collins looked at Peter. "Wait here. You'll be safe here."

Before Peter could say otherwise, Collins ran off, shouting instructions to the men around him.

"Let's get inside the main tent," said Tracey. "At least we'll get a good look at what's going on inside."

Peter nodded, and he followed Tracey around to the front of the tent as they heard more gunfire erupt in the background. Before them, under the large tent, sat a large array of electronic equipment. Techs manned screens and keyboards. They looked up from their monitors, their terrified expressions eerie in the dim illumination.

"What's going on out there?" The question came from a young woman with shoulder-length brown hair, around Marcy's age. Her face was white, and it wasn't just the illumination of her monitor. All eyes were on Peter and Tracey.

"We're under attack," said Peter.

The woman's eyes were wide as platters. "From what?"

Another loud roar answered the young technician's query.

"Is that a dinosaur?" asked a paunchy man in his thirties with sandy blonde hair, his glasses nearly falling off his face.

"I know what we're working on," declared Marcy, stepping forward from behind a table of laptops. "This land we're sitting on is abundant in an unclassified metal. Poseidon Tech is using it to focus the stabilization grid."

Peter and Tracey traded confused looks.

"By locking onto this vast deposit of ore, they'll be able to keep the island phased into our home dimension," said Marcy.

"That's how we're going to get home," said the man in the glasses. "This way there's no time pressure to make it through a brief window. They could hold the portal open indefinitely."

That last sentence sent a chill down Peter's spine. He looked at Tracey, his expression grave. "That's what they're here for."

Tracey looked pale, as if she'd seen a ghost. "Peter, there's something I have to tell you."

"What?"

"In the mission debriefing, before we landed on the island, Nielsen played audio from 207's flight recorder. Peter, I think something wants off this island."

He nodded. "That entity. The one that turned Mike Deluca into a monster."

"The one that offered to teach you how to use the death orb," added Tracey.

Marcy walked over to them. "I'm sure this is all just for the mission, to help get us off the island, like Randy said."

Randy nodded.

Tracey glowered. "I'm not so sure of that."

Nielsen came barreling into the main tent. "We're under attack! A dinosaur made it through the perimeter defense—big one, too. Collins wants us here in the center of base camp until it's over." He looked around the room and was stunned to see Peter and Tracey already inside the tent.

Peter shoved past him to look outside. Tracey was right beside him. Base camp was in a state of barely controlled chaos. The drilling for core samples ceased, and technicians flocked to the main tent as Collins and his team mobilized. The remaining weapons team hopped into their Humvees as the remaining Huey's blades began to turn.

Tracey pointed to the tree line to the south. "Look!" Bolts of light streaked into the jungle, trained on something they couldn't yet see from the main tent.

"That doesn't sound good," said Marcy, standing beside them.

"We'll be safe here," said Nielsen. "Collins is all over it. There's only one."

Peter turned on him. "Do you have any idea how large and dangerous a Spinosaurus is?"

"Peter, look!" Tracey gawked at something to the south as gunfire erupted. Several of the technicians darted up front for a look. A few remained inside the tent, cowering behind their laptops.

Peter turned in time to see the Huey rise into the air and fly south. He saw an enormous, hunched figure enter the clearing. It was long with a massive sail on its back. "That's got to be a twenty-footer," said Peter.

"Bigger," said Tracy.

Nielsen looked out the front of the main tent as Collins' team engaged the 'spine lizard.' He turned to Peter and Tracey. "You know what this thing is. Does it have a weakness? If it does, you need to tell Collins."

"It's thought to be largely aquatic," said Peter. "I encountered one in the river when I escaped the Zehhaki. The only reason I'm still alive is dumb luck. I got caught in the rapids, and it didn't follow me."

"Is it weaker on land?" asked Nielsen.

"It's definitely built for water," said Tracey. "It has a crocodilian bone structure. It uses its tail and webbed feet to propel itself through water."

"It must've followed us back from the river," said Peter.

"Or, we left a trail of breadcrumbs," said Tracey, glaring at Nielsen.

He shot her a sharp look. "What's that supposed to mean?"

"We dumped the Stegosaurus bodies in the river. Remember?"

"There's nothing we can do about it now," snapped Nielsen. "So, is it weaker on land?"

"I wouldn't say that," said Peter. Then he snapped his fingers, his eyes lighting up in an epiphany. "Crocodilian! It has nostrils on the top of its head. Tell your copter to focus its fire on the top of its head. If we can disrupt its breathing, it might go away."

Nielsen nodded and got on his radio. "Collins, it's Nielsen, come in." He was so excited, he forgot all about callsigns.

The radio crackled. "Chief, here."

"Our paleontologists said to concentrate fire on its nostrils on top of its head to disrupt its breathing."

"Copy that."

*

Nielsen watched as the Spinosaurus tore through the ground forces, roaring at the Humvees as they fired grenades at it. Its long, slender profile allowed it to dodge most of the fire. However, its sail took a few hits. In response, it bellowed at them in fury.

The Huey started firing at the top of its head. Streaks of light flew past its head, most missing their target. The large beast hunched and swerved, scooping its long snout into the melee and snatching up foot soldiers.

It pressed further and further into base camp, stomping on tents. Its massive sail was broken, blood glistening by the light of the moon and gunfire. Collins' team surrounded it, the Jeeps circling it, firing grenades. Each time it dipped its head to attack, they concentrated fire at the top of its head. One grenade made contact, wreathing its head in fire and smoke. It shook its head and staggered backward as the Huey barraged it with its minigun.

It whipped its tail about as it whirled around, catching one of the Humvees. The vehicle veered off, nearly flipping onto its side. As the hulking predator turned its body, its tail caught the gunner of the other Humvee, pulling him out of the mount.

Nielsen winced as he saw the Spinosaurus stomp on the gunner with a large, clawed foot. The massive lizard swooned as the other Humvee recovered, the gunner firing into its side. The Huey descended, coming in closer, taking advantage. Its minigun fired into its side. The dinosaur fell sideways, hitting the ground hard. It moaned, struggling to regain its footing, but Collins and his team moved in for the kill.

Nielsen turned to face the group. "We did it! Dr. Albanese, that was brilliant!" He looked around and saw the excited and relieved faces of his technicians, but he didn't see either of his paleontologists. Panic rose up within the project manager. "Where'd they go?"

"Who?" Marcy looked sheepish.

"You know who, our two paleontologists!"

Marcy shrugged her shoulders. "They left the tent."

The panic was replaced by annoyance. "Where'd they go? Go and find them. Congratulations are in order."

*

Marcy burst out of the tent, looking around. With all of the technicians inside the main tent and security out by the fallen Spinosaurus, base camp was empty. She strolled between the tents, hands casually in her pockets, her eyes darting back and forth. She squinted, rubbing her eyes as she saw them appear out of thin air. They slipped off Tracey's company-issued, light-bending camouflage blanket and got into a Jeep.

She stalked over to them. Peter looked over at her and muttered something to Tracey, who was shoving hand-held signal flares and a flare gun she found in the Jeep into her pack along with the camouflage blanket. Tracey looked up and frowned. Marcy thought they both looked like two children who were caught trying to cut class.

"What are you guys doing?"

"We have to go," said Peter. "There's something really important I need to do."

Marcy looked back over her shoulder. "Nielsen's looking for you two. Collins took the Spinosaurus down. We won."

Tracey got out of the Jeep and looked into Marcy's eyes. "Marcy, Peter set something in motion that he needs to correct. It could affect us all, even endanger this expedition. I'm going with him. He's going to need my help."

"But...Nielsen..."

Tracey smiled. "If he's really here to stabilize the portal, he won't be focused on us."

"Maybe I should come with you," offered Marcy.

Peter shook his head. "Too dangerous."

Tracey reached out and squeezed Marcy's arm. "You work for Poseidon Tech. Besides, we need you here to keep an eye on what he's doing. If our hunch is correct, Poseidon Tech's interest is in keeping the portal open indefinitely. They want to lay claim to this island."

Marcy shook her head. "I can't imagine why."

"Like you said, it's a major discovery. Maybe they plan on selling the rights to the island to the highest bidder. I don't know. Whatever the reason, it's above all of our paygrades."

Marcy looked as if she didn't want them to go. "If it's dangerous, maybe Collins can help you with whatever you have to do."

Peter shook his head. "He doesn't have the men to spare on a side mission he knows nothing about and, frankly, wouldn't believe if we explained it. His priority is securing the camp. Finding us was always secondary."

Marcy pouted. "You two, be careful. Make sure you're back in time for extraction."

"We'll do our best," said Peter.

"Be safe," said Tracey. "There may be other attacks on base camp."

"I'll stay in the main tent," said Marcy. "And, I'll keep an eye on Nielsen."

"Come on, Tracey," said Peter. "We have to go before they see us."

Tracey nodded. She hugged her friend. "Goodbye, Marcy."

Marcy's eyes welled up. "You make it sound so final."

Tracey rounded the Jeep and hopped back into it. Peter turned the ignition. The engine turned over, and Peter threw the Jeep into gear. Marcy watched as the Jeep pulled away, disappearing into the night.

She worried about her two friends. She hoped that whatever they had to do they'd be successful. She returned to the main tent, working on the cover story she was going to feed Nielsen.

ACT III

AWAKENING

CHAPTER 10

Jason strolled beside his deceased younger brother, Joey, as night gave way to dawn. The chorus of exotic frogs and the chittering of countless insects began to quiet with the brightening of the horizon, and warm rain fell.

"Where do I find Peter?" asked Jason.

Joey smiled up at him. "You won't have to. He's seeking out the Temple of the Simian King as we speak. I've seen to it." His little brow furrowed.

"What's wrong?" asked Jason.

"It's Peter," said Joey. "The poor man has carried the burden of two orbs with him, yet he only knows how to access one."

"The life orb."

Joey nodded. "You don't choose the orbs. They choose you. You have to be worthy of the power they offer."

"Hey, Peter's a good man. He saved my life. There's no one more worthy."

"That's not what I meant, Jason. He's perfect for wielding the life orb. It suits him. However, it's not in his constitution to wield the power of death."

It hadn't escaped Jason that his little brother was wielding a vocabulary well beyond his age. However, he was happy to see Joey. He didn't appear as an apparition or phantom now. He appeared just as he had in their childhood. When his little brother spoke, it wasn't just in words. He felt him in his mind and in his soul. He liked the sensation, and he fought back doubts and inconsistencies to allow this feeling to wash over him completely, even though in the very back of his mind, somewhere in his reptilian brain, he heard a faint voice of caution growing weaker and weaker, fading into the warmth Joey offered.

"So, who should wield it?" asked Jason.

Joey looked up at his big brother, beaming. "I think you're the perfect one to wield it."

Jason chortled. "You've got to be kidding. Me? I'm the worst person to have such a power."

"You're perfect, actually. You understand death. You respect it."

Jason's eyes welled up. It wasn't like him to be emotional. "I've missed you. I'm glad to see you again in this strange place." He looked around at the jungle, hesitating before speaking again. "Is this where people go after they die?"

"It's where I went. You were sent here to be with me again. You are alive, and I can be, too."

Jason scratched his head. "What...what do you mean, you can be too?"

Joey looked ahead as he strolled next to his big brother. "My body is being kept in the Temple of the Simian King. I need the power of the death orb to bring me back."

"But...that doesn't make sense. Why would the death orb bring you back?"

Joey pondered this question for a moment. "The only way I can explain it is that death put me here. That wolf pack..." he winced, "...it was horrible." He looked up at his brother, his eyes welling up and his expression searching, pleading. "They tore me apart, Jason. Like I was some kind of animal. They were death sent to me, to extinguish my life."

Jason audibly choked down his grief. His lips trembled as he croaked out, "I found them, Joey. I tried to kill them all to avenge you. I tried..." his eyes trailed off as he wiped away tears with the back of his hand, "...and I failed."

Joey gazed upon him, his eyes now strangely wide, impossibly so, anatomically speaking. They appeared as large pools threatening to drown Jason. The hunter allowed himself to be drawn in.

"You can bring me back, and we can be together again. We can get off this island and go home. Will you do that for me, Jason?"

Jason sobbed, hot tears mingling with the jungle rain as they streamed down his cheeks. "I'll do that for you, Joey. I won't let you down this time. I promise."

Joey smiled. "I know you won't. Your friends are in a cave up ahead. I have to go now, but I'll be there, at the Temple of the Simian King. When we meet there, we'll get Peter to pass the death orb onto you. He'll do it. He's a good man. It's too much power for one person, anyway. Absolute power..."

"Corrupts absolutely," said Jason, finishing the quote.

Joey was gone.

* * *

Susan watched the sunrise as Mary slept. They had walked for a couple of hours, but Mary was still weak. Susan had made sure her friend was hydrated, and then she selected a spot in a small cave not too far from the river for them to rest. Susan had tried to stay awake to keep watch, but fatigue had gotten the better of her. Fortunately, they passed the night without incident.

Mary began to stir, groaning as her eyes opened. She stretched out on the ground, arching her back as she yawned luxuriously. She smiled at Susan. "How long was I out?"

Susan shrugged. "I don't know, but you were out for a while. How do you feel?"

Mary rolled over on her side and propped herself up on her right elbow. "Better. Much better."

"You were exhausted and dehydrated," said Susan.

Mary stood up, brushing herself off. "So, what now?"

"Jason said he'd catch up with us," said Susan. "That's if he's still alive."

Mary smiled to herself. "He's alive. That guy has got nine lives."

"He's not as bad as he seems," said Susan. "He's actually pretty okay." She flushed after saying it.

Mary grinned. "Oh my God."

Susan looked at her sideways. "What?"

"You like him."

"He's okay."

Mary stepped closer to Susan, reading her face. "No, you like him. You *like* him."

"Come on," said Susan. "What're we, in middle school?"

Mary ignored the remark. She was genuinely fascinated by this development. "What happened between you two?"

Susan shrugged. "I don't know. He looked after me, made sure I was safe. He's actually pretty caring."

"Do you think he likes you, too?"

Susan averted her gaze. "I don't know. He's not my usual type, you know."

"Peter isn't my usual type," said Mary.

"Yeah, how did that happen, anyway?" asked Susan, turning the tables on Mary.

"I don't know. It just kind of did."

Susan looked down at the ground and back at Mary. "Do you love him?"

This time it was Mary who averted her gaze. "I don't know. He's a nice guy and all."

"But…"

"But…I don't know. Sometimes I just feel like we don't totally connect."

"What? Because of his…powers?"

"That's part of it, but there's something else. Sometimes, it's like he's holding back."

Susan looked around the cave and lowered her voice. "Have you two…"

"Oh, yeah," said Mary. "But it's like he's not there with me. Like he's off somewhere else."

"Thinking about someone else," said Susan, finishing her thought. "You know, I think he had it bad for Tracey Moran."

Mary nodded. "I know. But she kept him at a distance."

"And in you swooped," said Susan.

They shared a chuckle.

"Come on," said Mary. "You make me seem like some kind of predator."

"Maybe that's what he likes about you," offered Susan. "When you want something, you just go for it. He seems like the type of guy who follows the woman's lead."

Mary flashed a mischievous grin. "Yeah, not like Jason. Now there's a strong, take charge kind of guy."

Susan felt a twinge of annoyance, which must've been visible on her face, because Mary giggled.

"Oh, I'm only teasing," said Mary. "Jason is all yours."

"Gee, thanks." Susan managed an affable chuckle, but part of her wondered if Mary indeed had designs on Jason. After all, she did swoop in and grab Peter for herself. To make matters worse, her interest in Peter appeared to be fading, by Mary's own admission. Susan wondered if Jason was her next target.

"Someone say my name?"

Both women startled, having been engrossed in their discussion, and turned to find Jason standing at the mouth of the cave.

"Man, I caught you both off-guard," laughed the hunter. "What if I was a velociraptor, or something?"

"We were just about to make our move," teased Mary, flashing him a sly look.

The flirtation made Susan uncomfortable. Part of her was sure Mary was doing it to bust her chops. To her surprise, Jason appeared to ignore it. He walked over to Susan and asked, "Are you all right?"

Susan blushed a bit. "Yeah, we're okay. We had to stop walking. She was wiped out and very dehydrated."

Jason grinned at Mary. "This woman saved your life."

Mary smiled at Susan, and this time it appeared warm and genuine. "Don't I know it."

"It was nothing," said Susan.

"Nothing," chortled Jason.

"Nothing?" echoed Mary. "This chick took down a lizard man with a spear."

"You helped," added Susan.

"How did you find us?" asked Mary.

Jason outstretched his arms. "I'm a tracker, remember? I followed you right to this cave."

"What about the lizard men who were chasing you?" asked Susan.

He waved a hand at her. "We ran into some dinos, who helped considerably."

"So, what now?" asked Susan. "We got Mary back. Do we go help Hiu?"

He appeared lost in thought.

"Hey, I'm talking to you," snapped Susan.

Jason snapped out of whatever private moment he was having. "We have to find Peter."

"I thought he never came out of the lizard men's temple," said Mary.

Jason shook his head. "He's alive."

Susan found his certainty in that declaration strange. "How do you know this?"

Jason hesitated. "I found his tracks."

Mary's eye lit up. "Peter's tracks? Here? We have to find him."

"That's the plan," said Jason.

"What direction do they go in?" asked Mary.

Jason hesitated again. Susan found this to be strange, as it was a simple question.

"They head south."

"What about Hiu and the tribe?" pressed Susan.

"They left us to take care of their own," said Mary. "Now we have to take care of our own."

Susan acknowledged the relief she felt having been reunited with Jason. She imagined how Mary must've felt having been separated from Peter. Whatever doubt Mary expressed about their relationship appeared to vanish, at least for the moment.

"Let's go," said Jason. "Peter's out there, and he needs our help."

* * *

Peter kept alert as he drove the Jeep alongside the riverbank. Fortunately, they hadn't run into any predators. A few enormous crocodiles lounged together, but none showed any interest in the passing vehicle. He followed the mental map burned into his memory, and they made good time. "We should be there soon."

"What do we do once we get there?" asked Tracey.

"I awaken the Simians," said Peter.

"Are you sure this is a good idea?"

"It'll reset the island. Bring it back to where it was. Balance everything out."

Tracey sighed. "But—and I'm just playing devil's advocate here—you know that evolution is a progression shaped by specific selection pressures from the environment."

"Yeah. So?"

"So, these races had their time, and they died out for a reason. You brought one back, and look at the chaos it caused."

"So, I'm reinstating a selection pressure to bring about balance."

"You're playing God, Peter."

"Do you think I like this? Do you think I want this kind of responsibility?"

"So why do it?"

"Because for some reason these orbs chose me. I didn't ask for this. Maybe it's what I'm supposed to do."

Tracey shook her head. "You're not even supposed to be here, Pete."

"Aren't I? I don't know. None of this makes any sense to me."

Tracey turned in her seat to face him. "So, let's play this out. You change the selection pressure by reawakening the Simians, a race that was previously wiped out by a natural selection pressure. Now there are new selection pressures at play, you being one of them, all artificially put in place."

Peter paused, watching the road. He figured maybe she was right. "Tracey, do you believe in destiny?"

She laughed. "That's just silliness kids learn from storybooks."

Peter turned to look at her, arching his right eyebrow. "You mean stories about dinosaurs, ancient races, and magic orbs?"

"Okay, I see your point. Once you do this, are you leaving the island? Are you coming home?"

Peter smiled. "That's really why you came? To bring me home?"

Tracey's expression was grave. "Peter, that thing…that entity that you've been talking to…I think it brought us here. It wants off the island."

"Nazimaa," said Peter. "That's what it's called."

"Yeah, well, I'm pretty sure that's the voice I heard on the recording from 207's flight recorder." Tracey swallowed hard. "We can't let her get off this island."

"And now Poseidon Tech is zeroing in on the ore deposit below base camp to keep the portal to our home dimension open. That's going to be a problem." He chewed on his lip, deep in thought. "Maybe these Simians can help us with this Nazimaa."

"What makes you say that?"

"She's imprisoned there. Ghenga told me so. Maybe they were the ones who imprisoned her. Maybe they'll know how to contain her."

Tracey shook her head. "I don't know. Something doesn't sit right with me about this Ghenga character. I still don't know why he'd turn on his own people like that, and I don't buy into his story about saving them from themselves."

They drove on for a while in silence, each deep in thought about their predicament and their options. Peter wanted to restore balance to the island, and Tracey wanted to bring him home, even if he was with Mary now.

Peter looked up ahead. "Look. There." He pointed ahead.

A huge grin crept across Tracey's face. "I don't believe it."

Peter pulled up to Jason, Mary, and Susan. "Hey guys, need a lift?"

"Peter!" Mary cried out.

He stopped the Jeep, and he and Tracey stepped out. Everyone exchanged hugs and sentiments of relief. Peter related everything he and Tracey had been through, including Poseidon Tech's real purpose and the attack on base camp. Jason and Susan told them about how they rescued Mary.

Tracey stepped back, and Mary hugged Peter, showering affection on him. Peter didn't notice her uneasiness as he was too busy receiving a hero's welcome.

"So, we're really going to this Temple of the Simian King?" said Susan.

"It's the only way," said Peter. "I can feel it in my soul. It'll set things right."

"I agree," said Jason. "I know nature, and this island is out of balance. The lizard men will have the Umazoa for lunch."

"What about base camp?" asked Susan. "What about going home?"

"You can go any time," said Peter. "You don't have to follow me. In fact, you probably shouldn't."

"I can't exactly walk back on my own through a jungle infested with prehistoric monsters either," said Susan.

Jason threw an arm around her shoulders. "Once we finish this, I'll make sure you get back. I know you want to go home."

"What about you?" asked Susan, blushing. "Don't you want to go home?"

Jason took in a deep breath, puffing out his chest, and let it out slowly. "I don't know. I didn't exactly fit in back home. Here I can hunt all I want and not be regarded as a total piece of human garbage."

Susan appeared disappointed.

"Oh, I guess I'll go home," said Jason, sounding playful. "Why, if I didn't would you miss me?"

"You know, I just might," said Susan.

Jason smiled at her. "Good to know."

"All right," announced Peter, interrupting the moment, "everyone in the Jeep. I have another race to wake up."

"Hey, mate," said Jason, "I don't suppose you brought any additional weaponry with you."

Peter shook his head. "We had to get out of there fast."

They all piled into the Jeep. Tracey stood back, waiting for Mary to take the front passenger seat.

"You go ahead," said Mary, grinning impishly. "I'll sit in the back and cause trouble."

Tracey nodded and reclaimed her seat next to Peter. The others squeezed into the back. Somehow Susan ended up sitting in Jason's lap, but she didn't look like she minded.

Peter drove off, following the river south, keeping with the path marked on his cognitive map. They stopped a few times for water from the river and to relieve themselves in the bushes. Eventually, they reached a part of the jungle where the vegetation grew thick, and massive tree roots extending across the road precluded continuing in the Jeep.

Peter pulled to a stop. "We can't drive through this. We go the rest of the way on foot."

Everyone hopped out of the Jeep. Susan threw her arms up above her head, clasped her fingers together, and arched her back as she stretched. Mary rubbed her lower back, as the bumpy terrain played havoc with her spine.

Peter pointed in front of him. "It's this way. Be careful. Everyone, stay together and stay alert."

Jason strolled up to the front with Peter. He squatted on his haunches and scanned the ground.

"See any tracks we need to worry about?" asked Tracey.

Jason stood. "Nah."

Peter's eyes were closed. When he opened them, he looked up at the trees.

"What is it?" asked Tracey, looking up as well.

"We're not alone," said Peter. "We're being watched."

Small black furry shapes leapt amongst the canopy above, swinging from branch to branch. They called out in high pitched cries and howls.

"Gibbons," said Mary. "Or at least this island's version of them."

"Are they dangerous?" asked Susan, casting a wary eye at the canopy above.

"Not particularly to humans," said Mary. "But they're territorial."

"Beats a T. rex any day," said Jason, his eyes also cast upward.

A few of the gibbons swung to lower branches, looking down on the human party. They inflated their throats, like bull frogs, crying out as they deflated them.

"Those look like Siamang," said Mary. "They're endangered in our home dimension."

Jason counted tens of them. "They look like they're flourishing here."

"They live in monogamous pairs," explained Mary, her tone almost mocking. She looked at Susan, smirking. "Except when a group has multiple adult males."

"Sounds like some people I know," quipped Susan.

Jason noticed the exchanged and appeared amused. Peter was oblivious to the whole thing. His mind was on more important matters.

"They're patrolling," said Mary. "They're letting the others know we're here. We must be at the edge of their territory."

"What if they attack?" asked Tracey.

"Not likely," said Mary. "We're too big, and there are too many of us."

"Let's go," said Peter.

They entered into the jungle, staying close to the snaking river. This was new territory, and they had no idea what was in store for them. Driven by a grave sense of purpose, they pushed on toward the Temple of the Simian King.

CHAPTER 11

Peter and Jason took point, while the others followed behind. They crept through the bushes and small trees, jumping over large, above-ground roots and pushing aside thick vines. The gibbons hooted and whooped above, following them.

Jason scanned the ground and touched tree trunks, his fingers probing scratches and marks as they walked. "So, Peter, how've you been holding up?"

"I was captured, offered up as a sacrifice, was almost eaten by a Spinosaurus, and was swallowed whole by a Titanoboa. Other than that, I'm doing great."

"I guess your negotiations with the lizard men didn't go well."

Peter smirked. "That's an understatement."

"It's a good thing you have those orbs," pressed Jason. "I'm sure they saved your life."

"They did. The life orb did anyway."

"What about the death orb?" inquired Jason. "You haven't used that one yet?"

Peter shrugged. "I don't know how, and I'm not sure I want to learn."

"Why is that? If we get in a tight spot with a nasty dino or the lizard men, you could wipe them out," Jason snapped his fingers, "just like that."

"That's what I don't like about it," said Peter. "In fact, it straight-up terrifies me. It sounds too easy. Something that devastating shouldn't be so easy."

"Nothing easy about taking a life," said Jason. "Trust me. I know."

"The last person to wield it fancied himself a Death Lord," reminded Peter. "It consumed him."

"Maybe he was the wrong person to have it," offered Jason.

"Maybe," said Peter.

"You've been talking about balance and all...and yet you don't want to use the death orb's power. You've been focusing entirely on the life orb."

This hadn't occurred to Peter. "Do you think it's a mistake not learning to use it?"

Jason shrugged. "Maybe it's not meant to be wielded by the one who wields the life orb. Maybe that's the balance."

Peter furrowed his brow. "Interesting. That's entirely possible. I wonder who then would wield it to offer balance. It certainly wasn't Mike Deluca."

"Oh, definitely not that guy," chuckled Jason. "Who says that power has to be evil? Death is a natural part of life. Without it, there'd be population explosion, the devastation of entire ecosystems."

"That's true," said Peter. "Only the death orb is followed by an evil entity on this island."

Jason grew quiet. He shot Peter a sideways glance. "What do you mean?"

"Something evil offered to teach me how to use it."

"How do you know it's evil?"

Peter shrugged his shoulders. "It just feels evil. It's what communed with Mike Deluca and twisted him. Tracey thinks it made Flight 207 crash here. She thinks it brought *us* here."

"Why would it do that?"

"To get off the island." Peter hesitated. He and Jason had been on this island together for what felt like months or even years. In that time, Jason had only expressed a passing interest in the orbs and Peter's dominion over them. He found Jason's sudden interest peculiar. He decided to withhold the bit of information about Nazimaa being imprisoned in the Temple of the Simian King. No one, other than Tracey, needed to know about that. He planned on avoiding Nazimaa anyway, so he found it irrelevant.

"When you were left for dead by the Zehhaki, how did you recover?" asked Peter. He noticed Jason's demeanor change. It was a brief flash, a one-second micro-expression of emotion that was quickly covered up by Jason's cool veneer.

"I was exhausted and injured," said Jason. "I suppose I just needed a rest."

Their conversation was interrupted by a siamang who dropped down in front of them, blocking their path. It hung from a branch by one arm, its white-bearded face regarding Peter with great interest.

"Uh, Mary?"

Mary broke from the others and ran up next to Peter. "It's okay. He's just checking you out."

The trees and vines around them came alive with other siamangs, who hung out, observing the intruders into their territory.

Susan yelped, pressing herself up against Tracey for protection. Tracey put her arm around Susan in support, as a parent does to a frightened child.

One of the siamangs jumped onto Susan's shoulders, causing her to screech in terror. She whirled around and around, swinging her spear, and it circled her head, swinging from her shoulders. "Get it off me! Get it off me!"

Tracey backed away, startled and apparently uncertain of what to do.

Jason laughed out loud. "He likes you, hun."

"Calm down," said Mary, stepping toward Susan. "He's just curious."

"Curious?" squealed Susan, who now stood absolutely still and rigid, grimacing as the small primate used her as his own personal jungle gym. "He won't hurt me?"

"I don't think so," said Mary.

The siamang groped her, rifling through her pockets, grabbing her spear momentarily and letting it go. It grabbed the locket hanging around her neck.

"What are you doing?" cried Susan.

The siamang snatched the locket off her neck and leapt to a nearby vine.

"That's mine," demanded Susan. She dashed off after it, outraged.

"Susan, wait," cried Tracey after her.

"It has my kid's picture in it," shouted Susan over her shoulder.

*

Susan darted through the underbrush and hanging vines, pursuing the little thief who pilfered her locket. "Get back here, you little klepto!"

Branches hit her face, scratching her cheeks as she gained on the little crook, only for it to narrowly evade her grasp. It swung from vine to vine, staying low to the ground, stopping as if it waited for her to catch up, taunting her. Susan heard the others calling after her, but she was too livid to hear their warnings.

Suddenly, she burst into a clearing where a bunch of much larger primates all sat. She skidded to a stop in the dirt and stood still, placing her hands out defensively.

What looked like a small group of chimpanzees sat in a circle, each holding a rock. At their feet sat broader, flat stones with crushed nuts sitting on the surfaces. They had been cracking the shells of the nuts and eating until they were interrupted. The small young cringed behind their mothers. They all gazed at Susan with eyes that appeared all too human.

Forgetting about her locket, she started to back away when one of the chimpanzees cried out. Susan froze again. She heard her friends calling for her, searching the jungle. It dawned on her how far she'd separated from the group.

Now, most of the chimpanzees called out, and within seconds there was an answer. The jungle erupted with deeper calls and chest pounding—males. Bushes and branches rustled all around Susan as the larger males rushed into view, jumping up on tree trunks, pounding on them with their fists. They saw her as a threat.

Susan's skin went cold, and the primitive, fight-or-flight part of her brain cried out, 'Danger!' She was surrounded.

*

Peter ran forward with Jason, who clutched his knife, as the jungle around them exploded in percussion.

"That's chest beating and tree pounding," shouted Mary, running behind them with Tracey. "Those are larger primates. Susan's in trouble."

"She's invaded something's territory," panted Tracey, dashing alongside Mary.

"That's right," said Mary.

"Susan!" called Jason, desperate. "Susan, where are you?"

Peter closed his eyes and reached out with his senses, his chest glowing under his shirt. He could feel the jungle in his mind. He found Susan. "She's just ahead. Jason, she's surrounded."

Jason doubled his efforts. "Susan! Susan, get out of there!"

They slowed as they approached the clearing where Susan stood, surrounded by several male chimps. They glared at her, and she stood frozen.

"Susan!" cried Jason.

She turned and looked at Jason, her eyes wide and pleading. A single tear streamed down her cheek.

The chimpanzees rushed her, tackling her to the ground. They pulled at her clothes as she screamed.

Jason dashed forward, but Peter grabbed his arm. "Jason, no."

Jason turned on him, imploring him. "Do something, Peter! Use the death orb! Do it now!"

Peter closed his eyes and dug deep, reaching for that wall of frost within his chest. However, as he extended himself toward it, it only receded from him. It was too cold, too distant for him to even touch. He heard Mary and Tracey cry out.

He opened his eyes to find Susan being bitten and torn apart by the male chimpanzees.

Jason squared off with him, his eyes feral. "Give it to me! Give me the death orb!"

"I-I-I don't know how."

Before Peter could register what was happening, he felt the death orb leaving his body. He looked down at his chest in disbelief as it passed out of him and drifted across to Jason. "No, wait..." Off in the bushes he thought he saw a young boy smiling, extending his hand. It was as if he was pulling the death orb out of Peter's chest through sheer will. *Nazimaa.*

The death orb passed into Jason's chest, illuminating it with an icy blue glow. The hunter's eyes blazed white, his irises disappearing altogether as he was possessed with the power of death.

He turned on the chimpanzees that ravaged Susan's body and shouted at them. He tensed his body and a wave of blue energy emanated from his body, enveloping the murderous chimps. They simultaneously dropped like stones, crumpled on the ground, dead.

Something literally taken out of him, Peter dropped to the ground, feeling weak. Mary and Tracey were by his side, comforting him, asking him if he was all right.

Jason ran to Susan's gored body and knelt beside it, wailing. She was torn to pieces. Jason wept into his hands.

"Peter, what happened?" asked Mary. "What did he do to you?"

"He took the death orb," said Peter, gasping for breath. "He took it right out of my chest."

"How is that even possible?" asked Tracey.

Peter looked over to where the young boy had stood. He was gone. "Nazimaa. She helped him."

Jason stood and wheeled around, pointing an accusatory finger at Peter. His eyes were back to normal, but there was something different about him. "Why didn't you do something to save her?"

"I tried," muttered Peter. "I couldn't do it."

"You're weak," bellowed Jason. "You didn't deserve to wield the death orb. It wasn't meant for you."

Peter stood with the help of Mary and Tracey, who regarded Jason with suspicion and horror. "Is that why you were asking about the orbs? Why you were asking about the death orb?"

Jason's chest heaved. "You don't respect death. You treat it like an enemy, rather than the ally it could be."

"I-I'm sorry. I didn't..."

"And now Susan is dead because of you." Jason's face contorted with disgust. "You don't even have the power to bring her back."

Peter stepped forward to survey the remains of Susan. Mary and Tracey tried to stop him, but he shrugged them off. Susan was torn to pieces, beyond his power to bring her back. The primordial island had claimed her life for the second and final time.

"But I do," hissed Jason. "I can bring her back."

"No," demanded Mary, stepping forward.

Jason turned on her, eyes wild. "You don't think I can do it? You underestimate me."

"It doesn't matter if you can," said Tracey. "You shouldn't. You'd make her into a monster…"

"Like me?" said Jason, finishing her sentence.

"No, that's not what I meant," said Tracey, shaking her head.

Peter stepped in front of Jason, cutting him off from Tracey. "It's not right. She's gone. Anything you did would be a horrible facsimile of her. Don't disrespect her memory by doing something unnatural."

Jason recoiled from Peter's words, placing a hand in front of his face, like a vampire faced with a crucifix. When he dropped his hand, his eyes returned to normal. The orb in his chest dimmed, and his whole demeanor changed. He appeared less wild and more like himself. His face dripped with sweat. "She had a family. She was going to go home." His voice sounded small.

"It's my fault," said Peter. "She shouldn't have followed me here."

"That's not fair," demanded Mary. "She had no choice but to follow us." She pointed a finger at Jason. "Even you said this mission was essential."

Jason was calm, but the expression on his face was bitter, as if he had a foul taste in his mouth that he couldn't shake. "If Peter hadn't hogged all the power for himself, this wouldn't have happened. He was greedy, and he couldn't handle it."

Tracey balled her hands into fists. "No, don't you dare blame him. He didn't ask for any of this. He was only trying to do the right thing."

"You've been speaking to Nazimaa," said Peter to Jason. "Why didn't you tell me?"

Jason turned his back on them. "Because I knew how you'd react. After what happened with Mike Deluca, I knew you wouldn't trust me."

Peter laughed, but it was a piteous sound. "Wouldn't trust you? Jason, I trust you with my life. You're a good person."

Jason turned back, leveling his gaze at Peter. "Even now? Do you trust me now that I have the death orb?"

"Maybe you're right," said Peter. "Maybe you respect death enough to wield it. Look how you resisted being overcome by its power. You could use it for good."

"I know what I'm going to use it for," said Jason. "I'm going to the Temple of the Simian King, and I'm going to bring my little brother back."

Peter shook his head, sweating profusely. He looked wan. "No. I saw what you think is your brother. It's Nazimaa. She's a demon."

Jason stamped his foot. "No! It's Joey. I know it's him."

"She appeared to Mike Deluca as his deceased wife," said Peter. "She twisted and manipulated him, like she's doing to you now."

"No," insisted Jason. "I'm bringing my brother back. He's at the temple."

"Nazimaa's at the temple," said Peter. "She's imprisoned there. She wants you to free her so she can leave the island."

"Maybe you can use your death power to wipe out the lizard men," offered Mary. "Then we don't even have to go to this temple."

"That's not for you to decide," admonished Jason.

"Oh, come off it," said Mary. "You asked Peter if he could do it when he had the death orb. Now it's a bad idea?"

Peter stepped forward, looking Jason in the eye. "Come on, buddy. You have the death orb. I know you can use it responsibly. If anyone can do it, it's you. Let's think about this for a moment." He saw he had Jason's attention. "What do you think is the right thing to do? Not the right thing for you, but the right thing for all? For the island?"

Jason dropped his head. "I...I don't know what to make of any of this." He raised it again to look at Peter. "This must've been what you've been shouldering this whole time. I didn't realize...I'm sorry."

Peter felt relieved his friend was being reasonable. "We have plenty of time to discuss this. Maybe we need to rest." He looked up at the sky, but the canopy was so thick it was impossible to tell where the sun was. "We can camp here, scare up some food."

"Bury Susan," said Jason.

Peter nodded. "Yes. Bury Susan."

"What if there're more chimpanzees?" asked Tracey.

Mary shook her head. "No, this was that community's territory. It'll be a while before another community realizes it's unoccupied."

"I'll see that Susan gets buried," said Peter to Jason. "Why don't you see if you can hunt us some food?"

Jason nodded. He walked over to Susan's torn body, knelt by it, and paused as if deep in thought or even prayer. He gently lifted the hunting knife he lent her off the ground by her body, wiped each side of the blade on his pant leg, and sheathed it. He retrieved his own spear off the ground by Peter and walked off into the jungle.

"Is he going to be okay?" asked Mary, concerned.

"I hope so," said Peter.

"Do you think he'll become like Mike Deluca?" asked Tracey.

"Not if I have anything to say about it. I'll teach him how to manage it. Jason's a good guy."

"So was Mike Deluca, I'm sure," said Tracey.

Peter looked down at Susan's remains. "This thing…this Nazimaa preys on people's weaknesses. It feeds on their pain. Their grief."

"Well, it looks like we're not going to that temple now, so it's a non-issue," said Mary. "She won't be freed."

"Nazimaa won't stop trying to get at him," said Peter. "Especially now that he possesses the death orb. She won't stop until she bends him to her will."

"That's why she gave him the death orb," said Mary. "She knew it'd be easier to take it from Jason than you."

"How do we fight the spirit of a demon?" asked Tracey.

"We can't. We all have to get off this island," said Mary.

Peter frowned. "Negative. That would be extraordinarily dangerous, given the circumstances."

Tracey appeared upset. "But you promised. You said you were coming back with me."

Mary visibly bristled at Tracey's demeanor toward Peter. The chimpanzees weren't the only territorial ones. "I guess he didn't exactly tell you about us." She shot him a reproachful glance. "Must've slipped his mind."

"Actually, he did tell me," said Tracey. "Not that it's any of your business."

Mary squared off with Tracey. "*Actually*, it *is* my business."

Peter had had enough. "Will you two cut it out? One of our friends is dead, another just had a huge burden placed on him, making him a target for a demon, and all you two can do is bicker over me? Newsflash: I'm not anyone's property. I have a mind of my own. Neither of you own me. At this point, I don't want to have anything to do with either of you. Why don't you start a campfire while I bury Susan?"

"But…" offered both women in unison.

"But nothing. Leave me alone."

Mary stormed off, obviously displeased with her treatment.

Tracey lingered. "Pete…let me help you."

He averted his gaze. "I want to be left alone, Tracey. Seriously." He looked and saw her walk away from him, honoring his wish.

He surveyed the mess that was his friend Susan and couldn't help but feel guilty. Maybe Jason was right. Had he monopolized both orbs incorrectly? Did their powers need to be balanced out by being separated across two different people?

It took him about an hour to bury Susan. He had no tools and used his bare hands. He was covered in sweat and dirt, and he reeked of body odor. He resented both of the women in his life. He was tired of being viewed as weak. He was tired of being someone's property.

When he rejoined the others, Tracey and Mary both sat in front of a campfire. Peter saw an expended hand-held signal flare lying on the ground next to Tracey. She must've used it to ignite the kindling. Jason butchered some animal he had caught, handing chunks to Mary, who in turn skewered the bits with sharpened sticks.

Jason looked up from his cutting. "You're a right mess, mate."

Peter's shoulders slumped. "Tell me about it."

Neither of the women even looked at him, which was fine by him. "I'm going to wash up down by the river."

"Hold on a minute," said Jason. "Let me go with you."

Peter held up a hand. "I want to be alone."

"Let him be," said Mary, her tone bitter.

Jason shrugged. "Whatever you want, man."

Peter separated from the group, heading for the river. As he meandered through the jungle, he heard the current. He reached the riverbank and looked around. The coast appeared to be clear. At this point, he didn't even care if something jumped out and devoured him. He even welcomed it.

He stripped down, leaving his clothes in a bundle on the riverbank, and waded into the river. Sheltered from the sun by the dense canopy, the water was cool and refreshing. He waded in until the water was up to his chest. He splashed water on his face and then cupped his hands to douse the top of his head.

The Temple of the Simian King was close, but it looked as if they didn't need to go after all. Jason's facility with the death orb presented another option for them in dealing with the Zehhaki. Peter no longer had any qualms about wiping them out. Maybe Tracey was right, and he had no business awakening yet another race. There was no guarantee that the Simians would even be friendly. What if they also attacked the Umazoa?

While he felt relieved that he didn't have to awaken the Simians, he knew he and Jason could not leave the island. He had no idea how the orbs would function back in their home dimension. And, there was another problem still. Poseidon Tech appeared intent on keeping the portal between dimensions open. That meant that there'd be more expeditions to the island from the home dimension. They clearly sought to profit from it somehow. Would they charge rich people to come visit the island? How would other governments—like China or North Korea—handle the news that an uncharted interdimensional island suddenly appeared in relatively close proximity? Would there be a race to claim it?

Peter realized that the Zehhaki might be the least of the Umazoa's problems after all. The mad rush to claim the island would no doubt lead to some form of colonization. There might be the introduction of foreign disease that could wipe out their entire tribe. What if there were other tribes on the island?

And then there was the problem of Nazimaa. She was itching to leave the island. If she ever accomplished that, who knew what havoc she'd wreak in his home dimension? In fact, the portal was two-way. If kept open indefinitely, not only did his home dimension have access to this strange land, but this land and whatever inhabited it would have access to his home dimension. Besides a possible migration of dinosaurs to his home world, what if there were worse entities than Nazimaa wanting out of this world?

When he finished washing up, he waded back out of the river and put his clothes back on. They were drenched with sweat and dirt, but at least he was clean and refreshed underneath. He almost felt human again.

He re-entered the jungle and found his friends again. They looked as if they were finishing up their meal. Mary was licking her fingers. Tracey wiped her mouth with the back of her forearm.

Jason looked up at him and smiled. "I saved some for you, mate. It's not so bad. A little gamey, but edible."

"That sounds good," said Peter. He sat next to Jason, who handed him a skewer of cooked meat. "Should I even bother asking what this is?"

Jason winked at him. "I wouldn't."

Peter took a bite of the meat. It was chewy, but it wasn't bad. "So, how do you propose we handle the Zehhaki?"

Jason furrowed his brow. "You're asking if I should just wipe them out."

"Yeah, I guess."

"They died out for a reason," said Tracey, breaking her silence. "Maybe they should be sent back into retirement, in an evolutionary sense, of course."

Mary averted her gaze from the group. She was still obviously pissed off at Peter. She lay down, reaching back and tucking her hands behind her head, looking up at the canopy.

"I think the bigger threat, at the moment, is this demon," said Jason.

"I'm relieved you see it that way," said Peter. "She's obviously very manipulative."

Jason looked down at the ground. "She's definitely very persuasive. The whole time I knew she wasn't my little brother, Joey, but I didn't care. It felt good to be with him again, even though in the back of my mind I knew it wasn't right."

"So, how do you propose we handle her?" asked Tracey.

"Well, we sure as heck aren't freeing her," said Peter.

"But even imprisoned, she's still powerful," said Jason.

"Just wait till Poseidon Tech brings more people to this island," said Tracey.

"Just wait till she gets off and enters our dimension," said Peter.

"We have to deal with her," said Jason. "But how? I don't see any exorcists around here."

Peter took another bite of his mystery meat. The savory flavor was a welcome sensation in his mouth. "I think the real question is, why isn't she dead? She's imprisoned, but her spirit remains free to roam."

"Maybe she anchored her soul to an object, and that object needs to be destroyed," offered Tracey.

"How the hell do we know which object she's anchored to?" asked Jason.

Mary sat up looking exasperated. "You need to destroy her body. Duh."

"How do you figure that?" asked Tracey.

"She was mortal once," said Mary. "She's imprisoned. Death is her prison. That explains her connection to the death orb."

Jason arched both eyebrows. "She did say the death orb was the only thing that would free her."

Mary nodded. "Destroy the body, and she's gone for good."

"That's an interesting theory," said Peter. "But how do we know it holds water?"

They all exchanged looks. "We have to go to the Temple of the Simian King," they all said in almost perfect unison.

"Great," said Peter. "Just great. And, we have to do this without freeing her from her prison."

"What if I didn't go?" suggested Jason. "I'm the real danger. Just keep me away from her."

Peter nodded. "That's right. You can take Mary and Tracey back to base camp. They don't have to be a part of any of this. I'll handle this."

"By yourself?" Tracey was beside herself. "How do you expect to do this alone? Who knows what perils are in that temple? Remember the Temple of the Lizard Men? It was riddled with traps."

"Tracey, I can't ask you to come along."

"She's right," said Mary, making eye contact with Peter for the first time since their argument. "You can't do it alone. Another thing…we're assuming we need to keep Jason away from Nazimaa's body. What if we need the power of both of the orbs to destroy her body?"

Everyone looked at her, stunned at her insight. She flashed a snotty look at them. "You're not the only ones who play tabletop RPGs."

"That would make sense, if we were in a game," mused Peter. "The risk is too big. Having Jason there could be catastrophic."

"Not having him there could also be dangerous," said Mary.

Jason furrowed his brow. "Peter, Nazimaa told me she saw to it that you and I would both be there. She wants us both there."

"So, then maybe Mary and I should go to the temple," said Tracey. "Maybe the both of you need to stay away."

"Round and round we go," muttered Jason. "One thing's for sure…we can't just sit here debating this for all eternity."

"He's right," said Peter. "We need a plan that would cover all possibilities. I say we all go. If Jason and I prove to be a problem, we'll leave, and you two can destroy the body. This way, if we're both needed, we'll be there."

Jason smirked. "Better to have us and not need us than need us and not have us."

"Then it's settled," said Tracey. "After we rest, we go to the temple."

Everyone nodded their agreements.

"We take shifts on watch," said Jason.

"Neither of us should be awake alone," warned Peter. "I have a feeling Nazimaa's going to be paying us a visit, trying to manipulate us."

"Great," said Mary. "I'll take a shift with Jason. Tracey, you take a shift with Peter."

Peter felt hurt by her immediate pairing up with someone other than him. However, this was not the time or place to discuss whatever they were going through in their relationship. "Okay. Jason, you hunted. Get some rest. Tracey and I will take first shift."

Jason tipped his hat to Peter. "Much appreciated, friend." He stretched out, laid back with his hands folded behind his head, and was snoring within minutes. Peter figured he was wiped out, and it probably wasn't the first time Jason slept outdoors, in the open.

Mary followed suit, laying back and closing her eyes.

Peter sat across from Tracey in silence, keeping watch. Time passed slowly, and Peter began to feel the weight of his own exhaustion. At one point his eyelids grew heavy, and he found himself nodding off.

He startled when Tracey moved closer to him, he presumed to keep him awake. He didn't mind the thawing of the ice between them. She didn't appear as irritated over his protest.

She leaned in, speaking in low tones so as not to disturb the others. "If this Nazimaa comes to you, how will I know? Will I see her?"

Peter shrugged, answering in an equally low tone. "Honestly, I don't know. If I see her, I'll let you know."

"Please do. We can't have her corrupting you like she did Mike Deluca."

Peter glanced over at Jason, who was sawing wood. "Maybe his snoring will scare Nazimaa away."

He and Tracey shared a quiet chuckle. It was nice to hear her laugh. "Mary's pretty pissed at me."

Tracey smiled. "That's an understatement. First fight?"

"I guess...but truthfully, things aren't totally right between us."

Tracey cocked her head a little. Peter always found that mannerism adorable. "Really? How so?"

"I don't know. She's okay and all, but..."

"She's not for you."

"Yeah...I guess not. It was exciting and fun in the beginning, but she's not exactly...my cup of tea."

Tracey smiled, warming Peter's heart. "That's good to hear."

Taken by surprise, Peter stammered, "I'm glad to hear that."

Tracey shimmied closer to him, leaning in further till her hot breath caressed his face. He didn't mind. "I can't wait to get out of this place."

"I don't blame you."

"After this temple, we can leave together. Start over."

Peter looked down for a moment. "Tracey, I don't know if I can ever leave."

She looked stunned and disappointed. "Why?"

"I can't return to our dimension with this...curse. Who knows what would happen? Poseidon Tech would probably dissect me like some science experiment."

Tracey set her jaw. The campfire danced, reflected in her eyes. "I won't let that happen. I won't let them hurt you."

"You won't be able to protect me. And, I don't want to put you in danger. I've put you in enough danger as it is."

She locked eyes with him, adamant. "I'm not afraid of them. They will learn to fear me." A wicked grin crept across her face.

Peter recoiled from her. Her demeanor in that moment...it wasn't like her. Her confidence took on an arrogant tone. Something wasn't right. He looked across the campfire and saw Tracey sound asleep. *What the...?*

When he looked back at the person sitting next to him, it was a featureless figure with eyes black as tar. It flashed a toothy grin, its teeth sharp and jagged.

He scuttled away from it as it laughed at him, mocking him. He looked around to see if anyone had been woken by the commotion, but his friends were all sound asleep. "*You!* What do you want?"

It crawled toward him on all fours, its breathing raspy. "To walk the earth again, to leave this place."

Peter leveled his gaze at it. "I won't let that happen." He took a chance with what he said next. He figured she already knew they were coming for her. "We're going to destroy your body, and then we'll be rid of you."

It laughed at him. It was a bitter, derisive sound. "You will free me. It is inevitable. It is your destiny. It is why I've brought you here."

Peter closed his eyes, reaching out with his senses. He detected her, in front of him. She registered as something cold and dark, but powerful. When he opened his eyes, she was gone.

CHAPTER 12

Peter decided not to wake the others up. He had passed his test with flying colors, which is why Nazimaa had left. He did, however, feel violated. She had used his feelings for Tracey to torment him. He cursed himself for allowing himself to be drawn into it hook, line, and sinker. He cursed the fact that it wasn't real.

After an undefined period of time, when the fire died down, leaving behind glowing coals and embers, he decided to wake Jason up. He crept over to the hunter and reached out to shake him.

Jason's hand shot out, snatching Peter's wrist.

Peter, startled, nearly yelping. "You were awake?"

Jason smiled and winked at him. "No, but I'm a light sleeper."

"Yeah, well, it's your turn. I'm exhausted."

Jason sat up and looked over at Tracey, who was curled up on the ground, sound asleep. "I thought you weren't supposed to be left alone."

"Nazimaa came to test me," said Peter. "She posed as Tracey."

"What did she want?"

"I don't know. To torment me. She told me I was going to get her off this island. That it was why she brought me here."

Jason looked around, alert. "She's going to come for me, isn't she?"

"Probably. You should wake Mary up. I'm going to get some shut eye."

Jason nodded. He stood, brushing himself off. As he walked over to Mary, shaking her gently, Peter lay back and closed his eyes. Although he was rattled, he was totally and truly exhausted. Sleep took him quickly, and he drifted off into a dreamless oblivion.

*

When he opened his eyes, everyone else was gone. Peter sat up, rubbing his eyes. The campfire had been extinguished, the kindling smoking. The ground felt wet.

Jason burst out of the jungle clasping his spear. His shirt was out of his pants, his hair was a mess, and he looked panicked. "Jesus, Peter, you're finally awake."

Peter sat up, rubbing his eyes. He felt groggy. "What happened? What's wrong?"

"The girls are gone. I tried to wake you, but you wouldn't wake up."

Peter tried to stand. He felt woozy, and the jungle spun around him. "Where'd they go?"

Jason's eyes darted around their campsite. He looked like a madman. "I was visited by Nazimaa last night. She appeared as Joey, but I knew better. When she saw I wasn't taking the bait, she became enraged...and that's the last thing I remember."

"Three guesses where she's taken them."

Jason nodded. "Well, now we know she really wants us to go to the temple."

"The both of us," added Peter. "We have to go now."

"Agreed," said Jason. "She'll have two advantages: she'll be ready for us, and she has our friends."

"We'll have to be careful," said Peter.

"Come on," said Jason. "We'll come up with a plan as we go."

*

Peter pointed ahead. "We have to go this way."

"I know," said Jason. Peter looked at him, surprised. Jason pointed to his head. "She put the map in my brain, too. Just in case."

They traipsed through the jungle, careful not to stray too far from the river. They had to cut further into the jungle as the riverbank gave way to a rocky cliff that rose up between seventy-five and a hundred feet into the air, but neither was worried. They had an internal, cognitive navigation directing them.

"How did you resist her?" asked Peter.

"Nazimaa?"

Peter nodded.

Jason huffed. "You know, I'm not as weak-brained as everyone thinks I am."

Peter shot him a sideways look. "Oh, come on. I never said you were."

"You used to think I was a moron," said Jason. "When we first met."

Peter smirked back. "And you thought I was a geek."

"Still do," said Jason.

They both shared a chuckle.

"I know the difference between fantasy and reality," said Jason.

Peter raised both eyebrows. "She can be pretty convincing. She got me."

"Pretending to be Tracey?"

"Yup. It felt so..."

"Good?" offered Jason, finishing his thought.

Peter blushed. "I was going to say real, but yeah. It felt good."

"She really does care about you, you know. And I mean as more than a friend."

"I know," said Peter. "I've always felt the same way about her. It was just never reciprocated."

Jason pondered this idea as he swept hanging vines away with his right hand. "Did it ever occur to you that she wasn't in a good position to reciprocate?"

"What do you mean?"

"Well, the two of you worked together, right?"

"Yeah."

"Does the university have a no fraternizing rule?"

Peter shrugged his shoulders. "Between faculty and students. Not really between professors, although it's discouraged."

"You also have to think of it this way," said Jason. "What if it didn't work out? Then the two of you would be stuck working together. It would be awkward, to say the least."

Peter nodded. "That's exactly what she said. I guess there could be some truth to that."

Jason waved his hand in front of him, as if he was clearing an imaginary chalkboard. "Okay, let's look at it from an animalistic point of view."

"Okay..." Peter was unsure of where his friend was going with this.

"You know that animals have mating rituals, some very elaborate."

"Okay. Sure."

"Well, you know what happens if one little detail is off."

"The mating doesn't happen."

"Right. People aren't so different. We're all animals. There are certain requirements or conditions that have to be met before mating occurs."

"Okay..." Peter was sure Jason knew what these conditions were, and he was sure the hunter exploited them whenever possible.

"Timing is important. She likes you, but before now the timing wasn't right."

"It still might not be right," said Peter. "Now I'm with Mary."

"That is a complication," agreed Jason. "You have a big decision to make, assuming we all make it out of this alive."

"That's a big assumption."

The two men traded smiles. Peter had grown to like Jason. It was true, when they'd first met, he didn't like the man. The hunter reminded him of the jock douchebags that had always tormented him when he was younger. But there was more to Jason than met the eye, and they had become close friends. They'd saved each other's skins a few times whilst on the island.

"Why do you think Nazimaa separated the two orbs?" asked Peter. "Wouldn't the death orb be harmless with me?"

"I don't think she fears the death orb," said Jason. "I think she needs someone to access its power. She wouldn't have that if it remained with you."

"That makes sense," said Peter. "The question is, how is she going to make us use the orbs to free her?"

Jason's grin faded quickly from his face. He stopped dead in his tracks and extended his left arm out in front of Peter.

Peter stopped short. "What? What is it?" he whispered, his eyes searching all around them. Was it a dinosaur? Something else?"

Before Jason could respond, a hunting party of Zehhaki burst out of the vegetation, surrounding them. They flared their dewlaps, hissing at the two humans and jabbing at them with sharp spear tips.

"Stay close," said Jason, jabbing back at them with his own spear to create distance.

Peter went back-to-back with the hunter as the Zehhaki formed a semi-circle around them. "Use the death orb."

"Okay." Jason reached deep within himself, but that sensation he'd experienced when Susan was being mauled wasn't there. He even closed his eyes, focusing intently, but it was as if his focus had no target. He opened his eyes again. "Problem."

"What? What's wrong?"

"I can't feel it."

"What do you mean, you can't feel it? You felt it before."

"That was different."

"How was it different?"

"I have no idea."

The Zehhaki tightened the circle, pushing Peter and Jason to the cliff's edge. Peter heard the river flowing down below. "We're out of wiggle room."

Jason looked over his shoulder and saw the drop. "We're going to have to fight our way out."

"We could jump," offered Peter.

Jason looked back over his shoulder. "That's a big drop, man. I think we can fight our way out."

"Only you're armed," said Peter. He counted in his mind. "There's ten of them. They must've been following us."

Two rushed in, lunging with their spears. Jason pushed his spear tip into one Zehhaki's stomach, but he was stabbed simultaneously by the others. He cried out in pain.

Peter stumbled backwards, teetering on the edge of the rocky cliff. His heels knocked loose pebbles off the side, sending them falling to the river below. He reached out and grabbed Jason to steady himself, but it was too late. He stumbled backwards off the cliff, taking his friend with him.

After a few seconds of terrifying freefall, they plunged into the river. Peter turned head over heels underwater as the strong current rolled him. He quickly became disoriented, not knowing which way was up. He had also lost track of Jason.

He unfurled his body and kicked, breaching the surface and filling his lungs with much needed air. He bobbed up and down as the river took him south. He searched for Jason, wiping the water out of his eyes. However, the act of rubbing his eyes caused him to sink, and he needed to tread water just to stay afloat. As far as he could tell, Jason was nowhere to be found.

After the river snaked left and then right, the current slowed and Peter was able to breathe and regain his bearings. He looked around but didn't see anything. "Jason!" he called out. "Jason! Where are you?"

For a moment, he thought of the Spinosaurus, but he fought down panic. He needed to find his friend. He closed his eyes and reached out, harnessing the power of the life orb. He felt Jason. He was close. Peter opened his eyes and looked beneath him. He drew in a deep breath and dipped under the surface.

Closing his eyes, he used the life orb to locate his friend. Jason was rolling, unconscious, underwater. Peter didn't sense any large aquatic predators, which was encouraging. He reached out, grabbed Jason, and pulled him to the surface.

Peter gasped for air as he lay on his back, grabbing his friend. When he located Jason, he also felt that his lifeforce was weak and fading fast. Peter kicked his legs, swimming in a perpendicular line, making his way towards the eastern shore. Once again, the current turned his vector into a hypotenuse, only the current was weak and the angle more acute.

As he crawled onto shore, he dragged Jason with him. He knelt in the silt and pulled his friend, dragging him out of the water and onto the riverbed. He rolled Jason onto his back and placed an ear to his chest. Jason's sides bled out onto the silt, staining it crimson. He had suffered so many stab wounds.

Peter closed his eyes and summoned the power within him. He felt the life orb illuminate. It was a warm sensation. He felt Jason's lifeforce beneath him, growing smaller. He touched its essence with his power, infusing it. He pushed the water from out of his lungs and infused Jason's stopped heart with the power of life. He then repaired Jason's wounds from the inside out, first replenishing the damaged organs and then mending flesh and skin.

When Peter opened his eyes, Jason was sitting up. Peter smiled.

Jason rubbed his forehead. "My head is pounding."

"That's four you owe me now."

Jason grimaced as he struggled to stand. "Four? Wait…you're not counting that time with the Compys, are you?"

Peter smirked. "Of course I am."

Jason wagged a finger. "I had that under control. They were tiny little buggers. I would've taken them."

Peter laughed. "Good to have you back amongst the living…again."

"You were right," said Jason. "We should've jumped."

Peter didn't mention that he actually fell. He'd never live it down. "I think we can still make it to the temple fairly easily."

"Yeah, but now we know the lizard men are following us. They don't want us to make it."

"That was when I was going to awaken their rivals," explained Peter. "I'm not doing that now."

"Yeah, well you try explaining that to them." He looked around. "Dammit, I lost my spear."

Peter puffed his chest out and grinned. "We have all we need. We have the life and death orbs."

Jason shot Peter a weary glance. "Yeah, I just have to figure out how to use mine."

Peter shrugged his shoulders. "Maybe that's a good thing. If you don't know how to use it, you can't use it to free Nazimaa. Oh, and now you know how I feel. Isn't so easy, is it?"

Jason shook his head. "No, I guess not."

Peter pointed up ahead. "All we have to do is follow the river south."

"I know," reminded Jason, pointing his index finger to his temple. "I have the map, too. Remember? It's on the other side of the river. We'll have to cross it at some point."

They started to walk.

"How do you suppose Nazimaa dragged two unwilling women to the temple?" asked Peter.

"She *is* powerful," said Jason.

Peter wore a pained expression on his face. "I...I just don't understand this place. I can feel everything, but I don't understand any of it."

"You didn't feel that this wasn't an island," said Jason. "Maybe you're not as omnipotent as you thought."

"Omniscient," corrected Peter.

"Whatever."

Peter chuckled to himself. "I guess not."

"We do have one thing going for us, though."

"What's that?"

Jason winked. "We haven't run into any dinosaurs since we saw the gibbons."

Peter sighed. "I'm really sorry about Susan. If there was *anything* I could've done..."

Jason held up a hand, palm facing out. "Forget it. I totally get it, mate. It wasn't your fault."

Peter felt relieved. The last thing he wanted to do was lose Jason's friendship. The only thing was, he couldn't forget it. Susan was torn to pieces, and he was powerless to stop it. What if...?

"We'll save Tracey and Mary," said Jason, as if he had read Peter's mind. "We won't let anything happen to them."

Peter wondered if Jason *could* read his mind, having the other orb and all. Maybe they were now connected in some way, brothers in orbs. "How do we know they're still alive? How do we know Nazimaa didn't just kill them and cast their bodies into the jungle?"

"One, because she needs them alive to dangle in front of us. Two, I'd feel them."

This startled Peter. "What do you mean?"

"I *mean* I'd feel them. I can feel all the dead things around me, just as you feel all life. I can't feel them. Therefore, they must be alive."

"Fascinating," gasped Peter. "Do you think...?"

"I could awaken the dead as zombies?" said Jason, finishing Peter's thought. "Just like Mike Deluca? I'm not sure, and I'm not sure I want to find out."

"Agreed."

"Hey, do you think that we can get rid of these orbs, once we're done with all of this?"

"Like remove them from our bodies?" asked Peter.

Jason nodded. "Nazimaa pulled the death orb out of you. Maybe they can be removed, and we can be…"

"Normal," said Peter.

Jason flinched. "I've never used that word to describe myself before, but yes."

"Maybe it's possible," said Peter. "But first thing's first."

"Rescue the women," said Jason.

They trekked south, following the river. Peter and Jason cast nervous glances up at the cliffs to the west. They didn't see any Zehhaki following them. Peter reached out with his senses and confirmed it.

Eventually, they came to a point where the river snaked east, but across the river they saw what was undoubtedly the Temple of the Simian King. A large relief of a massive ape was carved into the side of the rock cliff. Its arms were raised above its head, its eyes wide, and its massive mouth complete with sharp teeth agape. The yawning mouth had to have been fifteen feet high, and within was pitch darkness. It was the entrance.

"Well, there it is," said Peter. "What's the plan?"

Jason scratched his head, surveying the area. "First, we have to cross the river."

"Okay…then what?"

"We know it's a trap. So, we spring the trap."

"That's not much of a plan," remarked Peter. "In fact, I don't even think that qualifies as a plan at all."

"Well, what's your idea, Einstein?"

"Don't call me that." Peter looked around, thinking. "We won't need torches, because I can sense anything living in there."

"And I can sense anything dead," added Jason.

"Right. I'm guessing there shouldn't be much of either in there. But, if it's anything like the Zehhaki temple, there'll be traps."

"Right, so we proceed with extreme caution."

"She'll be waiting for us," said Peter. "She'll threaten Mary and Tracey to bend us to her will."

"That does present a problem…What if only one of us goes in there? Say, me. When she finds me, I'll tell her you didn't survive. If she thinks you're dead, she won't be looking for you."

"That's not going to work."

"Why is that?" Jason appeared annoyed by Peter's immediate dismissal of his plan.

"Number one, she won't believe you. Number two, she's always found me before. I don't think I can hide from her."

Jason squinted in the hot sun, swatting a mosquito off the back of his neck. "Okay, so we don't hide from her. We let her lead us right to her body. Then, instead of helping free her, we destroy it."

"How do you propose we do that?" asked Peter. "We don't have any fire, and all you have is a hunting knife."

"If she's been entombed for a really long time, maybe she's like a mummy or something. Her body should be delicate. I bet it would crumble easily."

"I don't think she'll give us the chance to destroy it."

"She can't handle the both of us," said Jason. "We'll have to work as a team. Whichever of us can keep her attention, the other will destroy the body."

"How will we know who will do what?"

Jason shrugged his shoulders. "We won't. We'll have to wait and see how things unfold." He saw Peter's discomfort with the plan and added, "It's our only play."

Peter paced back and forth, mulling over all possible permutations, straining his brain for a real plan. He stopped pacing and met Jason's eyes. "I guess you're right. She'll try to manipulate us any way she can, play on our emotions. More specifically, our fears. It's what she does."

"We can't give in to her," agreed Jason. "Remember, whatever she presents as will be an illusion."

"Absolutely. I think if we hold on to that simple truth, we should be able to resist her and stay focused."

They both looked at the entrance across the river.

"Okay," said Jason. "Let's do this."

CHAPTER 13

Peter closed his eyes and felt for any life in the river. He sensed a few species of fish, but no large predators. They walked a bit north and waded into the river. They swam across, the current bending their trajectory, placing them just a bit south of the temple entrance on the other side.

They walked up to the entrance and exchanged nervous glances.

"Are you ready?" asked Jason.

Peter nodded, his expression grave. Truthfully, he was terrified beyond all belief, but he figured fear was healthy. It would keep him alert, prevent him from taking anything for granted. "Remember, until she's freed from her prison, we have the advantage. We have the orbs, but she'll try to trick us. She's very good at it."

Jason gave a solemn nod. "Got it. We'll have to help each other. If she tries to fool one of us, the other has to be his anchor to reality."

Peter nodded. "Okay. Let's go."

They entered the mouth of the cave and were immediately engulfed in darkness. Peter didn't need to close his eyes to focus. He reached out to sense Mary and Tracey. "I can feel them. They're beneath us, a level down."

Jason produced a small flashlight. "I can't feel jack squat."

"That's good," said Peter. "That means no zombies this time."

Up ahead was an open doorway, the room beyond it dimly lit. The light came from the ceiling of the cavern, and in the middle of the room sat what looked like the top of a large, leafless tree growing out of the floor. "Look," said Jason.

"I see it," said Peter. "Let's be careful."

They walked up to the doorway, careful not to cross the threshold. They inspected it carefully. Peter looked for any kind of crude mechanical trap while Jason checked the ground for prints.

"I don't see any obvious traps," said Peter.

Jason squatted down, looking at the floor within the room. He swept his flashlight beam back and forth. "There're prints. Two sets."

Peter nodded "Mary and Tracey. Nazimaa's a ghost, so she wouldn't leave tracks."

"Looks like the ladies walked in here," said Jason. "That doesn't make any sense."

"Nazimaa can probably control them. I think it's safe to step inside."

"You first," said Jason, making a sweeping gesture with his right hand.

Peter huffed. "Typical." He stepped into the room, bracing himself for projectiles, trap doors, and whatnot. However, much to his relief, nothing happened.

Jason stepped into the room and looked around. It appeared to be a natural cave located within the cliffs. "Check this out." He pointed his flashlight at crude cave paintings depicting large apes in various poses. Some depicted families composed of a large male, smaller female, and a few young. The young were painted in lighter colors.

Peter remembered a late-night nature show on television asserting that the young had lighter fur so the adults could better keep track of them. When they reached a certain age, their fur darkened.

Peter and Jason walked the perimeter of the cavern, taking in the paintings. The colorful scenes covered the walls.

"Look." Peter pointed at a depiction of several of the male apes (he guessed by their size and musculature) engaging in battle with green figures with tails and flared dewlaps. They clutched spears and threw rocks. "They fought the Zehhaki."

Jason passed Peter and stood in front of a depiction larger in scale than the others. "This must be the Simian King."

Peter caught up to him and saw exactly what Jason referred to. There was a throng of apes—male, female, and juvenile—all arranged in a semi-circle around a prominent ape, who stood alone at the center. He was slightly larger, clutching a club. He was a king holding court.

Peter turned to investigate the tree. It rose up, practically to the ceiling, where a hole in the center must've led up to the surface, as some sunlight passed through into the room.

"How long do you think that shaft is?" asked Jason.

"Those cliffs go up about fifty feet." Peter reached out to touch one of the tree branches. The wood was rough and hard.

Jason reached out and grabbed Peter by the arm, pulling him back.

"What?"

Jason pointed down. There was a large gap in the floor through which the top of the tree passed. The trunk and branches appeared to descend down to another level.

Peter ran his fingers along the bark of a branch. "This wood is petrified. This tree must be ancient."

Jason looked around the room, which was about one hundred feet across. "I don't see any other doorways."

Peter peered down into the hole. "I think we're supposed to climb down."

Jason sneered. "You've got to be kidding me." He shone his flashlight down.

Peter arched an eyebrow. "Hey, this temple was built by apes. Apes swing from trees. It's how they get around."

Jason peered down into the hole. "Yeah, well, I hope you know how to climb."

"How hard can it be?"

Jason slapped him on the back. "That's the spirit!" He stuck his small flashlight into his mouth and bit down. He leaned forward over the hole, reached out, and grabbed onto a branch. He swung over the hole, legs dangling. He switched his hands on the branch, turning to face Peter.

Peter smirked. "That's a good look for you. Natural."

"Ha, ha," he said, mouth full. "Get your ass out here. We're climbing down." Jason swung a leg up onto the branch he grasped. He pulled himself up so that he lay face down on the branch, balancing his body.

Peter took a few steps to the left, leaned over the hole, and grabbed onto a branch. He tried to swing out over the hole, but his grip wasn't tight and his body weight pulled him down. He dropped into the hole, crying out as he fell, and he landed hard on a branch below.

Jason took his flashlight out of his mouth with one hand while holding onto the branch with his other hand. "Peter! Are you all right?"

Peter gasped for air, moaning. The wind had been knocked out of him.

"Stay there. I'll come get you." Jason placed the flashlight back in his mouth and swung down, his legs dangling. He stretched his feet until they touched a branch below. He moved, hand over hand, until his feet were solidly on the branch. He walked his way towards the trunk and leaned his body up against it.

"It's dark down here," said Peter, sounding hoarse.

Jason pulled his flashlight out of his mouth. "Don't move. I'm coming down to get you." Jason shoved the light back in his mouth and lowered himself until he crouched on the branch. There was another one directly in front of him, but further down. He braced himself, leaned forward, and kicked out. He fell and caught the branch beneath him, the rough bark biting into his skin. He swung back and forth from the momentum of his jump.

Peter turned his body sideways, balancing himself on the branch. He looked around. Beneath him the trunk vanished into shadow, but there definitely appeared to be another level.

Jason swung down to another branch and shimmied his way out to where Peter lay on his stomach, his arms wrapped around his petrified branch.

Jason took the flashlight out of his mouth. The taste of metal lingered on his tongue. "Are you okay?"

"I think I broke a rib," croaked Peter.

"Okay, I'm going to help you." He looked down, shining his flashlight around. "A couple more branches and there's a floor. We can make it. We'll take it one branch at a time."

Peter's hands were sweaty. He wiped them on his pants, doing his best to dry them. He didn't want to slip and fall. It hurt when he inhaled, so he took shallow breaths. His anxiety didn't help his breathing or his palms.

"There's a branch right under mine. Do you see it?" Jason shone the light on it.

Peter nodded.

"Good. You're going to hold onto your branch tight and lower yourself until you're hanging. I want you to swing across and grab onto me. Wrap your arms and legs around me."

Peter shook his head. "I...I can't. Too hard."

Jason smiled at him. "Nah, you can do it. Just like swinging on the monkey bars at school. You *did* have a jungle gym at your school, right?"

Peter shook his head. "Not really. I was more of a freeze tag guy."

Jason's face fell. "Well, you're going to do what I said, just how I said it. Grab onto me until your feet touch the branch below and you can steady yourself."

Peter shook his head. "I can't. I can't do it. I'll fall."

Jason shook his head. "All right. Forget that. I have a better idea." He shone his light around beneath Peter. "I want you to hang down."

"Hang down?" It hurt to talk.

"Yeah, just hold on and hang there. I have an idea."

"I hang there, and then what?"

"The floor isn't that far away. It's actually pretty close."

"Are you sure?"

"Absolutely."

Peter nodded and shifted his body weight, sliding off the tree branch. He gripped the rough bark tightly this time and hung from the branch.

Jason looked down at him. "Sorry."

Peter's expression was quizzical. "For what?"

Jason fell backwards off his branch, grabbed it with his hands, and swung into Peter, kicking him with both feet. Peter lost his grip and fell inward, landing on the hard ground, narrowly avoiding the hole where the rest of the tree trunk emanated from. He wailed in pain as he felt several of his bones break. His head swam and his ears rang. He closed his eyes, focusing on his orb, harnessing its power to heal himself. He felt his multiple fractures heal and his tissues mend. The pounding headache subsided and the ringing in his ears ceased. When he opened his eyes, Jason was standing over him looking sheepish.

"What the hell was that?" asked Peter, his tone accusatory.

Jason extended a hand. "Let me help you up."

Peter took it, and Jason helped pull him to standing. Peter brushed himself off. When he saw Jason's grin, he lost control. He swung and decked his friend.

Jason reeled; his head snapped back. He righted himself, rubbing his jaw. "You pack quite a punch for a nerd."

"That hurt, you jerk."

Jason shrugged, smiling. "I had to get you down somehow without you falling into the hole below. I figured you'd heal yourself. No harm, no foul."

"Yeah, well it still hurt."

They looked around the cavern they stood in. Jason shone his light around. The tree trunk disappeared into another hole in the floor. It was pitch black inside, and a chilly breeze of stale air wafted out.

Jason swept his light around the cavern. Like the cavern above, this one also appeared to be naturally formed. The river outside likely once flowed through here, carving out the cave system they stood in. He startled when he saw seven-foot tall apes looming in the shadows. His hand went to his knife as he braced himself.

Peter chortled. "They're statues. They won't hurt you."

Jason relaxed. "That's a relief." He swept his beam of light across the statues. They lined each side of the cavern and appeared similar. Each wore armor made of bamboo and held a spear pointing straight up, the other end touching the ground. Their mouths hung open, baring sharp canine teeth.

"They look like warriors," said Peter. He walked up to a statue and touched it. A thick layer of dust came off onto his fingertips. "They're carved from stone." He looked down and saw that the spear and right leg of the statue merged with a rectangular base. "Interesting."

"What's interesting?"

"As impressive as these statues are, they aren't able to stand balanced on their own. They had to include a heavy base attached to one leg so the statue wouldn't tip over." Peter smiled. "The ancient Greeks were able to carve sculptures that were free-standing, but the Romans never mastered it."

Jason stared at him, his expression blank.

Peter snickered. "What, you've never been to a museum?"

"No, but I can climb a tree."

A hand reached out for Peter and grasped his shoulder. He jumped out of his skin, shrugging it off and shrinking back toward Jason, who drew his knife.

Jason shone the light directly in the creature's face and saw two large, black eyes and a flared dewlap. "It's a damned lizard man! They got here first!"

Peter saw the glint of a crystal ball in the creature's other hand. "No, wait. It's okay."

"The hell it is," snapped Jason, stepping in front of Peter, brandishing his hunting knife.

Peter stepped in front of Jason. "It's Ghenga, the one that helped me. The one that told me about this place."

Jason lowered his knife hand only a little, but his muscles were still tensed. "How the hell did he get down here?"

As if in answer, Ghenga held up clawed fingers and coiled his tail behind him.

"Relax," said Peter. "Some lizards climb trees. Iguanas use their claws and tail to climb." He stepped forward toward Ghenga, who swallowed, bobbing his dewlap.

"Peter, what are you doing?" Jason held his knife at the ready.

"I'm going to communicate. Watch."

Ghenga extended the crystal ball to Peter, who placed his hand on top of it, establishing the neural link with the Zehhaki.

'I am pleased to see you came.'

"We ran into some of your people, but we escaped. What are you doing here?" Peter answered out loud for Jason's benefit.

'I am here to help protect you against Nazimaa.'

Peter smiled. "We will need all the help we can get. She has our two friends."

'She is using them to make you free her.'

"Is there a way we can save them without freeing her?"

'You are here to awaken Simians first.'

Peter had forgotten that was the whole reason Ghenga directed him to find this place. It was no longer necessary. Peter cursed himself, realizing he should've broken the link before allowing his mind to drift to that new development.

'You must awaken Simians.'

"I must rescue my friends, first. Have you seen them?"

Ghenga exhibited a strange emotional display. He grew stiff and he extended his dewlap as far as it would go. 'It is more important to wake the Simians.'

"How? How do I awaken them?"

'First, you awaken their king. I will take you to his tomb.'

"Let me tell my friend." Peter broke the connection with Ghenga. He walked over to where Jason stood at the ready and pulled him aside. He leaned in, "Something's wrong."

"You're damned right something's wrong. You're talking to one of those things."

"He's demanding that I awaken the Simians, starting with their king."

Jason scowled. "Well, tell him we're not doing that anymore."

"He doesn't seem to want to listen."

"We don't have time for this," said Jason. "Do you think he'll help us or not?"

Peter turned and approached Ghenga again, who stood there, watching them talk with his large black pools for eyes. Peter placed his hand atop the crystal orb again.

'Will you awaken Simians now?'

"Will you help us save our friends? They're somewhere within this temple. Nazimaa has them."

'Stay away from Nazimaa. Awaken the Simians.'

Peter shook his head. "If my friends are in danger, I can't stay away. Will you help us?"

Ghenga pondered the dilemma for a moment. 'Yes. I will help you, and then you will awaken the Simians.'

"Okay," said Peter. He removed his hand from the crystal, severing the neural link. He wasn't entirely sure how to handle this. He really was here for Tracey and Mary. They had another method of dealing with the Zehhaki, but Peter was very careful not to let that notion enter his mind. Somehow, he didn't think Ghenga would approve of the hunter using the death orb to render his entire race extinct. In fact, that outcome was precisely what Ghenga was trying to avoid.

Peter was riddled with ambivalence. Ghenga wasn't like the others. He seemed reasonable and sincere. Surely, there must've been other Zehhaki like him. Peter suddenly felt guilty about what he and Jason were going to attempt. Good or bad, the Zehhaki hadn't asked to be reawakened, thrust into a world that had moved on without them. Then again, did they really belong here at this moment in time?

Peter knew that Charles Darwin rejected the notion of progression. Rather, he saw evolution as each species being best adapted to their environment. It didn't matter if the organism was single celled or as complex as humans. The Zehhaki, and the Simians for that matter, had been selected for extinction many moons ago. In nature, species modify, they don't go extinct and suddenly return through artificial means. Then again, in this place, in this dimension, Peter wondered if the laws of evolution even applied.

Jason was growing impatient. "So, what's the story? Time's a wasting."

Peter didn't want to get into the moral-ethical dilemma before them. "He'll help us. He knows Nazimaa better than either of us." Which was curious, as in his ventures into the Zehhaki temple and lair, he saw no reference to her, positive or negative. Then again, he hadn't spent as much time with the Zehhaki as he had the Umazoa, who also didn't reference her. Like Native American tribes, they prayed to multiple nature-based deities, and there were some they feared. The Umazoa didn't speak of those, likely out of some established taboo, so Peter hadn't learned much about them.

Jason nodded. "Okay, which way do we go?"

They all looked around. Ghenga, not comprehending their discussion, watched them. Then, picking up on the fact they were searching for a door, he joined them, running his clawed hands along the stone walls of the cavern.

Peter inspected the ape statues, tugging on spears and arms, looking for a mechanical lever of some sort. Jason inspected the ground. "Peter, I found something."

Peter looked away from a statue he was investigating. "What is it?"

"I think I found the girls' prints." He pointed with his finger. He walked slowly and cautiously, following them to the west wall of the cavern. "The prints end here."

"Then there must be a secret door," said Peter.

Jason traced his fingertips around the wall. "There's a faint painting of what looks like the Simian King depicted in the painting. If there's a door here, the edges must be seamless."

Peter started tugging more parts of the statues. He tried to shove one to see if it moved, but it was too heavy. Ghenga, realizing what he was doing, slipped his crystal orb into a pouch that hung from his belt and joined him, throwing his back into it. Peter saw the muscles in the Zehhaki's arms and legs flex, and he was surprised when the statue actually moved.

Jason wheeled around, responding to the sound of the statue's stone base grinding against the floor. "Brilliant!"

Peter and Ghenga pushed the statue until it swiveled, facing where Jason stood. After it wouldn't swivel any more, Peter and Ghenga stopped pushing. Sweating, Peter wiped his brow with his forearm, while the enlightened Zehhaki didn't appear fazed.

"Maybe to open the secret door we need to face all of the statues towards this area," offered Jason. "Just like in the cave painting."

Peter smiled. "I was thinking the exact same thing."

They teamed up, swiveling the heavy stone statues one-by-one until they all faced the spot where the tracks ended. It was grueling work, and Peter's back began to complain. When they finished moving the last statue into place, there was the grinding of stone and an area in the floor began to sink.

Peter, Jason, and Ghenga all ran up to the spot and saw the sinking stone form a staircase leading down.

Peter elbowed Jason. "You're getting sloppy. The door was in the floor."

Jason gawked in awe. "Amazing," he gasped.

Peter made a sweeping gesture with his hand towards the sunken staircase. "Your turn."

Jason nodded. He produced his flashlight, clicking it on, and unsheathed his knife. He cautiously descended the staircase one step at a time, shining the light down into the opening. Peter saw him vanish into the floor and decided to follow behind him. Ghenga followed behind Peter.

Peter ducked his head to avoid smacking his skull on the ceiling, and he found Jason standing in a room about seventy-five feet long and fifty feet wide. When he reached the bottom, he noticed a large stone altar occupying the middle of the room. In the closest, right corner sat a fire bowl with a good-sized flame dancing in it, illuminating the room. On the wall to the right were three cave paintings depicting different figures. In the furthest right corner lay the corpse of a large ape. In the furthest left corner stood a pedestal holding a small statue.

"What do you make of all this?" asked Jason, surveying the room. He switched his flashlight off to conserve the batteries, as the fire bowl produced enough light.

Ghenga stepped into the room. Peter stepped aside to make way for him when his right foot began to sink. Panicked, he lifted it, but the stone continued to sink several inches into the floor. "Oops."

Jason turned to face him. He looked down at the sunken stone panel. "What did you do?"

The grinding below partially masked grinding from above as a stone wheel slid across the exit to the cavern above, sealing them inside the room.

Peter stood there looking sheepish. "I didn't mean to…"

Ghenga looked around, his dewlap bobbing. The fire bowl reflected in his massive black eyes as the flame danced.

"Great," said Jason. "Now we're stuck."

Ghenga produced his crystal orb and held it out with both clawed hands. Peter placed his palm on top of it. "Ghenga, it would appear we're trapped."

Ghenga swallowed several times. 'We go forward.'

CHAPTER 14

Jason immediately strode to the opposite wall, running his fingers along it. "There's a seam." He traced it with his fingers. "There's a secret door here." He looked down at about waist level. He bent over, inspecting the stone. He blew dust out of a small hole. "This looks like…a keyhole."

Peter inspected the cave paintings on the wall to the right. He carefully wiped the dust away with his hand, causing some of it to go airborne. He sneezed, suddenly and loudly, startling Ghenga, who recoiled. The painting in the middle clearly depicted the Simian King. The one to its right depicted a female, as featured with large, bare breasts and a less muscled body. The painting to the left depicted a smaller ape, lighter in color, clad in bamboo armor—likely a juvenile. It held what appeared to be a torch. Peter figured it was the fire of youth, or something like that.

He looked underneath the paintings. Directly below each was a small tablet representation of the painting above it held fast in crude metal brackets. Under each tablet was a keyhole. "I found three more keyholes," said Peter, trying to tug the tablets free of their brackets. "They seem to unlock these tablets."

Jason was now standing over the large ape-like corpse in the corner. Although its frame was large, its flesh had atrophied and its skin was taut from desiccation. "We have a dead body here."

Peter's head jerked in its direction. "Is it going to be a problem?"

Jason closed his eyes, focusing. The death orb illuminated under his shirt, casting an icy blue light. His eyes opened. "No, it's dead, as in the not-moving variety."

Peter turned to find Ghenga inspecting the altar in the center of the room. The Zehhaki was particularly interested in the massive hourglass sitting on top. He picked it up, shaking it, shifting the black sand sitting at the bottom. He made to turn it over, but Peter stopped him.

Ghenga's body stiffened. Peter shook his head. "No, not yet."

Ghenga placed the hourglass back onto the altar. He produced his crystal orb. Peter lay his right palm on it, re-establishing the neural link.

"Not yet. Starting the timer may trigger something. I want to know everything we're dealing with before we set anything in motion."

Ghenga didn't answer. Rather, he backed away, bowing slightly in a gesture of deference.

Peter clapped his hands, rubbing his palms together. "Okay, let's think about this for a moment."

Jason shot him a look.

Peter noticed. "What?"

"Oh God," said Jason. "You're actually enjoying this."

Peter ignored the remark. He stepped back, surveying the room, his mind processing the materials before him. "I'm thinking we need to free the stone tablets under the cave paintings."

"Yeah, but what do we do with the tablets?" asked Jason. "I think we need to unlock this door here."

Peter nodded. "Yes, but we won't just find the key." When Jason answered his statement with a quizzical look, Peter chuckled. "We'll have to free these tablets, which we'll then use to reveal the key to that door. Trust me. I know how these things work."

Ghenga was inspecting the top of the altar. He ran his clawed fingers across the top.

Peter saw this and joined him. He looked down and saw three depressions matching the size of the stone tablets locked up under the cave paintings. "Here. We have to place the tablets in these slots. That should reveal the key to unlock that secret door."

Jason looked at the altar and nodded. He then looked around the room. "Got it. What are we looking for?"

"Anything that would reveal a key for one of the tablets," said Peter.

They each split up, searching a different part of the room. Jason stood over the corpse of the ape man, studying it. Ghenga went to investigate the statue on the pedestal. Peter walked over to get a closer look at the fire bowl.

Peter studied the fire bowl. "This fire bowl is empty. No logs, twigs, or any kind of discernable fuel. Yet, it burns."

"Maybe it's a magic fire," quipped Jason.

"Maybe it is," said Peter. He placed his right hand out over the fire palm down, and slowly lowered it. He felt heat on his palm. "It's definitely hot." He looked around, patting himself down, as if searching for something. He looked over at Jason. "Let me borrow your knife."

Jason looked over his shoulder, arching an eyebrow. "Why?"

"I want to see if this fire is hot."

Jason turned away from the curious corpse and handed Peter his hunting knife, handle first. Peter took it and placed the large blade into the fire. Within seconds, the blade began to glow red. Peter removed the blade and quickly touched it with the tip of his index finger. He pulled it away quickly. "It's definitely hot." He handed the knife back to Jason.

Ghenga was surveying the statue and the pedestal. Peter turned to see him touch the small figure, and it shifted, but it didn't move off the pedestal. "Hold on a minute, Ghenga."

Ghenga backed away, clawed hands up.

Peter crossed the room to get a better look. The statue was squat with curvy features. It appeared to depict large breasts and hips. "It's a fertility statue," said Peter. "Many cultures have them." He cocked his head sideways, studying how it sat on the pedestal. After Ghenga touched it, it sat crooked and something protruded from the bottom. The protrusion appeared to disappear into the pedestal.

"What do you have there?" asked Jason.

"Either it's going to lead us to a key, or it's going to trigger a booby trap."

Jason came over to have a closer look. "It looks like the statue comes off, but it has to be lifted up."

Peter wiped sweat from his brow that wasn't entirely due to the heat. His heart pounded inside his chest. "Okay, here goes nothing." He looked to Jason for any objection, and the hunter offered none. Ghenga just watched them both, standing back.

Peter reached out, grabbed the small fertility statue in his hands, and slowly pulled it up. He winced, anticipating anything from flying spears to poison gas. The statue lifted off the pedestal, revealing a long protuberance underneath its base. When Peter cleared the pedestal, he laughed out loud as he recognized the long, toothed structure beneath the statue. "Ladies and gentlemen, the first key."

Jason snatched the statue out of Peter's hands, inverting it so the key pointed up. "Great, let's open the secret door." He walked over to the door, lined the key up with the keyhole using the statue as a handle, and attempted to insert the key. He tried to push, pulled it out, studied the key and then the hole, and tried to force the key in again. "It's not working."

"I told you," Peter smirked. He took the key from Jason and walked over to the three cave paintings. He stood in front of the one depicting the female ape. "I bet it unlocks this tablet." He turned the statue in his hands, lining the key up with the keyhole beneath the stone tablet depicting the Simian female. He slid the key in and turned. The metal clamps holding the tablet snapped open, and Peter removed the tablet. "That's one tablet."

"Brilliant," gasped Jason.

"Thank you," said Peter, obviously pleased with himself. He walked the tablet over to the altar and lined it up with the slot opposite the cave painting of the Simian female. It fit perfectly. "One down, two to go."

They all started looking around the room again. Ghenga was particularly interested in the giant hour glass filled with the black sand, but he didn't dare touch it.

Peter looked between the corpse crumpled in the corner and the apparently magical fire. "We have a corpse, a fire..." he looked at Ghenga, "...and an hourglass." He looked back at the cave paintings, studying them.

"The young one is holding a torch," said Jason. "That must have something to do with the fire. Maybe we need to make a torch?"

They looked around the room. "There's nothing to use as a torch," said Peter. "No wood."

Jason snapped his fingers. He ripped the right sleeve of his shirt off and wrapped it around the blade of his hunting knife. He walked over to the fire bowl and shot Peter a dubious glance.

Peter nodded. "Do it."

Jason placed the blade wrapped in fabric into the fire. His shirt sleeve ignited. He pulled it out and held it up. "Okay, now what?"

"Hold it in front of the painting of the youth," said Peter.

Jason nodded and stepped in front of the painting. He held the torch up. "Now what?"

Peter got right in front of the painting, investigating it up close.

"What are you doing?" asked Jason.

"I'm looking for hidden writing." Peter pored over the cave wall, but there were no hidden messages revealed by the torch light.

Jason adjusted his grip on the knife handle as the fabric burned away, falling away from the blade. "Hurry, it's burning out."

Peter stepped back, getting a different perspective on the painting of the ape youth. "Hmmm...I don't see anything..."

Jason let the charred sleeve fall off the blade to the stone floor, where the fire extinguished, leaving behind a small puff of black smoke. "That's it. Want me to make another one?"

"Hold off," said Peter, scratching the stubble on his chin contemplatively. "I need to figure this one out."

"While you do that, I'll try and figure out the other clue." Jason stepped in front of the center painting depicting the Simian King. He scratched his jaw, deep in thought. "There's a corpse and a giant hour glass. Nothing in the paintings indicates time." He walked back over to the corpse and squatted on his haunches. He inspected the ape warrior's armor, made from bamboo. He fingered the individual shafts, searching for one that resembled a key.

Peter momentarily regarded the corpse, but he saw Jason searching it. So, he turned his attention to the hour glass. "Time..." he muttered to himself. "The passage of time..."

Jason stood up and moved the corpse. It was surprisingly light, after who knows how many decades or centuries of desiccation. There was no key behind the body. He stood back, stroking the stubble on his jawline, deep in thought. "There's something wrong with his jaw. It looks crooked."

Peter, lost in his own ruminations, ignored the observation. Jason unsheathed his hunting knife and slid it into the ape's mouth. It hit something hard inside. He smirked and pushed the knife in deeper, twisting the blade. He pried the mouth open, revealing sharp canine teeth, and reached inside. He pulled out a metal key. "I've got it!"

Peter was jerked out of his private calculations. When he saw his friend holding the key, he smiled. "Nice work."

Jason brought the key over to the painting of the Simian King and inserted it into the keyhole beneath its corresponding tablet. He turned the key, and the metal brackets holding the tablet below snapped open. He grabbed the tablet and held it up. "Eureka."

"Put it in the middle slot on the altar," said Peter, allowing his friend to do the honors.

Jason strode triumphantly over to the altar and placed the tablet with the carving of the Simian King in the center slot. "Perfect fit."

"That leaves one more key for one more tablet," said Peter. "The only clues remaining are the fire and the hour glass."

Peter and Jason stood over the hour glass. They each studied it from a different angle, while Ghenga looked on. Peter wondered how intelligent this 'thinking' lizard man actually was, as he didn't offer much in the way of help in solving the puzzles.

"Time," said Jason. "Something the young have plenty of."

Peter looked him dead in the eye. "Do you think we should turn the hour glass over?"

"I think we have to," said Jason. "It's a big hour glass. Maybe there's a key in the sand at the bottom."

"I just hope it doesn't set off a trap," said Peter.

"It's not connected to any mechanism," said Jason, lifting it off the altar.

"Yeah, but that doesn't rule out magic," said Peter.

"I don't think we have any other option," said Jason. "Unless you have any other ideas..."

Peter shook his head. "Go ahead. Do it."

Jason sighed deeply, steeling himself, and turned the hourglass over as Peter grimaced and Ghenga cringed. The black sand began to run down. Jason placed it back on the altar and stepped away.

They waited as the sand fell.

"Do you really think this is going to take an hour?" asked Jason.

"Possibly," said Peter.

"That's a long time to wait," said Jason. "Meanwhile, the girls are in danger."

Suddenly, Ghenga lunged forward, grabbed the hourglass, and smashed it on the ground. The glass shattered, and the black sand spilled out onto the stone floor.

"What the hell are you doing?" shouted Jason, reprimanding the lizard man.

Peter pointed at the broken time instrument on the floor. "Look." He squatted down, sifted through the sand, and produced a key. He stood, using the altar for support, and held the key up. "The final key."

Peter unlocked the brackets under the painting of the ape youngster and removed the tablet with the carving matching the painting. He walked it over to the altar and placed the tablet in the only vacant slot directly opposite its corresponding cave painting.

There was the grinding of stone coming from the front side of the altar. Peter, Jason, and Ghenga all backed away from it as the stone façade slid slowly into a slot in the floor just big enough to accommodate it, revealing a relief of a great flame with a large key floating above it. Behind the key and fire was a representation of the hidden door in the wall, the edges forming the exact same shape. The grinding stopped, and nothing else happened.

"Well, there's our key," said Peter.

"It's a carving of a key," said Jason. "Can't use that to open up the secret door."

Peter scrunched his nose and scratched his head. "I know. This must be a clue to finding the key that unlocks the door."

"I don't get it," said Jason, crouching to get a closer look at the relief. "It references the fire again."

They all turned to look at the mysterious fire bowl. Ghenga extended his orb, prompting Peter to lay his hands on it. When Peter obliged, Ghenga spoke wordlessly. 'Reach into fire.'

Peter shook his head. "It's hot. It set Jason's sleeve on fire."

'I will reach in.'

Peter was unsure of Ghenga's abilities or his vulnerabilities, so this time he stepped aside, deferring to the Zehhaki.

Ghenga slipped his crystal orb into his pouch and walked over to the fire bowl. He cocked his head sideways, examining the flame. He flared his dewlap a couple of times, swallowing hard, and he reached his hand into the fire. He held it there for a second, which led Peter to believe that maybe the Zehhaki was fire resistant, but then Ghenga yanked it out, crying out. He cradled his hand against his body.

Peter ran over to comfort him. "Are you all right? Let me see." He momentarily forgot that there was no neural link, so his words weren't comprehended. Ghenga shrank away from Peter, turning his body so that he faced away from him.

"Great," said Jason. "Any other ideas?"

Peter decided to give Ghenga his space for the moment. While he felt sympathy toward the lizard man, he was reminded that this was an alien figure from another dimension he just didn't fully understand.

"Fire...key..." muttered Peter. "The fire somehow produces the key, but I think we have to use something else in this chamber. The problem is, I think we've used everything."

Jason looked around. "Maybe we missed something." He walked around the room, checking the tablets in their slots on the altar, the now empty pedestal that once held the fertility statue, and the ape man corpse.

Peter turned around and around, taking everything in. He had missed something, probably some subtle detail. What would interact with the fire to produce a key?

Jason placed a hand on his hip. His fingers drifted to his empty pistol holster. "If only I had my gun. I could shoot the lock." Suddenly, his eyes lit up. He snapped his fingers. "I think I've got it!"

His outburst startled Ghenga. Peter jerked out of his thoughts. "What? What is it?"

Jason walked around the altar and stopped in front of the large hour glass lying broken on the stone floor. He squatted, scooped up some of the black sand into his hands, cupping them. He walked the black sand over to the magical fire and tossed it into the flames.

The flames rose, as if suddenly doused with accelerant, and they turned black. A key appeared, floating in the fire. Jason turned, beaming, looking triumphant.

"Son of a gun," whispered Peter, astonished.

Jason took a deep breath and reached into the fire. He grabbed the key and pulled it out, his hand and arm undamaged. He held the key up. "It isn't even hot." Behind him, the flames shrank and resumed their normal color.

"Let's try it in the lock," said Peter.

Jason nodded and stepped over to the secret door. He found the keyhole, slipped the key into it, and gave it a turn. They all heard the movement of tumblers, and the door began to slide open to the sound of stone grinding on stone. They each stood back, bracing themselves for whatever lay beyond the door.

As the door opened, Peter saw a long, dark corridor lying beyond. When the door had opened completely, the grinding stopped.

"It's dark in there," said Jason. "It looks like a tunnel."

Peter peeked inside. "It's long. We need a light."

Jason pulled out his flashlight. "I'll go first. Stay behind me."

Peter turned to Ghenga, who still cradled his arm. The crystal orb remained in its pouch. "Are you okay?"

Ghenga didn't answer. It was difficult to gauge his disposition. Reptiles weren't the most expressive animals.

"Okay, let's go." Jason entered the tunnel. It was narrow. Jason swept his flashlight beam back and forth. The tunnel was lined with desiccated Simian mummies in various standing, sitting, and lying positions. The air was dry and stale, and they kicked up dust as they walked.

"It's a catacomb," said Peter. "They buried their dead here."

"I know what a catacomb is," snapped Jason, pushing forward. Their footsteps echoed off the stone walls.

"Hey, that was good work in there," said Peter, keeping pace behind his friend. "Very clever."

"I thought about gunpowder," said Jason. "I remembered the black sand. I figured it was black for a reason."

"The ol' rifle above the bar," quipped Peter. If present, everything had its function.

"What?" Jason apparently didn't get the reference.

"You know...Chekhov's Gun...the story-telling device."

Jason rolled his eyes. "You are *such* a dork."

"Nothing. Never mind."

They heard grinding behind them. Each whipped around to find they were being sealed off from the Simian escape room they had just left.

"Onward," said Jason. He took a few steps and then stopped abruptly.

Peter came to a halt, Ghenga crashing into him from behind. "What? What is it?"

"Something doesn't feel right."

"We're in an ancient Simian temple surrounded by mummies. What could feel right about this?"

Jason turned to face Peter. "No. It's the orb."

"The death orb?"

Jason nodded. He looked down at his chest, and it began to glow under his shirt. The illumination cast the mummies in an eerie light, their eye socks and gaunt faces looking haunted.

"That's much better than a flashlight," said Peter.

"Something's happening," said Jason.

All around them, the mummies began to twitch and move. Necks and limbs jerked, hands and feet shot out in spasms. Eye sockets glowed.

"Can't you stop it?" asked Peter. "Use your orb."

Jason closed his eyes and focused. Peter and Ghenga watched as the mummified corpses around them began to reanimate.

Jason opened his eyes. "I can't stop it. It's Nazimaa. She's too powerful."

Peter and Jason exchanged terrified looks.

"Run," said Jason.

Peter nodded.

Jason broke into a sprint, Peter and Ghenga lagging behind him. Peter huffed and puffed, his lungs burning as the corpses jerked into motion, reaching out shriveled arms and hands for them. Peter shrugged them off as he zigzagged through the undead gauntlet.

In front of him, Jason was tackled to the ground by a mummified ape, and others immediately piled on top of him. Peter turned to look back over his shoulder, and he saw Ghenga seized by mummies. His path of escape narrowed in front of him as zombie ape men closed in on him. Large hands and long fingers pulled him down to the ground.

The apes mauled him, tearing his shirt and clawing at the orb in his chest. Nazimaa wanted the orbs, even if she had to rip it out of them with cold, dead hands. Peter pushed and kicked against his attackers as hands and bodies blocked out his vision. He had the sensation of suffocating under the pile on. He gasped, struggling to breathe. He heard Jason shouting and cursing.

Peter closed his eyes and felt the dim, cold presences of these mummies, much like the zombie cannibals Mike Deluca had created and controlled.

"Use your orb!" Peter cried out to Jason. "You can control them!"

"I'm trying...." he heard. "I can't do it!"

Fingers clawed at Peter's chest, sinking into his flesh, but not harming it. It reminded him of one of those weird late-night specials he saw on psychic surgery. The undead ape men were grasping the edges of the life orb, trying to pull it out of his chest.

Peter resisted, summoning the full strength of his inner power. He reached out, grasping at the icy life force that reanimated these apes. He concentrated, pushing the dark energy back. He felt Nazimaa pushing back against his power, and she was strong.

The life orb was now half out of his chest. He felt as if his life force was entangled with the orb, clinging to it. The resultant sensation was extreme pain, as if they were yanking his very heart and soul out of his body. Peter opened his eyes to find glowing eyes staring down at him as undead fingers pried the orb from his chest. He closed his eyes again, awaiting death, helpless to defend himself or prevent it.

Suddenly, Peter felt a wave of cold, black energy and everything stopped. He opened his eyes and saw the ape mummies frozen, staring down at him. It didn't make any sense. What had happened?

"Hurry!" shouted Jason. "She's too strong! I can't hold them forever!"

Peter pushed himself to standing and scrambled forward, shoving his way past inert ape men, bobbing and weaving through outstretched hands frozen in time. Up ahead, he saw Jason getting to his feet. Peter caught up to him and ushered him toward the far end of the tunnel, where another stone door blocked their exit.

"Hurry," grunted Jason, exerting himself over the mummies. "She's pushing back."

Peter frantically searched the end of the tunnel for a button, switch, or lever that would open the door. "I don't know how to open the door."

"Hurry," said Jason through gritted teeth, straining.

Peter turned to find the Simian mummies jerking back to motion in staccato movements. Nazimaa was disrupting Jason's signal to them. It was only a matter of seconds.

He turned back to focus on the stone door. He ran his fingers along its surface, but there wasn't a keyhole. "Dammit!" He looked at the walls around the door and saw nothing. He stepped back, slipping past Jason, who had his eyes squeezed shut, his body tense and rigid. He looked constipated. "Hurry, Peter!"

The mummies took uneven steps toward them, advancing slowly but steadily. Peter looked at the walls on either side of them and saw a large lever mounted up high on each side, ten feet back from the wall with the door. He jumped at one, latching onto it, pulling it down. It slid down and stopped. Nothing happened.

Peter ran across to the other wall and jumped, grabbing the other lever. He used his body weight to pull it down. However, he looked over his shoulder to find the other lever sliding up, back into place. When his current lever stopped dropping, nothing happened. "Crap. The levers have to be pulled down simultaneously." It made sense. An ape man would have the proper arm span to do it. However, Peter was no ape man.

He turned to find Jason swooning on his feet, hands out in front of him, holding the horde of mummies back. The more they advanced, the more he faltered.

Peter's mind raced, trying to figure out how to pull both levers simultaneously. He looked around him for anything he could use. The mummies were closing the distance, now only fifty feet away.

"Jason, I need your help!"

Jason snapped out of his focus and staggered over to Peter. He was soaked with sweat and panting. The mummies behind him started to regain fluidity to their movement.

"We need to pull these down simultaneously," said Peter.

Jason nodded.

They each stood under a lever and jumped up, pulling down on them. As they slid down, the stone door began to roll away. Peter saw the mummies closing in, reaching out for them, now only twenty-five feet away.

"Now!" cried Peter.

He and Jason let go of the levers and the door stopped rolling away. Almost immediately, it began to roll back into place. Peter slipped through the narrowing gap and into the next room. Jason darted over, the Simian mummies now clawing at his back. He wedged himself in the shrinking gap; Peter grabbed his arm and pulled him from the other side.

Jason slipped through in time as the stone wheel sealed off the gap, crushing reaching arms and severing grasping fingers. They heard the faint pounding of undead fists from the other side.

All around the room fire bowls erupted with fire at their presence, illuminating the room.

Exhausted, Jason's legs gave way, but Peter caught him, supporting him. He looked around the room. It was a larger room, a few hundred feet long and almost as many wide, with a massive statue of what could only be the Simian King on the far side of the room. The imposing figure loomed over a large stone sarcophagus, its chest puffed out, a spear in its right hand. It donned the bamboo armor seen on the corpse in the ancestral chamber, and on its head sat a crown. The statue stood on a raised platform. Statues of ape men warriors lined the sides of the burial chamber on very narrow cliffs.

Between the statue and where Peter and Jason stood was a large chasm. Several platforms jutted out of the void below about thirty to forty feet apart. Massive trees grew in between, with long branches and vines extending across, connecting the platforms above ground level.

"We have to hide," said Peter. "They'll pull the levers and be through in moments."

Jason nodded. Regaining some of his strength, he stood on his own. "Where's the lizard man?"

"He didn't make it. We have to hide, now."

They crossed the room to the edge of the platform on which they stood, looking down. "I can't see the bottom," said Jason.

Peter kicked a pebble off the edge, watching it fall. It vanished into darkness, and he didn't hear it hit bottom. The stone wheel grinded open behind them.

"We have to swing across," said Jason, eyeing the branches and vines, calculating a path to the massive statue of the Simian King.

"There's no way I'm making that," said Peter.

"You have to, mate."

Peter looked at the sides of the cavern. "I can climb across to the other side. I'll hold onto the statues for support."

Jason inspected the narrow shelf the statues stood on. "That's risky. If you fall, that'll be all she wrote."

"At least I stand a chance," insisted Peter. "If I try to monkey bar my way across, I'll definitely fall."

Jason nodded. "I'll draw their attention away from you and meet you there."

Peter nodded, and they parted ways—Jason approaching the first gap to the next platform, and Peter dashing to the narrow ledge on the right.

As the stone wheel opened up, the mummies from the catacombs poured through, spilling out into the regal burial chamber. As Peter cautiously looked over his shoulder, he wondered where Tracey and Mary were in all of this. There didn't appear to be any other doors to any other parts of the temple.

He took his first step onto the ledge, grabbing the ten-foot-tall statue of a Simian warrior around its waist. He carefully edged his left foot further left, and he slid his right foot onto the ledge. He swung himself around the statue, careful to cling to the sheer rock wall, pressing his cheek up against it as he shimmied out further.

*

Jason crouched, tensing his muscles in anticipation of a jump to the nearest tree branch, when he heard a commotion behind him. One part of his rational mind told him to jump and swing to the next platform. Another part told him that Simian mummies would likely be able to swing through the trees with ease, overtaking him within mere moments. Then, something tugged at the recesses of his mind, and that familiar wordless voice commanded him to turn around.

As the ape warrior mummies fanned out, Joey walked into the room. Two mummies followed, dragging Mary and Tracey. The women squirmed in their grips, but the mummies were too strong.

*

Peter saw Ghenga saunter into the room, followed by two mummies dragging Mary and Tracey. He understood now. It all made sense. When he had entered that sacred place in the Zehhaki city, where Ghenga had showed him the stored memories, he recalled being dragged out by the Zehhaki as if he didn't belong there. More importantly, he recalled their reaction to Ghenga—it was hostile, fearful even. He also understood why Ghenga had wanted him to go to this Temple of the Simian King. It had nothing to do with any balance of nature. He wanted Peter here with the life orb at the place of Nazimaa's captivity. He remembered Ghenga growing inpatient in the ancestral chamber and smashing the large hourglass with the black sand. Peter closed his eyes and reached out with his powers, and the familiar icy, dark presence confirmed it.

Ghenga was Nazimaa.

CHAPTER 15

Jason watched his little brother, Joey, enter the room with Mary and Tracey being dragged in behind him by Simian mummies. It didn't make any sense. He knew his brother was dead, he knew Joey's manifestation was a mind trick perpetrated by Nazimaa, yet he froze where he stood, feeling helpless.

'Jason,' said Joey in a wordless voice that was hollow, dry, and all too familiar. 'I told you we'd be together again.'

Jason shook his head, as if to clear it. His mind set off all kinds of alarms, warning him that what he saw before him was an illusion, a cruel manipulation. Yet, something tugged at his emotions, triggering grief and nostalgia in a wave that washed over him, drowning out the voices of reason. "You're…you're not real."

Joey stepped forward, away from the two mummies holding Tracey and Mary. 'I am real, and we can be together. You can help me.'

"No." Jason shook his head, defiant. "I don't believe you." However, memories began to replay in his head, memories of his childhood with Joey. The vignettes and the emotional responses they triggered tasted putrescent, like the stench of rotting flesh in the hot sun. "No! Stop it!"

Joey reached out a hand. Jason found his own hand reaching out to meet his brother's, though not of his volition. It was as if he was a passenger on a ride, watching but unable to steer the direction it was taking.

Their fingertips met, and the cavern around them melted away in Jason's mind's eye. Suddenly, they were in the woods of Alaska. The bare, rock walls morphed into the brilliant green unique to Alaskan flora. Snow blanketed the ground, and Jason saw his breath cloud up in the air in front of him with each exhalation. Yet, there wasn't an icy bite in the air. In fact, the only cold he felt welled up inside him, emanating from the death orb.

*

As Peter edged across the ledge, carefully negotiating his way around a second and third statue, he heard that icy wordless voice in his mind. 'Stop. Bring the life orb to me, or I will rend your friends limb from limb.'

Peter stopped where he was, pressing his face and chest against the cool rock. He turned his head, careful to maintain his balance. He saw Tracey and Mary held up by two massive ape mummies like rag dolls.

'No,' he answered. 'If you don't let them go, I'll throw myself off this ledge, and your precious life orb will be lost. You'll never escape captivity.'

Losing patience, Ghenga waved his hand and the mummies grabbed Mary and Tracey each by their wrists, holding them up in front of them. The women squirmed, trying to wriggle free. 'I will rip their arms from their sockets.'

'If I surrender to you, they're dead anyway,' said Peter. 'No deal.'

In a trick of the shadows, Ghenga transformed into a wraithlike figure, the top half that of a humanoid woman and the bottom half that of a serpent. Her eyes glowed yellow; the pupils were vertical slits. She was beautiful and horrific all at once.

'Let them go,' commanded Peter.

'You are in no position to give orders.' Nazimaa's eyes glowed brighter, and the mummies holding the women started to pull their arms apart slowly. Tracey cried out and Mary grunted, gritting her teeth.

He saw Jason just standing there, staring into space, hypnotized. He knew Nazimaa had already gotten to his friend.

Peter jutted his right hand out. 'Okay! Stop!'

Nazimaa's eyes dimmed.

'What do you want?' Peter asked the demon.

'Relinquish the orb, and I will let you all go unharmed.'

He knew if he did that, she'd be free—free to roam the land, and free to leave this dimension and enter his. She knew that he knew that. She also knew, deep down, he wouldn't allow Tracey and Mary to be harmed.

*

Jason watched in horror as the mummies, as well as Tracey and Mary, morphed into a pack of wolves and began to maul Joey. "No!" He stepped forward to grab his little brother, but the wolves snatched the boy first. They tore into him, savaging the poor kid all over again.

'Help me, Jason!' cried Joey, as the wolves sank their teeth into his small body, playing tug of war with him. Blood oozed out of Joey's mouth as he cried out for his big brother, as his coat and the flesh beneath was torn to shreds.

Jason dashed forward to try to help, but the wolves pushed him back. He felt helpless to do anything to save Joey.

'Use the orb!' cried Joey. 'Wipe them out in one shot! You can do it!'

Desperation and fury welled up inside Jason, just like when Susan was brutalized by the chimpanzees. It was all he needed to access the power of his death orb. He lashed out with his power, sending it out over the wolves in waves.

They recoiled from the dark energy, cringing and contorting. They whimpered and cried out in agony as Jason squelched their life forces. Simultaneously, Joey's wounds began to heal and his torn clothing mend.

Jason felt the satisfaction of vengeful bloodlust as he barraged the wolves with his dark energy. It was something he had always wished he could've done, but was unable to do—avenge Joey's death.

'Keep going,' pleaded Joey. 'I'm feeling...better. I'm coming back...we can be together...keep going.'

Jason wasn't going to let up. He didn't just want to kill these wolves. He wanted to obliterate them. He also wanted to bring Joey back, and it appeared the only way to accomplish both was to unleash the full power of the death orb. He reached deep inside himself and released a tsunami of death. It washed over the wolves, and they vanished in its wake, as did Joey.

Terrified he had made a fatal error, he ceased the attack, but it didn't matter. He felt the power recede, not just from around him, but from his own body. As the tides of death energy waned, Nazimaa stood in Joey's place, soaking it all up like a sponge. Jason looked down to see the death orb floating out of his chest and over to Nazimaa.

As she was still incorporeal, she was unable to absorb the orb as yet. However, her eyes burned within their sockets, and the death orb illuminated in response to its rightful master.

Jason felt an illness deep within him—once paused by Nazimaa—re-ignite. Fever engulfed him once more, and he felt his life slip from his body on the wings of delirium. The screams and cries of Tracey and Mary grew distant as oblivion consumed him.

*

Peter successfully turned his body so his back was to the wall in time to watch as Jason fell limp into Nazimaa's arms. She glared at Peter, her eyes flashing, and she tossed Jason's lifeless husk into the chasm.

"Nooooooo!" he shouted, feeling distraught and furious, enraged and helpless.

Nazimaa pointed a long, bony finger at Peter. 'Stay right there.'

With a wordless command, several of the Simian mummies bolted to Peter's side of the cavern on all fours, using their long arms to help propel them. They swung out over the ledge with great facility, using the statues like tree trunks. They closed in on Peter, who clung to the wall on the ledge only a few statues away.

He had half a mind to jump. It was the only thing he could do. He wouldn't stop Nazimaa, but he'd keep her imprisoned. He quickly summoned the conviction required, fueled by outrage and defiance. He leaned forward, jumping off the narrow ledge into the yawning chasm below.

However, he was too late. After a couple of seconds of freefall, he was snatched up by the swinging mummies and hauled back to the ledge. He cursed himself for pausing for even the briefest of moments. He hung over the chasm, dangling by his wrist, as one of the mummies gripped it tight with one massive hand, the other massive hand gripping the statue.

'Now, now. That wasn't very smart,' hissed the demon.

She hopped onto the back of one of the mummies, and it leapt, swinging from branch to branch until it reached the other side of the cavern. The mummies clutching Tracey and Mary also swung across, carrying their master's insurance policy, in case Peter had any other ideas.

They all waited at the foot of the statue of the Simian king as Peter's mummy carried him across, tossing him up in the air like a toy, only to be caught by another, and then another, as the mummies deftly swung from branch to branch.

At last, he was thrown to the ground at Nazimaa's feet on the other side. The demon loomed over him, and behind her the sculpture of her old nemesis loomed over her. Only this time, he posed no threat to her.

Nazimaa stroked the sarcophagus with a spectral finger and stood in front of the enormous statue of the Simian King, crushing her in effigy. 'Centuries ago, the Simian King faced me in battle. Despite my powers and cunning, he used his strength to subdue me before his god of power and light.

'His queen and daughter possessed the life and death orbs, the latter obtained by defeating the Zehhaki. They used the orbs to imprison me here to spend eternity under foot of the Simian King, my spirit cursed to roam the jungle.'

It all finally made sense to Peter. The Simian Queen, represented by the fertility statue, wielded the power of life. The daughter, who he had assumed was a son, bore fire, which could've symbolized destruction. The hour glass with the black sand represented the slipping away of time, impending mortality. She wielded the power of death.

Peter nodded, comprehending. "They buried the orbs in the Zehhaki caverns, far away from where you were imprisoned, to make sure you were never freed."

Nazimaa's thin lips curled into a ghastly smile. 'The orbs waited, protected by powerful magic, for those worthy to wield them again. In my current state, I was unable to reobtain them. The Umazoa, as you call them, emerged as the Zehhaki and Simians fell. They built a shrine over the Zehhaki ruins, completely unaware of what lay beneath and the history behind it. They made futile gestures of human sacrifice to appease their own pathetic deities.' The demon laughed derisively.

Peter frowned. "So, you had to wait for us to land on this island to unlock the orbs."

"She brought us here," said Tracey, her face twisted in anger and disgust. "She manipulated us from the start. Everything was to bring us to this moment, here and now."

'I have no need or desire to harm you or your friends. Use the life orb, set me free, and I will leave you in peace.'

"She's lying," hissed Tracey. "She wants to leave the island."

"Don't listen to her," spat Mary.

Peter remembered Mike Deluca's attempt to summon the support ships out in the surrounding ocean so he could bring Nazimaa off the island. He knew Tracey was right.

"Where is your body?" He was stalling for time.

Nazimaa gazed down upon her lifelike likeness. Her expression was that of self-pity and sorrow. 'Beneath the statue. For too long I have been imprisoned here, wandering the jungle a mere shadow.'

Peter marveled at her power as a 'mere shadow.' If she could breach his dimension and crash a plane as a ghost, he shuddered at what she could do if reawakened in corporeal form.

'No more talk. The time has come. You will awaken my body and release the orb or watch your friends die.'

Peter nodded. Tracey and Mary protested valiantly, but there was nothing he could do. His mind raced, searching for options, but none presented themselves.

Nazimaa gestured to the sarcophagus, and two of the Simian mummies toppled it over onto its side, revealing a stone staircase underneath that led into the ground. The lid of the sarcophagus dislodged, and the mummified body of the Simian King spilled out onto the ground. As large as the warrior mummies were, their king was even larger. Peter imagined the power and might such a specimen must've possessed in life, but now it was only an empty husk.

Nazimaa gestured to Peter. 'After you.'

Peter shot Tracey and Mary a dubious look, and he descended the staircase. At first it was dark, and he reached out to steady himself, but there was nothing to grab onto. Then, remembering his powers, he focused, causing his chest to glow. It was enough light to navigate the steep staircase successfully.

When he reached the bottom, Nazimaa slinked past him. Her army of Simian mummies, however, shoved him aside as they filled the burial chamber. Two of them dragged Tracey and Mary along. Fire bowls ignited around them, triggered by their presence, illuminating the room. It was a large room, about one hundred feet across and fifty feet wide. The floor was composed of stone tiles, and the walls were smooth with vast openings on either side midway. The walls bore crude cave paintings depicting the defeat of Nazimaa at the Simian King's hands. It was simultaneously a tribute to him and a rebuke to her.

"Boy, your defeat was a big deal to these Simians," chided Peter. "That's embarrassing."

'Silence.' She pointed a long, gaunt finger at the end of the room.

At the other end was a sarcophagus, plain and purposefully unadorned, surrounded by several fire bowls. On the wall behind the sarcophagus was a chiseled relief of the same sun deity depicted behind the large statue one level up. Peter realized it was likely this sun deity that maintained these magical fires, if one could believe in such a thing.

Natural curiosity won out over self-preservation. Peter, studying the paintings on the wall, made to step forward, but Nazimaa glided in front of him, blocking his path. Startled, he met her gaze and tried his best not to wither under its power. "What?"

She held up an index finger. 'Wait.' She gestured for the Simian mummies to step forward across the room, including the ones holding Tracey and Mary. They did as they were commanded. After progressing about twenty feet and stepping on strategically placed pressure plates, spears launched out of well-camouflaged holes in the cave paintings, impaling the two lead mummies. They staggered, clutching at the spear shafts lodged in various parts of their undead anatomy at multiple angles. Undead and undeterred, two others stepped in front of them and continued walking, triggering more pressure plates, causing boulders to roll out of the large openings in the walls, crushing them underneath.

Peter wasn't surprised. Of course this particular burial chamber was booby trapped. Whoever entombed this demon here wanted to make sure she remained undisturbed.

The remainder of the stretch leading to the plain sarcophagus was presided over by a statue of an armored warrior clutching a spear. When the remaining two uncrushed mummies and the two wounded by spears approached, it sprung to life, attacking them. At first, Peter thought it was a live Simian who had remained very still. However, when the mummies pounded on its exterior to no avail, he realized it was indeed a statue, but animated. It made quick work of the mummies, tearing them apart, reducing them to fractured bones and dust. The immediate threats vanquished, the Simian warrior resumed its pose, becoming statuesque once more.

Nazimaa turned to Peter, Tracey, and Mary. 'Only the bearer of the life orb can pass the final guardian. Then, you will infuse life into my corpse and bring me back, setting me free.'

"Don't do it, Peter," demanded Mary.

"She wants to leave this place," said Tracey. "We can't allow that."

Suddenly, both women clutched their heads and wailed in pain. They fell to their knees, writhing and flailing, crying out.

"Stop," said Peter. "Stop it. Release them. I'll do what you ask."

Just like that, the ladies were released from the demon's vice-like grip. Tracey and Mary panted on the floor, tears streaming down their cheeks. Blood trickled out of their nostrils. Tracey wiped hers on the back of her forearm while Mary sat up, glaring at Nazimaa, seething with rage.

The demon shadow swept a hand out, gesturing for Peter to progress. Her eyes flashed in menace for a brief moment before returning to their normal illumination.

Peter stepped tentatively, testing each tile on the floor. As he progressed, careful to avoid the tiles the mummies had triggered, he activated several other pressure plates. He winced, awaiting fast, pointy death, but nothing came. Apparently, the mummies had expended the mechanical traps. Peter carefully circumnavigated the massive boulders that had rolled across crushing two of Nazimaa's undead Simian minions. As he looked at either side of the room, he saw the massive channels from where the boulders originated.

At last, he was before the statue guardian, about twenty feet away. By all appearances, it was indeed a statue hewn from a gray stone in great detail. It stood upright, back rigid, clutching a spear. Peter took a deep breath, preparing to summon the power of the life orb, and stepped forward. After a few steps, it opened its eyes and sprang forward, pointing its spear at his face.

He quickly tapped into the power of the life orb, and his chest responded by glowing brightly. The statue guardian halted, falling just mere centimeters short of impaling Peter through his right eye. He closed his eyes, reaching out around him. He sensed the Simian guardian, its life force registering uniquely. It wasn't as warm as Tracey or Mary, and it wasn't as frigid as Nazimaa or the mummies.

Recognizing the aura emanating from Peter's chest, it stepped aside, allowing him passage to the sarcophagus. Peter opened his eyes and tentatively proceeded. As he passed the Simian guardian, he studied its face. It wore a stoic expression. Although animated, this statue was not imbued with actual life, but magic for a specific purpose.

When Peter reached the sarcophagus, he reached out with his power, sensing what lay inside, cold and inert. He felt Nazimaa's body, its aura vacant from having been abandoned so long ago. On Peter's radar, it registered as another object in the room, almost indistinguishable from the sarcophagus that housed it.

'Bring my body here. Awaken me, and you and your friends shall be spared.'

Anger flashed inside Peter. She hadn't spared Jason. Instead, she toyed with his grief and guilt for her own amusement, ripped his life from his body, and cast his empty husk into the void below so that Peter could never revive him. Her offers of mercy carried no meaning for him.

He closed his eyes and summoned the life orb's power. He felt it welling up inside of him like a hot spring. He released it on the corpse, infusing it. He felt Nazimaa's tissues mend and blood begin to coarse through its countless vessels...he felt Nazimaa's heart kickstart.

'No. What are you doing? Not yet. Bring it back here first.' The demon's wordless voice sounded panicked.

'No,' Peter replied within his mind.

In his mind's eye, he saw Nazimaa's ghost menace Tracey and Mary. 'I will smite them both!' However, her presence across the room faded as her spirit was recalled to her body. He both saw and felt her vanish from in front of Tracey and Mary. Suddenly, he sensed her inside the sarcophagus, only it was sealed. He heard a great shriek of fury from within, and the lid started to shift from pounding underneath.

Peter hadn't much time. He turned and ran back past the guardian, who briefly animated and then resumed its pose after he was fifteen feet away from it. He rounded the boulders as the sarcophagus lid shifted, stone scraping on stone.

"Where'd she go?" asked Tracey, looking around.

"She's in the sarcophagus," shouted Peter as he ran to them, "but not for long!"

Behind him, he heard a smash. Mary pointed in horror, and Tracey waved Peter forward, "Hurry! She's out!"

He looked over his shoulder to see Nazimaa sit up in her coffin. Her top half resembled that of a buxom young woman, and her chest glowed with the power of the death orb. As she lifted herself out of the coffin, he saw her lower serpentine half. She was beautiful and horrifying all at once. Not looking where he was going, he nearly crashed into Tracey and Mary.

"What do we do?" asked Tracey, panicked.

"She's alive," said Peter, "which means she can be killed. But..."

"There's always a *but*," said Mary.

"But, she wields the power of the death orb, which makes her nearly unstoppable."

They turned to find her advancing toward them. She waved her hands around, her chest glowing brighter, but as soon as she stepped within fifteen feet of the guardian statue, it animated. It immediately attacked her, interrupting what was likely going to be an attack that would've snuffed out all of their lives in one blast. She grappled with it, and they tussled, each pushing back against the other.

"That was lucky," said Mary.

"If she tries to use the death orb, I'll counter it with my orb," said Peter.

"And we'll try to kill her," said Tracey.

They all exchanged nods and dispersed. Peter went right, watching Nazimaa as she contended with the Simian statue. He waited for her chest to glow brighter and prepared to respond in kind, summoning his power. Nazimaa deftly dodged the statue guardian's spear thrusts, but she couldn't respond with counterattacks.

In the meantime, Tracey and Mary went left, searching for anything that could be used as a weapon. They scoured the ground, picking up stones. Their search was interrupted by grunts and howls from up above.

Peter turned to find the rest of the Simian mummies barrel down the staircase, answering their master's call. He turned and faced them, closing his eyes. He felt their cool, dark auras and reached out with his power, pressing against them, puncturing their outer shell and infusing them with the warmth of life.

*

Tracey saw Peter face the onslaught of Simian mummies, and she saw them halt in their tracks. They writhed under his power, their pallor fading, their dry skin and flesh repairing. She turned back to Nazimaa, whose chest was growing in illumination. In between dodging spear thrusts and wrestling with the statue guardian, she cast glances at Peter. Tracey's eyes darted to Peter, who appeared to swoon, swaying on his feet.

"She's hurting Peter," Tracey said to Mary.

They began to pick up any rocks they found around them, hurling them at Nazimaa. Most of the throws missed, bouncing off the statue guardian's stony exterior. However, Tracey used to pitch softball for the faculty team, and she was damned good at it. She picked up a softball sized stone sloughed off from the collision between the two massive boulders and wound up. She released the rock underhand, and it struck Nazimaa between the eyes, disrupting her focus. The demon's chest immediately dimmed, but the look Nazimaa shot Tracey was the stuff of nightmares.

"Oooh, she didn't like that," said Mary sardonically. "Nice pitch."

They moved closer to Nazimaa, preparing more stones for throwing. Tracey looked back at Peter. The mummies had already begun to turn. They sprouted black fur, and their musculature filled out. Their bodies convulsed as life rushed back into them.

Nazimaa and the statue guardian barreled past Tracey in a blur, as Nazimaa slammed the statue's back against one of the boulders.

"Damn, she's strong," said Mary, chucking a stone and hitting the demon in the back of the head.

Hurt from the blow, Nazimaa shook her head as the statue pushed back. However, Nazimaa side-stepped, throwing the statue guardian off-balance, and she snatched its spear from it hands. As it stumbled forward, she twirled the spear in the air and swung it down, connecting with the statue's head, knocking it clearly off its shoulders.

"Oh crap," said Tracey.

"That's not good," said Mary, pausing mid-throw.

Nazimaa's eyes burned like hot coals in her skull, and her chest illumination burned with hateful fury. Tracey pulled on Mary to run, but she felt something stop her cold. Icy fingers probed at her soul, as she felt her life begin to fade away from her body.

She heard a wordless voice in her mind, faint, calling to her. However, unlike the frigid sensation racking her soul, this voice was warm and familiar. It began to grow in volume and intensity until it filled her mind and chased away Nazimaa's dark tendrils. Tracey recognized the voice as Peter's.

She turned to find him squaring off with Nazimaa, his orb radiating in his chest and his eyes glowing bright like the sun, fixated on the demon. Confused, the now live Simians standing behind them watched the exchange in awe, pounding their chests and bouncing off the walls of the cavern. They appeared to recognize the demon. Tracey guessed this wasn't the first time they had seen this battle, only last time it was with different players.

Having been released from Nazimaa's frosty death grip, Mary gasped for air, recovering.

"Are you all right?" asked Tracey.

Mary nodded, panting. "I'm...okay...How...are you?"

"I'm okay." However, Tracey's heart was pounding in her chest, threatening to punch its way through. Peter and Nazimaa seemed to be locked in a stalemate, each canceling out the other's power.

"What do we do now?" asked Tracey.

"We kill this prehistoric bitch," said Mary. Before Tracey could stop her, Mary lunged at Nazimaa, rock in-hand, swinging it at the demon's head. However, Nazimaa cast the briefest glances her way, and Mary froze. Her body convulsed, and she dropped to the floor.

"Mary!" Tracey wanted to run over to her, but she thought better of it. It was too close to that monster, the new Death Lord.

She turned to Peter, her mind frantic, struggling to figure out how she should help. She didn't want to lose Peter, not again, and not to this prehistoric witch. She had returned to this horrifying place to bring him back because she loved him.

Suddenly, she felt another voice inside her mind, calling to her, instructing her to help Peter. Only this time, it wasn't Peter's voice. It was her own. She had an idea. She unslung her pack and unzipped it...

*

Peter leaned in toward Nazimaa, and she in toward him, as they locked in a high-stakes contest of opposing powers. Both of their eyes burned in their sockets, and the blinding illumination from each of their orbs—his golden and hers an icy blue—combined to bathe the room in an ethereal green light.

Peter looked around for Tracey, but she had vanished. He saw Mary lying still on the ground at Nazimaa's feet, and he became filled with a righteous rage. However, no matter how hard he pushed, he felt unable to budge the demon.

He caught something out of the corner of his eye, the briefest distortion in the surreal green light. It circumvented Nazimaa, passing behind her. Peter smiled as he sensed what it was—Tracey was hidden under some kind of light-bending camouflage blanket. He saw her hand reach out, visible, holding the red flare gun from the Jeep.

*

Tracey shrugged off part of her cover and held the flare gun to the back of the demon's head. She saw Peter glance over at her, a grin creeping across his face.

Nazimaa, sensing something amiss, turned her head. Her eyes widened and her mouth fell open in horror when she noticed Tracey—but it was too late.

Tracey rammed the red flare gun into the demon's mouth and fired. Nazimaa's mouth erupted in a bright red light. The wraith's hands gripped her face as she broke her standoff with Peter and staggered sideways, emitting a wordless shriek that caused Tracey and the now live Simians to cover their ears in agony.

Her attack disrupted, Peter capitalized on the opportunity and doubled his efforts, digging deep for the last of whatever reserves he had left. He felt his attack against Nazimaa amplify, pushing back her wave of cold death and darkness, his own inner force threatening to overtake her. He felt the demon's strength begin to yield under his, and he sensed her panic rising up inside her. The magnitude of his total power shook the cavern. The ground rumbled under their feet, shaking violently, but Peter kept his focus.

Nazimaa, however, staggered, losing her footing. Her power receded into her body, and the power of the life orb exploded in a bright flash of light.

*

The light-bending camouflage blanket (a la Poseidon Tech) fell from Tracey's shoulders as she felt wave after wave of Peter's power envelop her. She let the flare gun slip out of her hand, but she did not hear it hit the stone floor. As she embraced his energy, she felt her essence merge with his until they became one. She felt the power of the life orb as if it was in her own chest and intertwined with Peter's will, creating a synergy. She closed her eyes and felt the room. She felt Peter and the Simian warriors. She felt Peter's love and sacrifice, and she felt the Simians' fear and uncertainty. She also felt her own love, loyalty, and conviction, and fed it into Peter's power.

*

Peter's vision was white-washed. When his rods and cones recovered, he saw Nazimaa lying on the ground, her lips split, scorched, and bloody. Mary struggled to her feet, holding her head.

172

Peter ran over to Tracey, his face and body sweaty from exertion. "Are you all right?"

She nodded.

They were no longer one, but the feeling of their joining remained. He had never felt closer to her before in his life, and he knew she felt the same.

"I love you," she said, her voice strong but sweet.

They kissed each other deeply, their souls merging again. When they broke their embrace, Mary was beside them. Peter saw Nazimaa was standing again. She looked terrified, furious, and spent. Her eyes glowed, as did the death orb in her chest, and she gesticulated wildly, summoning the very worst of her dark power.

But nothing happened.

Peter turned to Tracey, astonished. "I didn't feel anything. Did you?"

Tracey shook her head, a smile creeping across her face. "I didn't either."

Mary smirked. "She's lost her power."

Peter turned on Nazimaa. "It won't work anymore. You're defeated. It's over."

"No!" croaked Nazimaa in torment, her mouth melted. Her eyes glowed and then dimmed. "No! It can't be! I am lord over death and darkness! Heel to!"

Tracey pulled up the corner of her mouth into a smirk. "Get over yourself."

Peter felt new presences behind him. He whirled around to find many more live Simians behind him, awakened in the catacombs by his explosion of life energy. Males and females all looked on, totally engrossed.

The crowd began to stir, and apes started to part, making way for something. Peter saw a massive figure wade through the crowd, its head and shoulders a head above the others. When it reached the front, Peter recognized what could only be the Simian King. On his right was his queen, and on his left was his daughter.

Peter leaned into Tracey and murmured. "I think I did it again."

Tracey nodded, stunned. "You woke up another race."

"So much for not interfering in the natural order," quipped Mary.

The Simian King regarded Peter, Tracey, and Mary, studying them with eyes that were all too human. He then shifted his gaze to Nazimaa. His expression changed when he looked upon her. His face contorted with anger, and he grunted. He slammed the butt of his spear into the ground and pounded his chest with his free hand.

Nazimaa froze, paralyzed with fear. Her humanoid face bore an expression of disbelief at history about to repeat itself.

The Simian King looked back at Peter, Tracey, and Mary, his expression softening. When his eyes settled on Peter's life orb, he bowed his head in reverence. The Simian Queen and her daughter, who had only been watching, stepped forward, extending their hands.

Peter felt a tugging sensation within his chest, but he didn't fight it. The life orb drifted out of his chest and floated across to the Simian Queen. She took it in her hands and pushed it into her own chest, her body absorbing it effortlessly.

Nazimaa cried out from behind them, but Peter didn't dare turn around. He already knew what had happened. The death orb drifted past him and Tracey. The Simian Princess reached out, accepted the orb, and absorbed it into her chest.

"The orbs have been returned to their rightful owners," murmured Peter.

The Simian King gestured for Peter and Tracey to leave the chamber. They all understood what he wanted.

"What about Nazimaa?" asked Mary.

Peter looked back. "She's toast. Let's get out of here."

As they walked to the back of the room where the staircase led up to the statue, Peter heard the Simian King grunt orders. The crowd erupted, rushing Nazimaa. Peter turned around in time to see them fall upon her, tearing her powerless mortal body apart.

CHAPTER 16

Having just survived the battle with a demon and having awoken yet another species on the "island," Peter and the two ladies walked along the river, back towards base camp. It was a long walk, and they currently slogged in silence, but the silence had nothing to do with exhaustion.

He and Tracey had shared a moment. The two had momentarily become one, and the intimate experience had left his mind reeling. It was the closest he had ever felt toward Tracey, and he still felt the wake of her presence in his mind.

However, since the temple, Mary was understandably quiet—not quite sullen, but withdrawn. She only looked ahead as she walked to his left, while Tracey on his right shot him furtive glances and smiles. A couple of times she walked close, and their fingertips touched on the verge of hand-holding. However, they each thought better of doing it with Mary present.

Peter broke the silence. "It's strange not having the orb inside me anymore. I feel detached from the island, cut off. Yet, it's a relief. Too much power and responsibility. I think it's in the right hands now." He hoped that was indeed true.

"Why do you think the Simians went extinct?" asked Tracey.

Peter shook his head. "I don't know. I hope we did the right thing by bringing them back."

"I guess that makes you the selection pressure for their return," said Mary, breaking the ice. "A selection pressure can be anything, really."

"Or anyone," added Peter. "Nazimaa brought me here. So, technically she was the selection pressure."

"It'll be up to the Simians to adapt and survive," said Mary. "Either they will, or they won't."

"Their very presence will be a selection pressure on the Zehhaki," said Peter. "Nazimaa was right about that. There needs to be balance."

"I wonder how the Umazoa are," said Tracey. "I wonder if Hiu rescued the others."

"I wonder if the Simians will be allies or competitors," said Peter.

"Who cares?" said Mary. "At this point, I want off this island."

"Do you think base camp will still be there?" asked Tracey. "What if the dinosaurs got to it, or they cleared out and returned home?"

Peter couldn't reach out with his powers to sense Poseidon Tech's presence because he no longer possessed the orb. He had actually grown accustomed to having access to its powers. A chill shot down his spine at the realization he was no longer 'indestructible,' nor could he heal his friends should they come to harm on the way back to base camp.

"Listen, about before…" began Mary, jerking Peter out of his worry.

"Mary…" began Tracey, her tone apologetic.

"No," insisted Mary, holding up a hand in front of her. "We need to talk about it. I'm not mad. Really."

"That's a relief," sighed Peter.

Mary looked at him for the first time since they had left the temple. "The truth is, you're a great guy, Peter…but, I don't know…"

"Maybe we're not right for each other," offered Peter, finishing her thought.

"Exactly. And it's no one's fault."

"No, of course not," said Peter.

Mary smiled at him and Tracey. "You two are obviously meant for each other. I think you two have something special. You always have."

Tracey smiled, glancing at Peter. "I think I always realized it. I was just afraid to acknowledge it. I didn't want to mess everything up."

Peter returned her smile. It was wonderful to hear her say it. "Geez, it only took an interdimensional island with dinosaurs, lizard men, ape warriors, and a demon…"

All three shared a laugh.

However, their revelry was cut short by movement in the jungle to their right. All three stopped dead in their tracks. Peter felt positively vulnerable without his orb.

"What is it?" whispered Tracey.

"I don't know," said Peter, breathless.

The vegetation all around them began to rustle and move. Large figures burst out into the clearing, surrounding Peter, Tracey, and Mary. The Simians surrounded them.

Peter took a deep breath, but his muscles remained tense. "They followed us."

"Why?" asked Mary, suspicious.

The Simians clutched spears, but they didn't point them at the humans. They waited, watching the party with uncannily human-like eyes and faces. The Simian King burst forth, bounding on his legs and arms, stopping short in front of the three humans.

Peter did his best not to flinch. He stood his ground as Tracey and Mary shrunk behind him. He didn't want to show fear, for in the jungle fear could be interpreted as weakness. This wasn't like when he awakened the Zehhaki, and he was in possession of the orb. He would not be viewed as a deity by the Simians.

The Simian King pounded his chest once with his right fist. Peter, taking a chance, did the same.

"What are you doing?" Tracey muttered, mortified by the gesture.

"I don't know," said Peter. It was the truth.

The Simian King grunted at them, trying to communicate. He gesticulated at the jungle all around them, and then he addressed the other Simians. Three massive males stepped forward right on cue. They each snatched up Peter, Tracey, and Mary and swung them onto their backs.

Peter's Simian mount grunted and it bounded back into the jungle. Peter clutched him tightly around the neck just in time to hang on. The Simian leapt, and they were suddenly airborne, swinging from branch to branch with such speed and grace it took Peter's breath away.

He closed his eyes as his stomach lurched. He was never one for amusement rides, and this was much worse. There were no seat belts or safety bars to keep him from plummeting to his death. In time, he opened his eyes and instantly regretted it. They were way up into the canopy. He looked down below, through breaks in the tree branches and leaves and saw a pack of tyrannosaurs roaming around beneath them. It was at that moment Peter realized they were being escorted safely through the jungle, carefully following the river back north as Peter, Tracey, and Mary had been observed doing.

Peter caught a flash of something in his peripheral vision. A blur flew right by him and collided with one of the Simians to his right. The ape cried out, losing its grip on its branch, nearly falling. Another blur zoomed past Peter, and he turned his head to see the wide wingspan and pointy head of a pterodactyl descending on him through a gap in the trees.

He braced himself, clinging to his Simian's neck, but he felt claws grip his torso. He was suddenly lifted from his Simian as it swung away, disappearing into the trees. Peter called out for help, but the flapping of a twelve-foot wingspan yanked him upward, taking his breath away.

He felt a large hand wrap around his ankle, yanking him out of the pterodactyl's grip, and another Simian slung him onto its back. It swung away posthaste as the winged predator pursued. Peter heard the shouts and cries of Tracey and Mary as he saw other pterodactyls descend upon them, attempting to snatch them away.

Other Simians punched and swatted at the airborne attackers, roaring in fury. The canopy erupted in a feeding frenzy, and Peter hung on for dear life. His Simian made an abrupt turn to evade a winged attacker, and Peter lost his grip. He slid off its back, falling through the canopy. In his freefall he saw a pterodactyl diving right for him. Another Simian reached out and snatched him from its beak as it snapped closed, just missing him. The winged reptile collided with a tree trunk, but Peter didn't get the chance to see what happened to it as he was immediately whisked away. The Simians threw him around like a ragdoll, passing him back and forth, keeping him out of harm's way as they contended with the winged scourge.

After a few minutes, the Simians had put enough distance between them and the pterodactyls, and the canopy was once again safe for passage. While making stops on long tree branches up high, Peter caught glimpses of the other Simians. He saw Tracey for a brief moment, and then Mary. He was thankful they were safe. They spent the rest of the day swinging through the trees until Peter's Simian stopped at the edge of a clearing. It grunted at him.

Peter hoisted himself up on its shoulders and had a look. Tracey and Mary each landed on a nearby tree on the back of their escorts.

"It's base camp," said Tracey. "The Simians took us back."

"It looks deserted," said Mary.

It was true. Peter didn't see any sign of activity. The tents remained upright and intact, and the land vehicles appeared unharmed, but there wasn't a soul to be found.

"The helicopter is gone," said Tracey, crestfallen.

"They left us," said Mary, bitter.

"We don't know that," said Peter. He noticed the Simians waited, listening to their discussion, though he doubted they comprehended it. Peter held a hand out in front of his escort's face and pointed his finger down to the ground.

With a jolt that nearly sent Peter flying off its back, the Simian swung down, descending the tree, finally landing on the ground. Peter barely hung on for dear life. Tracey and Mary landed next to him on their Simians.

They each slid off their escort's back. Peter was relieved to have his feet planted on terra firma. He stepped forward, his eyes searching the camp.

A diminutive figure stepped out of the main tent, looking around. It appeared to be one of the Umazoa. Peter squinted, trying to determine who it was. "It's Hiu!" Then other tribespeople stepped out.

"He did it," gasped Mary. "He saved his tribe."

"Let's go say hello," said Peter. He turned to his escort and pounded his chest. "Thank you."

The ape warrior returned the gesture, and then he grunted at the others. They immediately dispersed, leaping into the trees and disappearing into the canopy.

Peter smiled, watching them vanish. They seemed like a good species. Maybe there was hope for this place yet. "Let's go."

He, Tracey, and Mary strolled into camp. They were quickly spotted by one of the Umazoa, who sounded the alarm. Within seconds, they were surrounded. Men, women, and children all took turns embracing each of them, fussing over them in a true hero's welcome.

"Thank you...yes, nice to see you..." Peter looked around to see if any Poseidon Tech staff were present. He saw Hiu approach, smiling, arms held out wide in front of him. Marcy and Collins were with him.

The others parted as Hiu embraced Peter first, chattering on in Umazoan. He touched Peter on his arms and chest, apparently looking for wounds. His expression turned to concern when he saw Peter's chest sans orb. Hiu pulled his shirt open, practically sticking his head inside. "Where it?"

"Gone," answered Peter. "Nazimaa gone. Dead."

This pleased Hiu, as he laughed raucously and embraced Peter again. He then kissed and embraced Tracey and Mary, greeting them as prodigal children returned. His joy faded as he looked around. He turned to Peter once more. "Where hunter?"

Peter's smile withered, and he shook his head.

Hiu bowed his head in respect and grief.

"We thought you left us," said Tracey, hugging Marcy.

"Not a chance," said Collins, shaking Peter's hand. "Marcy wouldn't leave without you."

"You stayed too," said Peter.

Collins shrugged. "I was contracted to bring everyone back safely. I didn't want to get sued for breach of contract."

They all shared a laugh.

"So, that means we're getting off this damned island?" asked Mary.

Collins nodded. "A chopper is on its way to pick us up."

"Thank you," said Peter.

"Don't mention it," said Collins. He pointed to Marcy. "You should've seen her stand up to Nielsen."

"He must be pissed," said Tracey to Marcy.

Marcy smirked. "I think he was impressed."

"How did you know we'd come back? That you'd ever see us again?" asked Tracey.

Marcy shot a glance at Peter. "I knew you'd bring him back. I just had a feeling."

Within minutes, a chopper arrived. Hiu and his tribe, having never seen a contraption like that before, startled and practically ran away. Peter and the others reassured them, and they reluctantly stayed but never took their eyes off the magic flying machine. Hiu nearly fell over when he saw a human hop out.

Nielsen ran over to the group. "Excellent! You're back." He looked around at the group. "Where's Jason and Susan?"

"They died saving our lives," said Peter.

"We have to go," said Nielsen. "HQ is sending a fresh team to guard base camp. We're keeping the portal open."

"About that..." said Peter.

"We'll discuss your concerns when we return back to our dimension," insisted Nielsen. "There'll be a full debriefing."

Peter nodded. He said his goodbyes to everyone. He didn't have time to tell Hiu about the Simians, nor did he have time to ask about the Zehhaki. It would all have to work itself out—natural selection.

He hopped into the chopper with the others, and they took off, heading for the offshore oil rig. Peter looked out the window as the island dropped beneath him, shrinking as they flew away. The island remained in view, the portal containment field holding up. However, as they flew further away from it, the sky resumed its familiar blue. He was in his home dimension again.

It was an odd sensation, leaving the island behind. He didn't know why, but he felt ambivalent about it.

* * *

In the cafeteria, Peter dove into a ham sandwich with Swiss and mustard. He never thought a ham sandwich could taste so good. The others also dove in, stuffing their faces like ravenous beasts. Peter took a long draw off his can of ginger ale, which tasted amazing.

Nielsen watched, smiling, apparently pleased they enjoyed the refreshments provided by Poseidon Tech. "Eat and drink up. We head back home in a few hours, after a full debriefing."

"Can I take a shower?" asked Mary. "God, I'm dying for a shower."

"I think we have time for that," said Nielsen.

"Fresh underwear," blurted Peter with his mouth full. "I'd give my right arm for a fresh pair of underwear."

Home. While initially a strange concept, with the island behind him (left in another dimension) a feeling of normalcy began to wash over him. He wanted to see his parents and his friends. He enjoyed the filtered air in the cafeteria, the feel of the metal tables, and the halogen lighting. It was real.

He wasn't sure if he was just compartmentalizing it all in his mind, but his experience on the island was beginning to feel like the vague memory of a distant fever dream. He looked over at Tracey, who was downing an ice-cold beer. She was real, and now their relationship was real. Prior to the island, the notion of romantic involvement with Tracey was a mere fantasy. Ironically, actual fantasy made their relationship real.

The whole experience with the dinosaurs, orbs, demons, lizard and ape men...it all reminded him of one of those Saturday morning cartoons from the 1980s he liked to stream on the internet. It was like a tabletop RPG come to life. No one was going to believe it. Then again, thanks to the non-disclosure agreement he had signed, he wouldn't be able to tell anyone anyway.

He'd get to tell Nielsen everything when he was done gorging on deli sandwiches. Then again, maybe Nielsen didn't have to know every little detail.

CHAPTER 17

Peter heard the doorbell ring as he just about finished setting up the game. Tracey and a few of their old faculty gamer friends sat around the dining room table. Everyone was smiling and laughing, drinking cold beer, and munching on handfuls of chips and popcorn.

He stood up. "I'll be right back."

Peter crossed the dining room and living room to the front door. When he answered it, his face fell.

"Hi, Dr. Albanese," said David Lennox, smiling.

"I'm busy right now."

Lennox chuckled affably. "I just need a few minutes of your time, and then I'll leave you alone."

"I'm not interested."

"Peter, you don't even know why I'm here."

"It's 'Dr. Albanese.' And I can hazard an educated guess."

"Just a few minutes. I promise."

Peter sighed and stepped aside, allowing Lennox to enter.

Tracey stepped into the living room smiling. "Who is it, Peter?" her smile faded when she saw David Lennox standing in their living room.

"Oh good! You're both here," said Lennox.

"What do you want? We have company," snapped Tracey.

"Just a few minutes of your time," said Lennox.

Peter waved him over to another room off the living room. "Let's step into the den."

Lennox nodded and followed Peter into the den. Tracey followed, closing the door behind them.

David Lennox looked around at the room lined with mahogany bookcases. In the center sat a mahogany desk, with two plush leather chairs positioned in front of it. To the right was an eighty-six-inch television mounted on the wall. "You have a lovely home. I see you've put your stipend to good use."

Peter turned around and leaned on his desk. "What do you want, Mr. Lennox?"

Lennox chose to remain standing and cleared his throat. "Poseidon Tech is going to be expanding operations on the island. There are other interested parties."

"Other governments?" said Peter.

Lennox didn't confirm or deny it. Instead, he flashed his signature smarmy grin. "We need guides. Those with obvious experience on the island. You two, of course, would be paid handsomely."

"Forget it," said Tracey.

Lennox's grin grew wider. "Don't you want to know how much?"

"No," said Peter. "We're perfectly happy with our current arrangement."

Lennox nodded, his smile waning only slightly. "You're living the high life now. It takes money to maintain this sort of lifestyle."

"We'll do just fine," insisted Peter. "Now, if that is all..."

"How about scientific curiosity?"

"Fully satiated. I know all I'll ever want to know about dinosaurs."

Lennox leveled his gaze at Peter. "It's a shame. This is all going to go public. The greatest scientific discovery in the history of mankind, and you don't want to be part of it?"

"We _were_ a part of it," said Tracey.

"Not officially," reminded Lennox. "Why don't you enjoy your time in the sun, take your fifteen minutes? Parlay it into something else you want to do. You could finance more digs."

"That island, which is actually more of a continent, is dangerous," demanded Peter. "Who knows what else lurks in that dimension undiscovered?"

"Discovery is fraught with danger," said Lennox. "The moon landing was extremely dangerous, executed with less technology than exists in your cell phone. Yet, it was a tremendous achievement."

Peter only glared at him.

Lennox chuckled to himself. "Okay. Point taken." He reached into the right breast pocket of his designer suit and produced a stiff, off-white business card. "In case you should change your mind."

Peter accepted it and guided Lennox out of the den. They crossed the living room, and Peter held the front door open. Lennox stepped outside. He turned to say something. "Remember your non-disclosure..." but Peter closed the door in his face.

He sighed. "That felt good. Shall we return to our guests?"

Tracey smiled. "Yes, let's."

They returned to the dining room table. Tracey took her seat, and Peter took his. He looked at his friends from over his Game Master screen and cleared his throat. Everyone grew quiet. They all watched him as they sipped beers and rolled polyhedral dice in their trays, practicing. Miniature game pieces sat haphazardly on a well-worn gridded game board.

"Okay," he began. "Your airplane experiences quite a bit of turbulence as it flies through a massive storm. Lightning flashes outside your window. Suddenly, the plane drops, the cabin loses pressure, and oxygen masks drop from the ceiling. You black out and regain consciousness. You're on the ground, the torn fuselage open to the night sky.

"Most of the passengers have died, leaving you as the only survivors. Raindrops fall through the opening above you. As you look around and begin to process your predicament, you realize you've landed on an uncharted island.

"Off to the right, you see trees moving in the moonlight." Peter contorted his face and raised his arms, pulling them close to his body for dramatic effect. "A massive Tyrannosaurus rex steps out into the clearing, sniffing the air. It smells its next meal and turns in your direction, letting out a deafening roar.

"Another emerges from the jungle at the other end of the plane, zeroing in on your location. It begins to snatch bodies from their seats, rending flesh from bone. It tosses the fresh meat into the back of its mouth as blood runs down its jowls. Strapped into your seat, you look on in horror."

Peter unconsciously fingered Lennox's business card behind the screen, pulling at the corner with his index finger, bending it and letting it snap back.

"What do you do?"

THE END

 SEVEREDPRESS

facebook.com/severedpress
twitter.com/severedpress

CHECK OUT OTHER GREAT DINOSAUR BOOKS

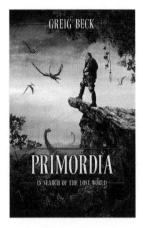

PRIMORDIA
by **Greig Beck**

Ben Cartwright, former soldier, home to mourn the loss of his father stumbles upon cryptic letters from the past between the author, Arthur Conan Doyle and his great, great grandfather who vanished while exploring the Amazon jungle in 1908.

Amazingly, these letters lead Ben to believe that his ancestor's expedition was the basis for Doyle's fantastical tale of a lost world inhabited by long extinct creatures. As Ben digs some more he finds clues to the whereabouts of a lost notebook that might contain a map to a place that is home to creatures that would rewrite everything known about history, biology and evolution.

But other parties now know about the notebook, and will do anything to obtain it. For Ben and his friends, it becomes a race against time and against ruthless rivals.

In the remotest corners of Venezuela, along winding river trails known only to lost tribes, and through near impenetrable jungle, Ben and his novice team find a forbidden place more terrifying and dangerous than anything they could ever have imagined.

PANGAEA EXILES
by **Jeff Brackett**

Tried and convicted for his crimes, Sean Barrow is sent into temporal exile—banished to a time so far before recorded history that there is no chance that he, or any other criminal sent back, has any chance of altering history.

Now Sean must find a way to survive more than 200 million years in the past, in a world populated by monstrous creatures that would rend him limb from limb if they got the chance. And that's just his fellow prisoners.

The dinosaurs are almost as bad.

 SEVEREDPRESS

⬤ facebook.com/severedpress

⬤ twitter.com/severedpress

CHECK OUT OTHER GREAT DINOSAUR BOOKS

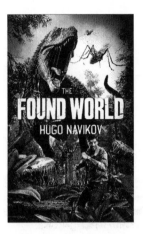

THE FOUND WORLD
by **Hugo Navikov**

A powerful global cabal wants adventurer Brett Russell to retrieve a superweapon stolen by the scientist who built it. To entice him to travel underneath one of the most dangerous volcanoes on Earth to find the scientist, this shadowy organization will pay him the only thing he cares about: information that will allow him to avenge his family's murder.

But before he can get paid, he and his team must enter an underground hellscape of killer plants, giant insects, terrifying dinosaurs, and an army of other predators never previously seen by man.

At the end of this journey awaits a revelation that could alter the fate of mankind ... if they can make it back from this horrifying found world.

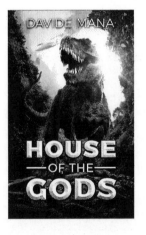

HOUSE OF THE GODS
by **Davide Mana**

High above the steamy jungle of the Amazon basin, rise the flat plateaus known as the Tepui, the House of the Gods. Lost worlds of unknown beauty, a naturalistic wonder, each an ecology onto itself, shunned by the local tribes for centuries. The House of the Gods was not made for men.

But now, the crew and passengers of a small charter plane are about to find what was hidden for sixty million years.

Lost on an island in the clouds 10.000 feet above the jungle, surrounded by dinosaurs, hunted by mysterious mercenaries, the survivors of Sligo Air flight 001 will quickly learn the only rule of life on Earth: Extinction.

 SEVEREDPRESS

 facebook.com/severedpress
 twitter.com/severedpress

CHECK OUT OTHER GREAT DINOSAUR BOOKS

FLIPSIDE
by JAKE BIBLE

The year is 2046 and dinosaurs are real.

Time bubbles across the world, many as large as one hundred square miles, turn like clockwork, revealing prehistoric landscapes from the Cretaceous Period.

They reveal the Flipside.

Now, thirty years after the first Turn, the clockwork is breaking down as one of the world's powers has decided to exploit the phenomenon for their own gain, possibly destroying everything then and now in the process.

A MAN OUT OF TIME
by Christopher Laflan

Five years after the Chinese Axis detonated an unknown weapon of mass destruction off the southern coast of the United States, Special Ops Sergeant John Crider and the members of Shadow Company have finally captured what they all hope will lead to the end of the war. Unfortunately, the population within the United States is no longer sustainable. In an effort to stabilize the economy, the government enacts the Cryonics Act. One hundred years in suspended animation, all debt forgiven, and a chance at a less crowded future are too good to pass up for John and his young daughter.

Except not everything always goes as planned as Sergeant John Crider finds himself pitted against a land of prehistoric monsters genetically resurrected from the fossil record, murderous inhabitants, and a future he never wanted.

Printed in Great Britain
by Amazon

55948033R00108